Y0-BOB-519

Intersections/Fast Forward

Angel N

Intersections

May you find something of pleasure & of inspiration in these pages.

Sheila S

Sheila Scobba Banning

Library of Congress Control Number: 2009906518
ISBN: Hardcover 978-1-4415-5129-0
Softcover 978-1-4415-5128-3

This book was printed in the United States of America.

To order additional copies of this book, contact:
Xlibris Corporation
1-888-795-4274
www.Xlibris.com
Orders@Xlibris.com
65564

CONTENTS

Intersections

Fast Forward

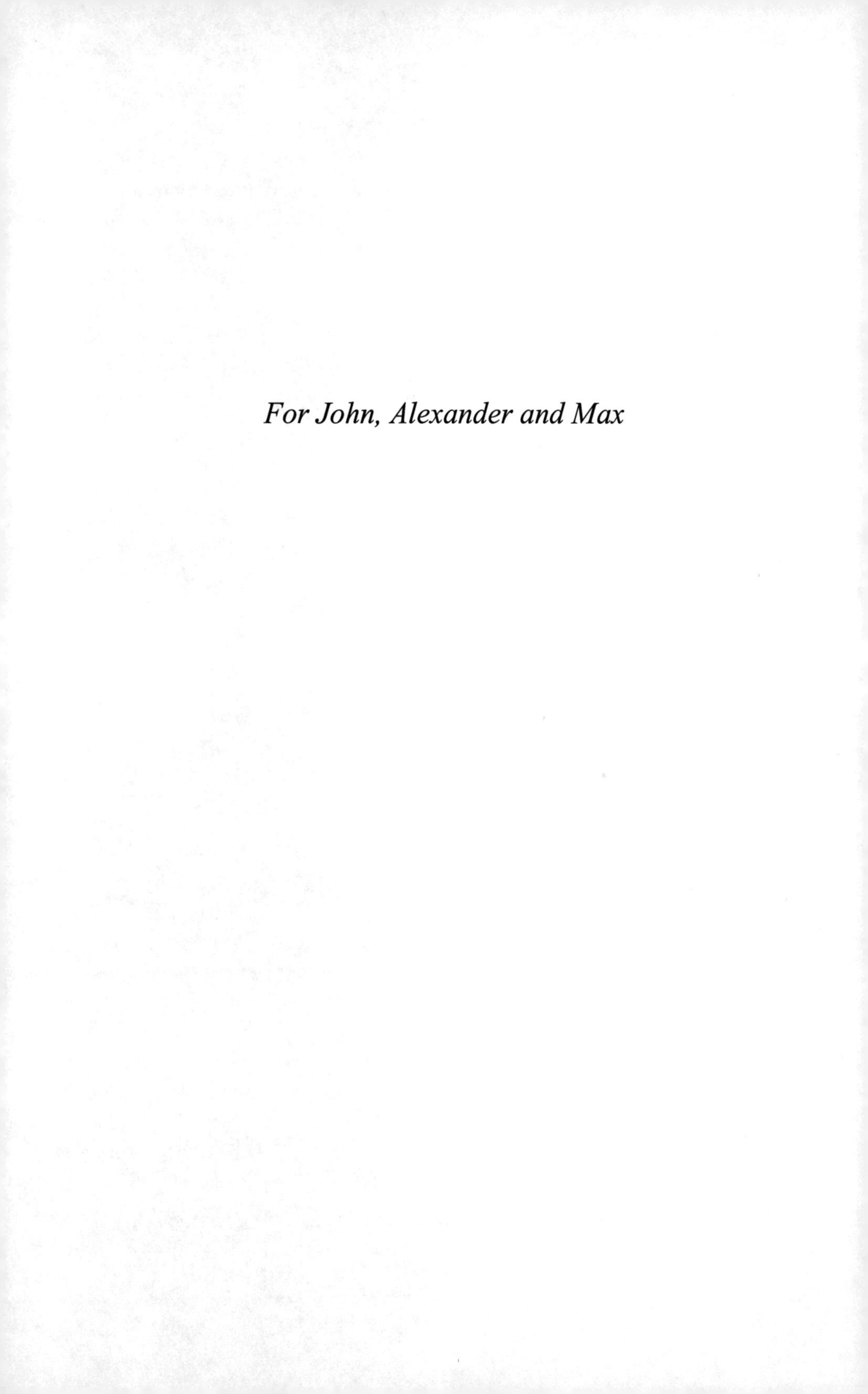

For John, Alexander and Max

Acknowledgments

I would like to thank the following people whose lives as writers and readers have intersected mine: John Billheimer, Bob Brownstein, Anne Cheilek, Mark Coggins, Ann Hillesland, Jan Austin, Lexy Gilmore, Teri Hessel, Barrie Moore, Jeanese Snyder, Lee Berger, Dale Boone, Todd Capurso, Dorothy Fadiman, Pamela Rose, Andres Velasquez, Lydia Esposito, Craig Haladay, Debbie Prentice, and Ellen Sussman and the rest of the original writing group.

Author photo by Suzanne Becker Bronk

GPS

"*At the next intersection, make a left.*"

Lorraine looked up from the map at the announcement from the GPS lady and turned toward her husband. "You aren't going to follow *those* directions are you?"

David shrugged. "Why not? Let's see where it takes us." He glanced over at her and laughed. "We set it for most direct route, right? Maybe she knows something we don't."

He made the left onto Washington as Lorraine frowned at the map, blocking the last rays of the setting sun with her right hand. Washington Road did connect to an expressway on the other side of the park, but it didn't look like a timesaving choice.

"We're going to be late."

"Maybe we'll be early."

Lorraine had teased him about buying the car just for the GPS. He had looked at plenty of cars, from zippy midlife-crisis models to SUVs, but the low-mileage beemer with the unbelievable bargain price won him over. The twitchy little man selling the car could have been the brother of the proverbial little old lady from Pasadena. Not only had he driven the car only around town, but after a fender bender on a one-way street, he immediately put the car on the market. The drive to his mechanic to have it checked out was all the convincing David needed. He was sold at the first instruction to turn.

Lorraine was less enamored of the GPS lady than he was, however. There was something about her tone that irritated Lorraine. The usual directions for turns and instructions for upcoming intersections were delivered in a soothing contralto, but sometimes the inflection seemed a bit strident. And when they reached their destination, she always sounded entirely too smug for Lorraine's liking.

"*In six-hundred feet, keep to the left.*"

They veered slightly, following the branch of the road that would not connect to the expressway. The trees on either side of the road shivered in a sudden gust of wind and tiny drops of rain began to bead on the windshield. Muffled plinking on the sunroof gave the impression of tapping fingers. The last of the day clung to the horizon in a pale blue glow, then dimmed and vanished. Lorraine turned on the reading light and adjusted the map in the spot of brightness.

"This road goes over the hill! That can't be right."

David squinted over at the map as if he could read it from that distance, then punched the button on the GPS menu a couple times, switching it to map display mode. They appeared as a tiny green triangle moving along a thin red line.

"Look, it's going to the freeway."

"Over the hill?" Lorraine checked her watch, none too subtly. "How long?"

"Twenty minutes. Maybe thirty."

"Well . . ." He punched the button again and blipped through the menu. "It's twenty miles to the freeway this way, but their new house is in that gated place up above, right? We'll might be a little late, but we're skipping the commute traffic through the City. Maybe this is a shortcut."

"I don't think there's an onramp from this road. I don't see anything on this map."

"It's probably too new. That's the advantage of GPS, they update it all the time."

Lorraine shot him a look but didn't say anything.

The rain picked up and David flipped on the wipers. The headlights illuminated the surrounding scenery in strobe flashes as they wound through the woods: a massive trunk, a cluster of moving shrubs, the retinal reflections of something about to cross the road.

"I'm always surprised by how dark it is in the hills, even in the daytime." Lorraine scanned the edges of the road ahead at the furthest reaches of the beams. She thought the local deer would have sought shelter by now, but better safe than sorry.

"Yeah, it's hard to believe that we're surrounded by hundreds of thousands of people." David glanced into the blackness of the review mirror. "You'd think we were the only people on earth."

"*At the next intersection, make a right.*"

"There is *no* intersection on this map!"

David squinted at the GPS screen, slowing as he scrolled to the map again. "There isn't on this map, either." He returned to the direction screen. It listed their next turn as just "unincorporated county" without a street name.

"You know why the GPS has a woman's voice?" Lorraine nudged her husband. "Because when they tested the first prototypes on pilots years ago, the male test subjects apparently didn't respond well to taking direction from another man."

"But they've had some woman telling them what to do since they were born, right?"

He smirked and she swatted his arm. Lorraine noticed a slightly larger than usual break in the trees as they passed.

"*If possible, make a U-turn!*"

David braked automatically in response, then continued. "Oh, well, that must have been the right turn."

"Now tell me she didn't sound strident just then!"

"She didn't sound strident just then. She sounded exactly the same as she always does. She's a *computer*. *You* sound strident."

Lorraine crossed her arms and stared pointedly out her side window. David accelerated in response. The rain that had started with sprinkles and gusts whipped itself into a frenzied downpour. The GPS screen went blank as the computer recalculated their position from where they should have been to where they actually were. Leaves began to catch in the wipers and small branches torn from the canopy above scratched across the hood.

As David reached for the menu button to change the screen, a sound like an explosion filled the car and a tree dropped onto the road ahead of them. He stood on the brake and gripped the wheel as the vibration from the antilock brake system shook the car. At the last moment when it looked like they weren't going to stop in time, he spun the wheel hard to the left.

They came to a rest up against the tree, branches smashed into Lorraine's window with leaves pressed flat against it like the hands of an angry mob. The only sound was the soft thunk of the wipers and the staccato rain. They exchanged a look and blew out their held breath together.

David took off his glasses and rubbed his eyes with the heels of his hands. "Do we have any water?"

Lorraine picked up the bottle in the cup holder and shook it, then handed it to him.

"I guess we should have listened to her after all," he said and drained the bottle. "Well, let's see if we're stuck."

David put the car in reverse and the tires spun on wet leaves and mud. He alternated between low and reverse, rocking the car back and forth to gain some traction.

"Do you want me to get out and push?"

"I've almost got it. Maybe if I put the blanket from the trunk under the back tires. Slide over and hit the gas when I tell you to."

Rain swept in with the wind as soon as he cracked the door, and David had to lean on it hard just to get out. Lorraine had to pull her straight skirt up to her waist to get enough maneuverability to climb over the center console. She left the door ajar so she could hear David when he called.

The trunk popped open but didn't close.

"David?"

Lorraine stared into the rearview mirror as if it were a crystal ball. She watched and waited, but nothing changed. Finally she had to open the door and step out. She was soaked instantly.

"David!"

"What?"

The voice came from behind her and very close. She jumped.

"Sorry. I decided to put a piece under the front tires, too. Drive forward as much as you can, then stop."

He vanished behind the car and Lorraine closed the door. She shifted into gear and pressed the accelerator. The car moved just slightly away from the tree.

"Stop!"

David reappeared beside the car and yanked the door open. “Slide over.”

This time the forward backward motion picked up momentum like a pendulum until the car was freed. David winced as the bigger branches scraped the side of the car with the unmistakable whine of metal being gouged. The image of a man with a hook and a couple out parking flashed in Lorraine’s memory for an instant. When the car was facing back the way it had come, the GPS screen showed their location again.

Lorraine shivered and cranked up the heater. “So much for the party.”

“*At the next intersection, make a left.*”

They were moving slowly enough this time to see the gravel road. David made the turn and Lorraine turned so quickly in her seat to face him, her wet skirt squeaked against the leather seat.

“Where are you going? We might as well go back the way we came.”

“The freeway will be faster anyway.”

“*What* freeway?”

The bumpy single lane opened abruptly onto a smooth unlined blacktop. Lorraine turned on the reading light to examine the map again. “Wait. I think this is a fire access road. The old estate that was here before it became open space must have had it put in.”

“See? We’ll be there in no time. If it weren’t for the trees, we could probably see their house from here.”

The blacktop was cracked but in surprisingly good shape otherwise. The canopy nearly blocked out the sky, and as the wind died down, the rain seemed more nuisance than threat. Lorraine put the map away and turned out the light as the road climbed steeply through a series of gentle curves.

“We’d better go downhill pretty soon if this is really going to hit the freeway.”

She crossed her arms against the chill of her wet clothes. Even with the heater going full blast she could feel the involuntary tremors passing through her.

“Look, we’ve crested.”

The downhill was steep and straight. The lights from the valley floor began to appear in flashes through the trees.

"*In three hundred feet, enter the freeway.*"

They both looked at the GPS screen. The arrow showed the road they were on nearly perpendicular to the freeway with a slight angle to the right of an onramp.

"That can't be right."

The added acceleration from the steep incline made the city lights flicker faster and faster through the leaves. The road seemed to curve to the right ahead, just as the screen indicated, and David braked slightly to make the turn. The car went into a skid and broke through a damaged guardrail as the road veered sharply to the left. They shot out of the cover of trees and into the air, civilization spread out far below with the bright red snake of the freeway arcing around the lights of the new development directly beneath them.

"*You have arrived!*"

###

Landscape

As a gardener, I am an experimental Darwinian. I throw plants together with only passing regard for their requirements then see what survives and what thrives. I love to be surrounded by flowers, but my idea of gardening is putting in a drip system and whacking back the growth once in awhile. Fussy plants that wilt at the slightest chill or attract peculiar molds until they fade into a limp Camille routine hold no appeal for me. Retrieving a plant from the brink of destruction again and again, knowing that the brink is the best it can ever do, sucks more out of you than one plant can replace. Give me the tenacious of the plant kingdom every time.

I haven't even been able to think about the yard all week; haven't been able to think about anything. When I looked out the window, all I could see was my own reflection. Today I can finally see through the pane to the back yard where alternating sections of dark green, light green, silver, lavender, and red with occasional spikes of deep burgundy make the yard look dappled with impressionist light and shadow even in full sun. I take up my lopsided wicker basket with the clippers and gloves heavy in one end and walk outside. After all, weeds never rest.

"Weed" is just a label given to any plant that grows where it isn't wanted. Walking between patches of translucent lime-green echeveria and family clusters of more opaque hens and chicks, I find nothing to pull up. These fleshy, drought-resistant succulents grow up shoulder-to-shoulder in tight packs like a band of Irish-Catholic brothers. If they let an intruder infiltrate their ranks, I figure it was invited. I stoop to retrieve some leaves trapped in the crocodile jaws of the aloe and drop them into my basket. An irregular stretch of reddish dragon's blood offers spotty resistance to the insurgence of ice plant sweeping up from the fence. Up close, the individual plants appear distinctly artificial. The echeveria could be points of jello sculpture, the port-colored mum-shaped heads on tall stalks are clearly plastic, and the string-of-pearls might be discarded pop-beads. Even the bloom spikes sent up by the succulents every year look more like primitive signal devices than flowers. You have to know succulents to know they're real.

I break off a damaged spike and drop it into the basket on my arm. Last night Michael started talking about getting married again. It was probably a mistake to use the word "unnecessary" when what I meant was that I'm happy with the way things are. The topic took me by surprise, though; he hasn't said anything about marriage in years. I guess my reaction came across as negative, but what does he expect? I've lived in this house *with him* for longer than I've lived anywhere else, ever. Shouldn't that be enough?

Ten years can alter a landscape dramatically. The day I pulled up to the front of the house with my life in a U-Haul, the lawn was lush green with a couple fairy rings over by the border hedge. Michael helped me carry boxes and clothes into the house and showed me where he'd made room for my desk and the art deco dresser I used as a file cabinet. After everything was moved in and the truck had been returned, we took a break in the late afternoon shade of the backyard. Over sweating bottles of beer we established the ground rules of living together, trying to begin with shared expectations.

Michael had lived with someone before me, and it had ended badly. Shouting, tears, I'm guessing even broken pottery was involved. He wanted to be sure I knew what I was getting into, wanted to be sure I was sure. His concern was very sweet, but I had nothing to add to the conversation.

"I live in the present," I said when he pressed me. "We'll deal with the future when it gets here. Why worry about what hasn't happened?"

If things didn't work out, there wouldn't be any big scene. Time passes, circumstances change, you adapt. I had lived alone before, and I could move again. What else was there to say? He shook his head and smiled at me as if I would get the punch line later, shifted the discussion to concrete details like cooking and cleaning and squeezing the toothpaste.

Following the stepping stones that look like a partially submerged sea serpent over to the corner, I see that the succulents on the side of the house are greeting spring with a vengeance. From the mound of lavender rosettes with blade-shaped petals spread to the size of salad plates hs sprung a forest of narrow stems as much as two feet tall. Each one holds eight or ten clusters of tiny yellow stars. I moved one plant back here from the front just a couple years ago, cut it off from an overgrown section and stuck it in the new location without any preparation besides digging a hole. I watered it, watched it lose a lot of petals and shrink back to a single tiny know on a big stem. A few months later it started sending out new stems, then exploded in all directions to fill the corner. Succulents are surface rooters. Dig them up, move them around like so much furniture, and still they grow and bloom. Some even do better under harsh conditions, rising to the challenge like a thumbed nose in the face of deprivation.

Michael had no pets when we met, but our third summer together he decided we should have a dog. He grew up with a golden retriever that was his only consolation when his parents split up. The dog went with him as he shuttled back and forth between his mom and dad, and it became the element that defined home for him. If we were a family, we should have a dog.

"I like the same kind of dogs as children," I told him, "other people's."

He swore I'd learn to love having a dog and said he would do all the work. Dogs are okay in small doses, but the constant need for attention, the slavish devotion, make me feel claustrophobic after awhile. Dogs are the ultimate passive/aggressive manipulators—they quiver at the sound of your voice, live for only your presence, but it's all done to squeeze more response out of you. Dogs are affection junkies. Cats, on the other hand, don't need you. I'm not saying you're just a warm place to nap that includes meal service; they do enjoy your company. Sometimes. When a cat showers you with affection, it's a compliment. The action is a choice, not a compulsion. Cats always hold a little bit in reserve.

"What about a cat?" I asked Michael.

His compromise was to get both a dog and a cat. He chose an energetic mixed breed pup at the pound and named her Ginger for her hair color and spicy personality. He played with her and trained her initially as promised, and I gave her the occasional scratch behind the ears. Of course she started following me around the instant she grew out of her leggy adolescence. Ginger had the instincts of a retriever, and whichever of my socks happened to land on the top of the laundry was carefully ferried from room to room all day long as she mooned in my wake.

"See, I knew you'd come around!"

Michael would grin and nudge me every time the dog leaned against my legs as I stood at the stove or tripped me as I tried to leave a room. In his logic of love, if the dog loved me, I must love the dog. For Michael, dogs were like relationship super-glue.

The kitten ballooned into a twenty pound former tom who brought me gifts of not quite dead birds and left beautifully dissected mice outside the bedroom door. Bluto refused to acknowledge the absence of his testicles and continued to take on all comers in defense of his territory, usually outside our bedroom window at three in the morning. Shrieking at about the pitch and volume you'd expect from a woman being knifed would launch me upright with an adrenaline surge before I was even awake. Heart thudding audibly, I'd mutter dire threats out the open window.

"You'd make a good muff! . . ."

In weak moments, I'd resort to throwing shoes. Even when I managed to hit him, Bluto would ignore me, Ginger would try desperately to get outside to retrieve the shoe, and Michael would sleep through it all.

"Paper doesn't make a relationship permanent," I told him when he proposed that year for the first time. "Look at your parents. Look at mine."

"We're not them! We're not even like them. I love you. I want to be with you forever."

"Go far enough into the future, and everything, everyone is gone. Now is forever, Michael. I love you now."

The next spring I planted calla lilies.

Bulbs are pretty low-maintenance, as flowers go. A little food, a little cleaning up, and you don't actually have to divide the bulbs if you don't want to. The calla lilies have grown to fill the entire southwest corner of the back yard, and tall bearded irises in tactile yellows and violets have formed tight communities up against the house. I've even got some gladiolas standing sentry at the corners where the succulents meet the irises. The yard welcomed the colorful strangers more readily than I did, the low and high, the seasonal and perpetual accommodating each other gracefully. When the bulb flowers rise up each year to form a brilliant skyline above the undulating field of succulents, I watch them with an awed sense of witnessing both creation and reincarnation.

Pulling limp petal remains from the side of my rust iris, I am drawn to the full bloom above. I stroke the surface with one finger. This is Michael's favorite, the one he says is the color of my eyes, although I know he's making that up.

"Look, right there!" he always says, holding up a mirror and angling my head until the sun is almost in my face. "See?"

I do look, but I end up laughing at what I can't see. My eyes are just brown, not this iridescent caramel with flecks of gold and copper. This color in velvet or a moire silk could be considered obscene in some states. I still don't know what Michael sees, but this iris is how he sees me.

I have refused the comfort of walking the yard this week. The fragrance, the palette, even the sound of the breeze through the leaves were more than I could take. I learned early to adapt to change, but that doesn't mean I enjoy it. Against the back fence, in the corner not filled with calla lilies, I've been shaping a jade tree, pruning it as if it were an overgrown bonsai. This plant is not quite five years old, but it's almost as tall as I am and has a trunk the size of my leg. Between the bulbous teardrop leaves, miniature white bouquets are beginning to appear. succulents don't need much water, but they accept abundance when it is offered and expand to fill your expectations. I have thinned the plant a little at a time from its beginning in a two-inch pot, studying the growth pattern of the branches and cutting with care. When certain side shoots and extra leaves are removed, windows through the plant open up and the branch knuckles show.

The jade reminds me of an ancient knarled oak clinging to the same hillside for hundreds of years with a stubborn resilience. Of course, my version would melt like the Wicked Witch if it had to face a hard frost. Last December when we got the unexpected freeze three nights in a row, I covered it with plastic and even bought one of those smudge pots they use in orange groves. When the wind picked up, I ran out to be sure the tent was not making contact with the jade, providing an opportunity for damage. My absence woke Michael, and without a word he stood beside me at three in the morning propping up the plastic. My jade tree has frailties, but they are directly linked to what makes it special. It was worth saving.

My mother never had succulents. She had a huge traditional garden full of perfumed flowers and towering shrubs. At least, I think it was huge. A fuzzy image of a gold-lit tea party in the midst of lilacs and roses is one of the few memories I have of my parents. Everything moves in slow motion in the image I replay, and it feels like I have all the time in the world to pour cups of tea for that smiling man and woman.

If the scene is more imagination that reality, the details embellished from some story told to me by the aunt who raised me after they were gone, I don't want to know. This is how I want to remember them.

Running away from the jade tree along the side fence is a stretch of bare ground where I tore up a patch of ice plant last week. I stoop to crumble a clump of sun-warmed soil, rubbing it to nothing between my thumb and fingers. Seven isn't very old for a cat, really, but attitude takes its toll. I like to think seven years living in the suburban jungle was worth more to Bluto than twenty sitting inside with his nose pressed to the window. Ginger stayed under the bed for the first five days after we buried her feline companion, but yesterday she came out and ate a few bites. And Michael . . . well, Michael wants to get married.

I've delayed planting here until I was sure what I wanted. The weathered gray of the fence calls out for a dramatic contrast, something vibrant, like Bluto. Now I know just the thing, an apricot rose bush with soft petals in his muted orange but with the same prickly hazards if you handle it wrong. I've never tried to grow roses, but caring for them is something I can learn. Even if it takes forever.

###

The Net

```
The first thing I will do when I see you
is rip off your panties and bury my tongue
in the wettest part of you. I will devour
you until you moan with pleasure, and
then . . .

You finish.
```

Jessica felt the wave of heat creeping up from her chest and noticed her hands were actually trembling. She started to feel faint, concentrated on taking slow deep breaths as she blinked to keep the e-mail on her screen in focus. She had a client meeting in two hours, a proposal that needed serious revision, but she could not stop rereading Adam's latest message. He had never been this specific, this graphic, and the image drove out all the rest of her thoughts. She couldn't picture the project layout. All she could see was the scene he had created. Now was the time to put an end to it.

```
What panties?
```

She hit send, then deleted both his mail and her response. She covered her face with her hands, resting her elbows on the desk and leaning over her keyboard as if in prayer. Putting an end to it would have been saying, "Enough." or "Please stop." or better yet, no response at all.

"Idiot!" she cursed herself.

"But I swear I haven't even done anything stupid yet today!"

Mark was standing in the entrance to her cubicle, holding out his hands, palms up, and grinning. Jessica turned her chair and threw a pen at him, feeling a tiny rush at the realization that he had just missed seeing Adam's message.

"Everything isn't about you. I just screwed up . . . some text I was editing."

"So you're the idiot?"

"Apparently so. And I'll be the unemployed idiot if I don't get my act together. I'm not ready for my eleven o'clock."

"How about lunch?"

Jessica patted her mouth and frowned. "I can feel my lips moving. Is no sound coming out? I am be*hind*."

"Well, you're certainly being an ass, but you still have to eat, especially if you're going to be out of work. Come get me after your meeting."

She gave in just to get him to leave and tried to focus on the proposal. It should have been no more than fifteen or twenty minutes of finessing, but she kept seeing words like *devour* and *tongue* and *wet*, and had to read every line over and over again to make sure she wasn't actually including them in the text. Jessica glanced at the clock at the top of her screen. She wanted to check her mail again. She needed to see his response. There just wasn't time. She printed a hard copy and hurried to the conference room, forcing herself not to look back at her computer.

The meeting ran long, as expected, and Mark was loitering in the hall outside, pretending to be engrossed by the equations on the white board. He caught Jessica's eye as she walked out and tapped his watch when her clients weren't looking. He trailed in their wake as she walked them to the door.

Mark was her office spouse. She had picked up the term from one of those titillating articles that the serious newspapers were including more and more in an attempt to compete with the tabloids. Epidemic Sexless Marriage! Thongs for Preteens! Office Coupling! The feature had been half legitimate sociological study and half cautionary tale. The academic foundation was built on the natural pairing off and intimacy that often develops between people working together. The author chose to extrapolate increased risk factors for office romance, but Jessica ignored the hysteria. She found the whole idea amusing. It provided a label for the sort of bickering, teasing relationship she had with Mark. Once when he complained to his wife about a particularly irritating exchange, she said they sounded like an old married couple.

"If you were that hungry, you should have gone without me."

Mark waved off the suggestion. "They should have been done half an hour ago. Sushi?"

Jessica looked past him to her cubical. "I have to . . . (check my mail) get my purse. I'll be right back."

She brought up her e-mail, glancing over her shoulder in case Mark popped in. Adam's response was there.

> I can't wait to see you Friday. And you'd better not be kidding about the panties.

She hit delete just as Mark walked in.

"I meant lunch *today.* Give it up, Jess. You're such a grind. You can't work on an empty stomach, anyway."

He grabbed her arm and steered her out the door, hesitating just long enough for her to grab her purse from the bottom drawer. She became very aware of the pressure of his fingers on her biceps, his thumb on her inner arm. This thing with Adam had put her into some sort of hyper-arousal state, and it seemed to be rubbing off on the people around her. The kid at Starbucks had been flirting with her yesterday, her vet had engaged in all sorts of innuendo-laden banter with her while taking the cat's temperature last week, and three total strangers had handed her their phone numbers Saturday night, two of them women. Maybe she was emitting pheromones. Maybe she was just eroticizing everything, tinting all interactions with the same sensation she experienced reading Adam's messages. And now Mark's hand on her arm felt like an invitation.

Adam's hands gripping her thighs, head between her legs, red patent spike heels marking his shoulders as she

"Whatever it is can't be related to work. Nothing you're working on is that absorbing."

"What?' Jessica looked a Mark. "Sorry. What were you saying?"

Variations on the theme of Adam in a hotel room with assorted toys, props, and paraphernalia kept playing in her mind like the trailer for some high-concept indie film. She was two days away from seeing him, and the increasing distraction had rendered her virtually useless in the real world. Her only hope was that finally being with him would put an end to it, like a cymbal crash at the end of a concert.

It had started simply enough with a dream. Nearly every man Jessica had ever known had made a guest appearance in an erotic dream at one time or another, along with some she didn't know at all. She knew enough of psychology and brain chemistry to read nothing more into these visitations than perhaps a reminder that she hadn't talked to Jeff in too long, or that Evan's birthday was coming up. Then last month she had included a reference to her latest dream in one of her regular e-mails to Adam.

> Details, please? C'mon, throw me a bone here.

His response had been to the one line about the dream. She knew trying to interpret the emotional content of e-mail is the cause of more misunderstanding and flame wars than the content, itself, but it was hard not to read into Adam's request a sense of urgency and level of interest she hadn't anticipated.

> After a meeting in the City. Your room, a couple neckties, and that hotel ice that leaves tiny holes in the cubes as it melts.

Days passed without a response, and she wondered if she had gone too far. He eventually wrote from Las Vegas to ask if she had seen the underwater Cirque show, and Jessica assumed he had just reverted to their usual pattern of communication without giving the salacious nature of her last message a second thought. They had been friends for so long, they could go months without speaking or writing and yet never feel out of touch. Still, she couldn't help but worry about the shift in tone their last exchange had taken. Hard to judge someone's reaction to a conversation that only existed on-line. Not that Adam had ever been that easy to read.

Jessica still remembered the first time she met him. He was on stage, bathed in the perfect golden-pink light of a musical number. Even in full make-up, he was the most "male" person she had ever seen. Part of it was the role, but only part. He exuded sexuality the way some people are funny—effortlessly and automatically. She considered taking a class in the drama department just to meet him, to see if he was so compelling in person. Everything Jessica did was held to her exacting standards of practicality and efficiency. She had served as secretary or treasurer for so many different organizations she just accepted it as her natural role. Even her relationships with men, dating or otherwise, received the same rational scrutiny. But this, this—chemical attraction was new. Then one Friday night she answered the door as her roommate was changing for a date. And there he was.

"You must be Jess. I'm Adam."

He looked directly into her eyes and took her hand in both of his. A little buzz ran up her arm, as if she had held her fingers too close to the metal prongs while plugging in the lamp. In person he was much better and far worse. High cheekbones, deep-set eyes so dark they seemed black. Just a hint of musky cologne.

"Well, if I must be, then I guess I am."

Carrie walked out of the bedroom and Jessica watched the two of them leave for the first date of what would eventually turn into a marriage.

"Jess? Hello?"

Mark was waving his hand in front of her face. She blinked, then smiled.

"Okay, I'm *really* sorry." She glanced at her watch. "Maybe we should just head back."

"You've hardly eaten anything! What's up?" He lowered his voice. "Can I do anything?"

Jessica burst out laughing. He sounded so earnest, was obviously concerned, but picturing what he was offering to do without realizing it was too much. Mark looked so hurt she stopped immediately and reached across the table to touch his wrist.

"I'm not laughing at you."

"Well, you can't be laughing with me, 'cause I'm not laughing."

She squeezed his wrist then clasped his fingers. "I know I'm preoccupied, but it's something I have to deal with myself. I promise, it's nothing terminal, no deaths in the family, not even financial disaster. It's . . . frustrating more than anything. Okay?"

He leaned forward and raised her hand off the table with both his. "Okay. For now."

She couldn't break eye contact and his hands felt unusually warm. He excused himself and let go only after a prolonged silence. Jessica watched him turn the corner to the men's room and wanted to scream. Was it just a halo effect from her building desire for Adam, or was Mark really responding to her with a lot more than friendship?

Lifting her purse onto her lap, she crossed her legs and leaned back against the vinyl booth. She tensed her muscles and shifted the weight of the bag to a better position. Her breathing had just accelerated into soft staccato gasps when Mark reappeared at the end of the room. It was going to be close, but she didn't want to stop. She looked out the window, tracking him out of the corner of her eye, then covered the moan she couldn't quite stifle by jangling her keys and dropping her purse heavily onto the seat next to her as she began to slide out.

"My turn." Jessica skirted Mark without looking at him and moved away as quickly as she could without drawing attention. She saw the line at the women's restroom and ducked into the men's room instead, locking the door behind her. The face in the mirror was flushed, pupils dilated.

"You have got to get a grip!"

She counted ten slow, deep breaths in and out, then patted her face and chest with a damp paper towel. Adam gave her a hard time about using the men's room once.

"Look. Two single-person restrooms with locking doors. One has a line, one doesn't. What difference can it possibly make?"

"This one has a picture of a little man on it, Jess." He put on a mock stern expression.

She squinted up at the icon as she held the door for him to exit before she entered. "I don't see a penis, just arms and legs. I've got those."

Adam's laughter filled the hallway. He teased her, but obviously enjoyed and even appreciated her quirks. His relationship with Carrie had lasted five years, and while she grew more distant from both of them, Adam and Jessica remained friends.

He had gone into business, not acting, and had risen quickly to become VP of sales in first one tech company then another, each either bigger or sexier than the last. Adam traveled extensively and had relocated to Seattle, but he usually managed to have lunch or dinner with Jessica a couple times a year through the ups and downs of various dating disasters and longer term relationships for each of them. Somehow they were never both unattached at the same time. The sexual tension joined them for every meal, sitting quietly between them unaddressed and undiscussed. Until Jessica told him about the dream.

"Jess?"

The knocking on the door broke her reverie. She rolled her eyes at herself in the mirror and checked her watch.

"I know you're in there. Are you okay?"

"Geeze, can't a girl get a little privacy around here?"

Mark did an exaggerated double-take and stepped back.

"Oh, excuse me, sir. I must have the wrong door."

Jessica smacked him on the arm and left the restaurant ahead of him.

The drive back was nearly normal. Jessica forced herself to concentrate on what Mark was saying and reined in her free-range fantasies. Knowing that she could check her mail in five minutes had a calming effect.

Mark flashed his keycard and held the door to the building for her, then hesitated before they parted ways in the lobby.

"Jess . . ."

"I know."

She ran to her cubicle and pulled up her mail screen. Thirty-two messages, none from Adam. Not that there should be. Not that she was expecting more. He had sent the last message, and that wasn't more than a couple hours ago. Jessica got a cup of coffee and started to work on the All Company meeting presentation, but each set of bullet points was like an opportunity to list all the things she wanted to do or have done to her. It gave her a whole new perspective on Power Point. After the introduction and overview were finished, Jessica started checking her mail after each slide she finished. After two pointless hours, she grabbed her bag and left without talking to anyone.

```
Anything you want me to bring? Or wear?
Or do?
```

He wouldn't get the message before morning, maybe not even before he left, but just sending the words out into the ether relieved her anxiety at not hearing from him. She had deleted all the mail he sent to her work address, but if she could get a reply like the one about the panties sent to her home address, she could reread it and savor his phrases over and over, hearing them in his voice.

The response came back almost immediately.

```
Had to work late tonight. I have this
tremendous erection just thinking about
you right now.
```

Jessica abandoned all pretense that resistance was an option. That they were just going to have lunch. That she cared at all that he was married.

```
I have been wet for three weeks. Or is it
longer?
```

Almost a year had passed since she had seen Adam in person. They were both passing through O'Hare on their way to or from meetings East, and he was waiting for her at the gate. As always, he looked better than everyone around him, even though he was dressed casually in jeans and a button-down shirt with the sleeves rolled up. But the jeans were form-fitting and the shirt was tailored and made of Egyptian cotton the color of a Santa Fe sunset. His smile spread as she approached, and his eyes never left her face. The sight of him made her salivate.

After an enthusiastic hug and kiss, they walked arm in arm to the nearest bar, a watering hole too small to even be claimed by one of the ubiquitous airport chains. Adam ordered a bottle of champagne.

"What are we celebrating?"

"Winged flight! Old friends! A two-million dollar contract.! Your luminous face!"

Jessica laughed and held up her hands in surrender. In manic mode Adam reverted to his actor training and swept all around him into the show. "That's reason enough for me."

They talked life updates and movies and books and Broadway while they polished off the bottle and started a second. When she started to object, Adam said, "Hey, we're not driving!" Eventually, the conversation turned to relationships.

"How is Sarah? Didn't you just have an anniversary? I seem to recall standing on a beach in Maui about a year ago."

"How can you even remember that?" Adam shook his head. "I barely remember my own birthday. It must be one of those sex-linked things."

"You always remember my birthday."

He reached for her hand and took it in both of his, a familiar gesture that still made her a little dizzy. Or maybe it was the champagne.

"That's different."

They stayed that way, gazing into each other's eyes and the air shifted around them like the drop in barometric pressure preceding a storm. The moment was broken by a sweaty businessman with an unwieldy bag who staggered into the table. They both leaned back and picked up their glasses.

"So when will I be watching your wedding?"

Jessica shrugged. "I have high standards." She smiled at what she wasn't saying. "These days I'd settle for a good sexual outlet."

"Well, I'd be happy to watch that, too!"

They laughed, but their conversation was charged with more than affection. When Adam placed his hand on Jessica's back as they left the bar, she jumped. Neither one commented.

As the last call for her flight was announced, they shared an awkward embrace. Before she could board the plane, though, Adam shouted her name. He grabbed her in a real hug, turning his head to run his lips from just below her ear, across her neck, finishing with a kiss that felt more like a beginning. They parted without a word, and by the time the plane landed, Jessica had written off the whole thing as an alcohol-induced anomaly.

> Must be longer—I'd say it's been years of foreplay. Is there anything you want me to bring?

Jessica touched the screen, running her fingers across the words as if they were part of Adam.

> How about champagne? ;)

She called in sick the next day and went shopping just to get out of the house. Away from the computer. She could barely accomplish something as simple as ordering coffee; there was no way she could get any work done. The day passed in a haze of department stores and espresso and imagined sexual acrobatics with the edges blurred together so it was difficult to determine where the fantasies ended and real time began.

"This is crazy! Think about something besides sex!"

Jessica was berating her reflection in the Nordstrom mirror when a toilet flushed behind her. A flustered older woman scurried past her and out the door without washing her hands or making eye contact.

"Great. Now I'm reduced to scaring little old ladies in public facilities. Not to mention talking to mirrors." She checked under all the stalls, then pointed at her other self. "You are *not* like this."

Jessica willed herself not to look at the computer for an hour after she got home, then she broke down and sent one final message.

```
Tomorrow. (!)
```

Even knowing there would be no response, she checked her mail at eight and at nine. She checked again at nine-thirty and nine-forty five and ten. At ten-fifteen Jessica went to bed after rereading Adam's message about his tremendous erection. When her bladder prodded her out of bed at four in the morning, she tossed and turned and couldn't get back to sleep until she went to the computer and checked for new messages one more time.

The hotel lobby was all gilt and plush burgundy. Adam was sitting beneath a large potted palm tree ignoring the newspaper folded in his lap as he watched the traffic flow through the revolving door. He stood when he recognized her, letting the paper drop to the floor, and walked to intercept her. Jessica had been smiling since she parked the car, but the smile faded as she picked up speed to reach him. She could actually hear her pulse, a pounding louder than the ambient noise. She had a fleeting thought that she should be alarmed, but it was driven out by her need to get her hands on Adam. They did not embrace so much as merge, every possible surface pressed together, each wrapped around the other. When she opened her eyes, she saw that they had captured the attention of a small audience.

"You're shivering," Adam said as they separated just enough to move toward the elevators.

"Hurry," was all she could say.

Later Jessica wouldn't be able to remember anything of the ride in the elevator or the walk down the hall to the room. When the door closed behind them, she dropped her purse as Adam propelled her backward, lifting her onto the bed and beginning exactly as he had promised. She clutched the bedspread for traction with both hands, so hard was Adam driving against her. She was momentarily grateful for the soundproofing in luxury hotels before her sensible self was subsumed by another wave of climax. When he finally entered her after some measureless amount of time, she caught snapshots in the dresser mirror of knees and hands and intertwined bodies as they shed their clothes then shifted configuration again and again. Like flashes of strobe on a dance floor, the images were blurred in motion. Half the time she wasn't even sure which parts belonged to her. At the end, Jessica was pushing off the bed to balance on her shoulders looking up into Adam's face with her ankles crossed behind his head as he moved with her, holding back, making her wait, until the speed and force and tension made her beg him to finish. When the orgasm finally hit, she nearly blacked out.

"You better not be sleeping." Jessica ran her hand up Adam's leg and across his torso, pausing only at his belly button before coming to rest just below his right nipple. He was even more beautiful without clothes. She tried to decide if there was any part of him she hadn't tasted yet so she could start there next. Maybe after some room service.

Adam rolled over and pulled her into his arms, resting his head on her breasts. They had each taken a brief interlude in the bathroom before returning to bed for a little recovery. Jessica had not even been tempted to speak to her reflection, and took that as a very good sign. Something in the silence had shifted, though, from the smug contentment of post-coital exhaustion to something less relaxed, something waiting.

She ran her fingers through his unruly hair. "Are you okay?"

"Yes. No. I don't know. I'm really conflicted."

He propped himself on one elbow and looked at her with the moist eyes and deeply pained expression that could only be achieved by someone trained in The Method. He could not have achieved a faster chill with the bucket holding the champagne.

"What?"

Adam laced his fingers through hers. "There has always been something between us. Something amazing. Nothing can change that." He dropped his eyes. "But this isn't fair to Sarah."

Jessica dug around for the anger she thought she should feel, but couldn't find it. "You might have mentioned this at some point in the last couple weeks."

"I know. I'm sorry. It's just . . . I thought it would be okay. Because it's us."

She released his hand to hug him, then started collecting her clothes and putting them on in the order she found them, first a red shoe, then the black camisole, then the print skirt.

"You don't have to go."

She looked at him for a long time. He didn't look any less appealing forlorn and torn up than he had earnest and predatory. In fact, the whole conversation seemed to be stimulating for him as she watched. Or maybe that was just from watching her reverse strip tease.

"Yes. I do."

He got up and pulled on his pants, not saying anything until she was dressed and walking toward the door. He came up behind her and wrapped his arms around her just as she reached for the handle.

"I love you."

The looped film of fantasy sex scenes she had been replaying for days was now inter cut with real scenes, and those were even better. Playing simultaneously on her mental split-screen was every conversation they had had about relationships over all the years they had known each other. With the exception of one instance where he dated two women at the same time who thought he wasn't seeing anyone else, he had always been honest with his lovers and girl friends and wives. And he had been faithful in his marriages. Adam's reaction wasn't really a surprise. The surprise was that she had wanted him so badly she was willing, even eager, to forget everything else.

"I know."

Jessica drove home on automatic as she tried to pin down her emotions. Anger finally showed up, but at her own decision to ignore the obvious as much as at Adam's sudden shift. Hurt was there too, but oddly enough, all her feelings were trumped by an overwhelming desire to see him again. Everything else paled next to the memory of her building excitement as their messages became more detailed, the sensory overload when they finally connected. She was perplexed by her own reactions.

There were five messages on her machine, but none from Adam. Two were from Mark, clearly worried about her unexplained absence from work. Her e-mail was full of the usual spam that seemed to defy the filter along with half a dozen from Mark. Nothing new from Adam. She needed to figure out what was going on, started to write a garbled dissertation on deception and desire and fantasy. Spun theories about e-mail and lowered inhibitions, but she deleted it without even filling in the address. Jessica read Mark's mail just for distraction.

> Miss Perfect Organization would never blow off work without a good reason. Whatever you're going through, you don't have to do it alone.

She read the last message twice, then smiled. It had been sent just twenty minutes before.

> Have you ever been so completely consumed with desire that nothing else mattered? Had the best possible feelings come from wanting the wrong person in the worst way?

The response came back within minutes.

> Jess! Thank god you're okay!
> Everyone has chosen the wrong person at some point. You can't let it ruin your life. Do you want to tell me what's going on?
>
> Have you ever spent three weeks in a constant state of arousal? Have you ever had sex so fabulous you blacked out?
>
> Like most guys, I spent my entire adolescence in a constant state of arousal. :-)
> And I hope you won't think less of me if I admit the answer to question number 2 is "no".
>
> Nothing could lower you in my esteem. From time to time, I even see you in my dreams . . . .

###

Blue Juice

If she hadn't come back, I would have been fine. Really. I always wear long sleeves, but my hands look good. I was nowhere near resorting to my knuckles. I was only using veins no one could see, hadn't blown out any capillaries, still had a job. Sort of. She was the last thing I expected. Sophia. Sophia of the eyes I couldn't read. Sophia of the mouth that started as an intoxicating curve and ended in a hard line. For one more chance I would do anything.

Heroin wasn't my first drug of choice, it was just the fastest route to what I wanted. Which was oblivion. I considered becoming a Buddhist monk, but that road to nothingness is way too long. And winding. My introduction to opiates was surprising. Kind of like meeting a celebrity and having her ask for your autograph. You're naturally suspicious, but the flattery is too much to resist. So you don't.

Everyone has bad days. Lots of people have entire years that aren't so hot. Some black streaks last for decades. But you can get used to that burden, hunch your shoulders into the gloom and keep going. Real devastation comes from a single moment, watching what your life used to be shatter into whatever is left. And then you look for the way out.

My accountant gave me my first fix. I thought heroin was some kind of urban youth thing. Street culture, needle exchange programs and all that. Turns out there's this whole suburban circus of tightrope walkers tiptoeing overhead all the time right out in plain view. Hey, you pay your bills and show up at work and really, who cares what gets you through the day? Unless it's nicotine. Then you have to go outside or stand in little penned—in areas in airports and amusement parks.

Sophia might as well have been an opiate, the effect she had on me pretty much from the beginning. She would rest her fingers on my wrist and lean close in noisy restaurants, and I would watch her lips shaping glossy circles like blowing red kisses. Seeing her across the room made it hard to hear conversation around me. Sophia would turn, catch my eye, and give me a look that said no one else existed. Just knowing I might see her made my heart stutter in patterns that both disturbed and excited me. Like a tango performed by that Irish river guy. I didn't know it was even possible to feel like that. I wasn't quite sure if it was good or bad, I wasn't even sure those terms applied. I just knew I didn't want it to stop.

You can read all the descriptions of shooting up ever written. You can look at movies of the sweat and shakes and ratcheting vomit of withdrawal so graphic you feel it yourself, have to run, barely make the call to Ralph in time. It's all just words and pictures. Words and pictures like valentines are to love. If you haven't lived it, those two dimensions never translate to three. So here I am, waiting my turn, sitting next to a woman so enormous she hangs in folds over herself like the drapes in a renaissance painting. I have to look away to keep from calling her Jaba. George Lucas forgive me. The other side isn't any better. An old guy, skin stretched thin until it's almost transparent, tears running down his face from pain so excruciating it has rendered him silent. Whether the pain is physical or existential, I couldn't say.

When Sophia left, I developed hysterical blindness. Not the visual kind, the emotional kind. I couldn't see people anymore, couldn't feel them, couldn't feel anything but the whistling chasm edged with shards where my heart used to be. My so-called friends actually tried to set me up with dates, as if doing some twenty-five-year-old blonde for a few hours/days/weeks could fill that hole. That's the difference between like and love, between high and addiction. At some point it isn't a scale anymore, it's an absolute. On-off. One-zero. Life-death.

Naltrexone is an opiate blocker. It hooks up to the same sites endorphins would if they hadn't already been shoved out by heroin, which is so efficient at sucking up to those sites that the endorphin manufacturing process shuts down entirely. Hence that whole withdrawal thing. This clinic has the Evelyn Woods version of detox. No methadone, no meetings, just a little nap and an intravenous chemical flush. Boom! Just like that, you'rc clean! Apparently there's some follow-up naltrexone to keep those receptors from screaming for their missing sweetheart, but I think I can live with that.

I don't think it's just linguistic coincidence that heroine and heroin sound exactly alike. Some women, you let them in, let them drive your story, and it's just like a needle. Pop pop pop, under the skin, into the blood, slamming the heart until you're sure you can't take anymore but you still can't get enough and you keep pushing, keep trying, do whatever it takes to be with her. Because it isn't your story anymore.

Technically, this is an experimental treatment of last resort, and I don't qualify. Technically. Like so many things in life,though, this technicality responded well to cash. Sophia doesn't know and isn't going to. One step, one afternoon, one IRA cashed in, and I'm back to where I was when I met her. Or that neighborhood, anyway.

Disappointment was the reason she said she left. She was disappointed in me. I was a disappointment. I didn't say enough. Or I said too much. Or maybe I just said all the wrong things. Hell, I don't know. Disappointment isn't like anger or hurt, something big you can actually identify and fix. Disappointment is more like resentment, a steady dripdripdrip of negative that eats away at a relationship until a hole is worn right through and all the love leaks out.

They showed me a film of the procedure before they took my money. The stuff in the tubes running all around and into the guy was the color of some artificially enhanced popsicle or one of those girlie turquoise rum drinks that comes with an umbrella. Made calling it a chemical cocktail seem more actual than metaphorical. But he woke up like the desire had been nothing more than a bad dream, like the need and the hurt and the want and the pure relentless joy were all imaginary. It's a cheap trick ending for a movie, but jesus! Just think if you could do it in real life.

In a few hours, that'll be me. The new me. Me post—blue juice salvation. I hope it works, for Sophia. I hope it works for Sophia.

###

Less is More

Larry stood at the intersection he crossed at least twice a day. The same intersection he drove through on the days he didn't work. The intersection he used to call "walk and don't walk," but the joke sounded stale even to him after three years. At first it seemed like a gift to be able to walk to work, like he had won the lottery. When the position opened up at the new location in downtown Mountain View, he couldn't believe his luck. Now each morning as he watched the trains blow by and waited for the signal at Central, the disbelief remained. Only the luck had changed.

Walk sign is on. Walk sign is on. Walk sign is on.

The Central/Castro signal is one of those talking ones where some guy gives you instructions about crossing the street. Larry wondered how they determined which ones would talk. Traffic speed? Proximity to a railroad crossing? Census information indicating at least one blind person in the neighborhood? That possibility gave him the willies—a little too Big Brother. Mostly he just stirred the voice into the background noise as he trudged across with his head bent as if gale forces blew down Castro toward the distant Bay.

It's funny how you can think your life is just fine, pretty good, even, until somebody else offers an unsought second opinion. Like one of those magnifying mirrors, some people reflect back the big gaping pores that you had managed to avoid examining too closely. Larry owned a condo, took vacations, ate out all the time. He had plenty of friends when he wanted company and nobody to bother him when he didn't. Isn't that the perfect life? Maybe he wasn't going to cure cancer anytime soon, but that hadn't exactly been the prediction next to his yearbook photo, either. At their twentieth reunion, Ariel, a former cheerleader who looked better than nature intended, grilled Larry like a prosecutor. At the end of the evening after enough mai tais for the whole squad, she told Larry she was sorry he was still alone.

Technical writing is the sort of job you can't explain to anyone who doesn't actually do it. "You write manuals?" Sometimes. "So *you're* the guy making up directions I can't follow for my software installation?" I hope not. "Are you a programmer?" No. Larry didn't so much choose this job as wash up against it. He had to work at something after college, and job by job, company by company, this was where the flow left him. He hardly knew how he came to be here, why should anyone else understand what he did? Maybe all jobs are indecipherable to the uninitiated. Maybe everyone toils in shadow, unknown and unknowable.

Some people live in their work, see it as home and family and reason for being. That might be okay—if you find the perfect career, love what you do. If you just occupy a cubicle, though, shuffle paper or widgets or words, that attitude is a recipe for certain despair. Larry looked upon people like that with a mixture of derision and sympathy. He knew better than to mistake any job for his actual life. But he also knew what it was to long for complete immersion in something, to have your identity easily defined. To be able to label yourself to strangers when asked what you do. Manager. Engineer. Artist. Father.

About the time Larry reached the midpoint of the intersection, the message always changed. It was crackly and garbled and even if the speaker weren't broken, the new line seemed redundant—what did you need to know at that point in the road?—so he had never really listened to it. Today, though, the voice was clear.

Less is more. Less is more. Less is more.

He stopped in the intersection and looked around. The couple walking ahead of him was deep in conversation and all the cars had their windows up. The source of the sound was hard to place; the voice came from everywhere and nowhere, like traffic sounds or God. A car honked and he jogged the rest of the way across.

The message at Central faded as Larry's morning filled with minutia from the freshly minted Ph.D. whose diploma not only qualified him to write code, but apparently rendered him an expert in grammar, typography and aesthetics as well. Interpersonal relations must have been left out of the curriculum, however, and he was scorned by the other engineers and despised by the nontechnical staff. Larry had called him a puckered sphincter once and the name stuck. Now everyone referred to the guy as PS. Arrogance was usually a quality Larry valued, because it was mostly just self-confidence that had been mislabeled by the jealous. In this case, however, the word didn't even scratch the surface. About once a week Larry considered telling his supervisor that somebody needed to have a talk with the guy before his career flamed out in the first stage, but today wasn't one of those days. It was hard to have sympathy for anyone who didn't get the concept of white space.

Lunch couldn't come too soon, but it didn't anyway. Larry started to walk home to eat leftovers and read the paper, but halfway there, the memory of the intersection engulfed him like a following sea. *Less is more. Less is more. Less is more.* His belly felt full of helium. He just didn't want to hear it again. Larry stopped dead on the sidewalk, forcing a man behind him to swerve suddenly and give him a hard look, then pivoted like a cadet on parade drill and walked through the first open door. It was a bar he had never set foot in during daylight. At 1:00 in the afternoon the tables were empty and the three old guys at the bar were definitely drinking their lunch. They shouted "Norm!" in unison as Larry entered, laughing at their own joke before returning to what sounded like an old ongoing argument. They looked more like retired professors than bar flies, all in wool sweaters and wire rim glasses and sitting in order from completely bald to full beard and pony tail. They looked like a hair replacement ad. Larry sat at the end of the bar angled slightly away from them.

"Uh . . ." he scanned the chalkboard wedged in between the whiskey shelf and the world beer collection when the girl behind the bar put a napkin and a bowl of peanuts in front of him. It was a short list. "I'll have the reuben. And an Anchor Steam."

When she came back with the beer, he looked at her more carefully. Maybe it was the eyebrow ring and tattoo that subtracted a decade from the first impression, but she had definitely seen the seventies, if not part of the sixties. Her hair was a color Pantone hadn't catalogued, and her mouth turned up at one corner like her world came with a laugh track and better writers than yours.

"Have you ever crossed the Central intersection?"

Her eyebrows shot up; he wanted to take it back but it was too late. At least she didn't back slowly away.

"Is that anything like the Maginot Line?"

He spit beer onto the bar. The emeritus trio grinned and toasted.

"I'm sorry, I never do that. I mean, I don't . . ."

She smiled and waved it off. "Unfair advantage. I usually go the other direction down Castro. Why?"

"This morning the signal said, 'Less is more.'" She twitched the pierced eyebrow up in a way he had always envied in others.

"Did I say that out loud?"

She laughed and shook her head. "I'll get your reuben."

The sandwich was better than expected, but it was delivered by a pink-faced fat guy in an apron. Larry was pretty sure he had scared off the bartender. She made him think of Lisa, not so much how she looked, but the way she looked at things. Lisa had that same sort of secret smile and playful wit, but she looked like a Ralph Lauren model, icy blond and expensively dressed. Hitchcock would have loved her. Larry had. He still did. Sometimes, though, love isn't enough. Larry should have told that to Ariel.

Larry's mind wandered during the All-Hands meeting that afternoon. *Less is more. Less is more. Less is more.* Not exactly the current company philosophy. Although it could be one of those obscure marketing campaigns where all you remembered was the catch phrase. Tight as government budgets always were, maybe the city council had gotten corporate sponsorship for the traffic signals. This crossing brought to you by Mini Cooper.

The CTO was test-driving his new customer presentation, and just as he hit the climax where the graphics demonstrating their chip's superiority were displayed, Larry realized the guy was using the old Power Point slides. After having Larry spend most of the week revising the whole presentation and half the night before redoing all the graphs, they used the original set anyway. His eyes hit the ceiling so hard he was sure it was audible. Over-thinking was a common problem, but confusing motion with progress was even worse. Larry had been with a lot of startups, and he thought this was going to be the one. In the Valley you had a startup the way men in other parts of the country had a mistress. First it was all infatuation and promises, knowing that you'd finally found the real thing. Then there were disappointments, unexpected details, things that didn't add up. Finally there were recriminations and self-doubt and a substantially reduced bank account. Was it optimism or masochism that brought that light of belief back again and again? Or was it just the wanting?

At first Larry and Lisa wanted the same things. They came together so fast it felt like picking up where they'd left off in a past life. They liked the same movies, traded favorite books, sat together in silence for hours. Sometimes Lisa would catch him watching her from across the room, and in response she would send him one of her complicated smiles, not the least bit self-conscious. He asked her to move in with him after only two months. After four more months of explaining in vain all the qualities that made her hard to live with, Lisa relented.

The company meeting stretched to approach infinity, as if they were being sucked into a black hole. Larry kept checking the clock to make sure the hands were moving. The Chief Scientist was introducing the new celebrity engineer they'd snared with stock options and a refrigerator full of Red Bull. Watching the guy's lips move as he droned on, Larry could have sworn he said, "Less is more." *Less is more.* Less what? Wanting less, having less, being less? More what? More rewarding, more fulfilling, more enlightened? For awhile Larry had had more than he believed was possible.

No contraceptive method short of sterilization is 100 percent effective. There's this cultural math bias that automatically rounds up anything over 99, but that's just wishful thinking. Even if the failure rate is only one in a thousand, that one might be you. On Friday afternoons Lisa usually got home first, then met Larry at the door with some froufy cocktail with way too many ingredients tarting up the alcohol. Her "drink of the week." She knew he preferred beer, but it had become one of those running domestic jokes that took on sentimental value through repetition. When he walked into silence that Friday almost a year ago, even though Lisa's car was home, his saliva dried up and his throat constricted. She was sitting in the living room with a half-empty bottle of wine and full glass, staring at the corner of the ceiling the way cats do, intently focused on something you can't see. She didn't look at him right away, and when she did, he started to cry.

"I'm pregnant."

Larry blew out the breath he didn't realize he'd been holding. "Thank God! I thought you were dying. Or leaving."

Her eyes changed, the line of her mouth shifted. He knew he had said the wrong thing, but he had no idea why or how to fix it. Losing her was unthinkable; anything else seemed manageable. He watched his future flash before him in scenes involving baseball and school plays and tried not to smile. When Lisa told him she was going away for the weekend to think, he said, "Okay." What he thought was, "Marry me."

The best thing about a Friday afternoon All-Hands was the complete lack of expectation for productivity afterwards. In the nineties there would have been beer and pizza, but Larry thought the slow slide into the weekend was even better. He could buy his own beer. And he really felt no compelling need to socialize with his coworkers. Or maybe he was just getting old. At five o'clock, a good two hours earlier than usual, Larry grabbed his bag and jacket and headed home.

"Hey!"

The sound registered, but Larry didn't turn.

"It's not 'less is more'."

That stopped him, and he turned back toward the bar he'd been in earlier. The bartender grinned at him from the door and went back inside. Larry hesitated, almost kept going, then followed her in.

Now half the tables were full and a waitress scurried back and forth refilling drinks and slaking the week's end thirst of the growing crowd. Larry took a seat next to the three professors, mentally calculating how long they had been there. The bartender put an Anchor Steam down in front of him.

"Bless the Pope."

"What?"

She laughed. "The signal says, 'Bless the Pope.' I checked."

"Aw, she's just pullin' your leg," the bald one in the faded red sweater broke in. "It says 'Press for more' in case you need extra time."

The middle drunk with the not quite conceded hairline whacked his companion on the arm. "When *you* cross it says, 'Useless dope!'"

The man with the beard and long hair snickered and toasted. "Good one, Bob. Wait, I know! It's 'Trestle load' if there's a train in the station. Or maybe just 'Cross Castro' if there's not."

The three men exchanged assorted hand gestures of a congratulatory nature while Larry and the bartender looked on. She shook her head and shrugged, offering Larry an almost wistful smile.

"Well, it sounded like Bless the Pope to me."

He nodded in response and took a drink. "Less is more. Bless the Pope. Those are close. Useless dope is pretty good, too."

"Dress the poor!"

"Fearless hope!"

"Restless whore!"

"Senseless chores!"

Not only were the three regulars shouting out alternative interpretations, but the rest of the seated customers and the row standing behind them had joined in. It was like some drunken poetry slam or bad linguistic jazz.

"Witless bore!"

It went on and on, variations on a theme of three syllables with "ess" and a long "o" and occasionally even a traffic-related subject. By the time it wound down, Larry had drained two more beers and had ordered a burger. He had a couple more beers for dessert. Afternoon became evening became night, but from Larry's chair time had slowed to polaroids. He could see words like cartoon balloons. When he looked at the regulars, all the years they had been there and all the years they would continue to sit there were woven together in a continuous cord. And the bartender. The bartender poured and served and laughed and chatted and occasionally drank from a glass behind the bar. Her hair went from magenta to aubergine to something seen only in sunsets and vampire movies and the light glinted off her eyebrow ring like it was excalibur.

When it felt like time was moving fast enough that he might be able to make it home, Larry piled assorted bills on the bar and drained his last glass. Before he could slide off the stool, a soft hand grasped his wrist. The bartender leaned over the bar and looked into his eyes.

"You shouldn't believe everything you hear from traffic signals. Less is *not* more! *More* is more! Anyone who tells you otherwise is a coward. Or he wants something you've got."

She searched his face, then suddenly shifted forward far enough to be nose to nose. Just when it seemed she would kiss him, she smiled a big, joyful smile and touched a finger to his lips before spinning away to respond to the call of the waitress.

Larry sat frozen for moments, trying to gauge his grasp of reality. He could still feel her fingerprints on his lips and wrist, so he was sure it had happened. He edged through the bodies and walked out the door with only a slight deviation from a straight line. Not having to drive to work wasn't the only advantage of his home's location. It was early by Friday night standards, not much after ten, and Castro was humming with pedestrians and cars, street musicians and dog walkers, first dates and couples pushing strollers.

The Monday after Lisa had the abortion, Larry had rushed to get home. She had insisted on going alone, told him it was easier that way.

He brought flowers and her favorite chinese take-out and planned to spend the evening reestablishing the equilibrium of their relationship. Early as it was, he wasn't really surprised that her car wasn't there. He was surprised that none of her belongings were, either. Everything was gone—all the clothes, the make-up, her dishes and furniture. It was as if she had been deleted from his life.

The envelope on the glass coffee table lay apart from all the books and magazines as if they were just as afraid to touch it as he was. When he finally read it, there was nothing in it he didn't know. He could have written it himself if he hadn't been trying so hard all along to write a different version of their story. Larry waited as long as he could before he gave in and tried to contact her by e-mail. His message bounced.

Larry stood at the intersection of Castro and Central waiting once again for the light to change. Is less more? Maybe we should dress the poor and the whores, press the door, test the score, ask for more, bless the Pope and stress for hope. Maybe all those things were true for someone. Larry watched the signal flash as the man appeared. It didn't matter what the garbled part said, he realized. The important message was the first one.

Walk sign is on. Walk sign is on. Walk sign is on.

Larry stepped off the curb and started across the street.

###

In A Yellow Wood

Callie stared openly at the woman in the next check-out line. Her dishwater hair hung in a limp ponytail and the lines on her face put her on the other side of forty. She had that look of surrender on her face, an expression of blank defeat that, combined with the blue-tinge under her eyes, said she had given up all hope of sleep. The little pink bundle strapped to her chest like the creature from *Alien* told the rest of the story. "There but for the grace of contraception go I," thought Callie.

Two months after her forty-third birthday, Callie's period did not arrive on schedule. Because her reproductive cycle had been relentlessly predictable for more than thirty years, her first thought was menopause. Her second thought was panic. Diapers and spit-up and sleep deprivation of the magnitude used to break hostages were more than a decade behind her. Callie didn't say anything to anyone. She knew her husband would just tell her to do whatever she wanted. No need to get everyone all stirred up over a false alarm. When a week had passed, she started to picture their lives with a newborn inserted into the already complicated balance of school and soccer and work and ballet and piano and karate. She also remembered how it felt to be nudged from the inside as if sharing a private joke, to hold a new person she had made, personally, out of nothing. And then there was that milky warm baby smell. The next day her period came on with a vengeance, and she didn't replay the infant scenario again.

In the exit line from the parking lot, Callie was behind the zombie mom waiting to make a left. The gray clouds overhead sent a few warning drops before letting loose a downpour. Traffic hesitated as everyone turned on lights and wipers. Callie turned right, watching her otherself disappear around a corner in the rearview mirror.

These close encounters with her parallel selves had been happening a lot lately. Last week it was a potter at the craft faire. A smiling woman draped in wildly colored silks sat surrounded by vessels in shades of lavender, sage, and violet. Callie smiled back and remembered how much she used to love the feel of the slip, forming bowls like holding life in her hands, and the sense of time suspended as the wheel and the world would spin spin spin.

Callie had always been artistic but never called herself an artist. Even in college, those suspended adolescent years of few responsibilities and perfectly elastic ties, she already knew she lacked the obsession required to make art her life. Her interests were many and varied, and she refused to commit. Instead she worked in frenzied bursts of creativity, making all her Christmas gifts one year, selling a few pieces to an artisan gallery another, taking the blue ribbon at a juried show. Her jobs became more demanding, and so did her relationships. She was promoted, got married, had children. The call of the clay and the glaze and the kiln faded. After her second baby was born, Callie sold her supplies and used the kiln she couldn't quite part with to store Christmas ornaments.

At the end of the show, Callie passed the potter's booth again on the way out. A tall bearded man was helping the woman wrap the display pieces in newspaper and stack boxes to ferry to the parking lot. They touched each other often as they talked, a conversation about dinner and driving back over the hill. Callie had closed her eyes and smelled the ocean, and for a moment the fogdamp breath of solitude and quiet creation from that other life filled her. Then she opened her eyes and went home.

The mailman was walking up the driveway just as Callie pulled in. He handed her a bundle of letters and magazines as she stepped out of the car, and she shoved the whole stack into the grocery bag without looking at it, running to get out of the rain. When the perishables were safely stored, she flipped through the water-spotted mail. After she'd put aside the bright greeting card envelopes she wasn't ready to open, the only thing left not advertising or bills was her alumni magazine. She had never joined the Alumni Association, hadn't been to a reunion, couldn't have sent them more than fifty bucks in all the years since graduation, and yet, no matter where she lived, they always found her. She had a theory that if the FBI contracted out to college alumni associations, no one would ever go missing.

The Class Notes section was always the best part. Once in awhile there was someone there she was actually interested in reading about, but more often than not it was the usual suspects in a parade of wedding announcements, baby pictures (in tiny football jerseys, of course,) job promotions, major relocations and international adventures with a few national awards thrown in for good measure. It made sense, really. After all, who would want to share their failed marriages, infertility struggles, downsizing layoffs, eldercare burdens and suburban rut with everyone who ever set foot on campus?

Callie skimmed through to the obituaries at the end. The quarter-page photo in the middle of the text stopped her. Robert Anderson, an emeritus professor from the psychology department, had died after a long illness. He had just finished rewriting his classic textbook, the one that was the standard introductory course in every major university. The picture next to the obit showed him standing at a white board beside a smiling woman with salt-and-pepper spiky hair and dark-framed glasses.

The year Callie had spent editing his first rewrite was one of her best jobs ever. She was the only undergraduate in the group, but Dr. Anderson treated her just the same as his grad students. When she took his cognitive psych class, he told her she had insight and a facility with language and encouraged her to apply for the Ph.D. program. The world of academia was a familiar and comfortable place for Callie. She imagined living out her life on campus, never leaving but simply changing roles from undergraduate to grad student to assistant professor to professor, maybe changing schools but always safely cocooned by the university. The more she pictured it, the finer the line between comfort and suffocation seemed to become. When she told Dr. Anderson she wasn't even taking the GRE, he was sympathetic but obviously disappointed. He shook her hand at graduation, and she sent him a Christmas card for a couple years, but she never saw him again.

The rain hammered on the roof in a steady flow that might have been soothing if it weren't for the syncopated bongo drip in the down spouts. Callie stood at the kitchen window watching drops splatter across the back patio like it was being strafed. Water streaming down the glass blurred her reflection and gave back the long waves of hair she'd cut off almost two decades before. She had an hour till the kids came home, a pile of bills, and e-mail that hadn't been read for three days, but she couldn't make herself move. The cold wet always made Callie feel dense and slow, as if the change were more about gravity than weather. The year she'd spent in Seattle had practically made her suicidal. Within a month of moving, she was convinced the caffeine stop on every corner was intentional urban planning—the antidepressant equivalent of fluoridating the water.

It wasn't nearly enough for her, though. The entire episode would have been a nightmare if she hadn't met Greg.

Greg was impervious to the weather, both physically and emotionally. He ran and hiked rain or shine, and when he smiled, which was often, everyone near him seemed illuminated. They knew a few people in common, hung out at the same coffee house, so Callie had noticed him even before they were introduced. She found him incredibly irritating. She hated her job, hated her apartment, hated her life. And she really hated attempts to jolly her out of her foul mood, which was just the sort of thing someone like Greg would do. The first time they had a conversation alone, she braced herself for a relentlessly chirpy diatribe about making lemonade, but Greg talked about the summer he spent in the jungles of Ecuador and his plans for a "third-world bank" to make small business loans in transitional countries.

Callie discovered that closing the drapes and spending every free hour in bed could be at least as uplifting as a trip to the beach. When the job offer she'd been waiting for in the Bay Area came through, Greg asked her to go with him to Mexico instead. She told him to give her six months. She cut her hair, bought two new suits and moved to San Jose. Three weeks later she met her husband. Callie still got postcards from Greg once or twice a year, never from the same place.

The house felt too small, as if it were shrinking in the storm. Callie paced aimlessly from one room to the next, watering a plant, adjusting a picture frame, not quite able to focus or land. She finally flopped on the couch and turned on the television. One of those news magazine shows was on, with the interviewer questioning experts about the newly available vaccine to prevent cervical cancer. A polished blonde in a scarlet suit, the CEO of a national women's organization, was speaking in support of the vaccine. Callie recognized her as her successor at the women's shelter.

When they offered Callie the regional directorship, she was thirty-five years old with two kids under five. She loved her work with the local network, had managed to structure her childcare and work time so she had the perfect balance—barely. Her husband told her to do whatever she wanted. Callie turned down the promotion and took a part-time position instead. Two years later her position was eliminated. She didn't send out any resumes.

Callie believed in living consciously. It had practically been her motto. In every decision from the little ones, like what to wear, to the big ones, like having kids, she was certain she had made a thoughtful choice. In the year since her pregnancy scare, though, she had begun to wonder how much of what she thought was chosen direction had been more like floating with the current. Maybe her life hadn't been a powerful ship whose course she directed but merely an engineless, rudderless piece of driftwood that only looked purposeful because it moved so fast. Perhaps it had always been the case that she didn't so much make things happen as have things happen to her. Or was it as simple as choosing the path *more* traveled-by every single time the road diverged?

The rain grew quiet and then stopped. The trees and the eaves dripped in time with the down spouts. Callie turned off the television and listened for the sound of the car in the driveway. Allie and Josh would be bickering when they walked in, more out of habit than for any particular reason. They would have bags of books and the cake they'd picked up on the way home. Josh had her eyes and smile, and Allie favored her father, dark wavy hair and perfect cheek bones. Callie had spent ten years tending her children like a garden. She loved watching them when they weren't looking, seeing the infant and the toddler nested within the teenager like those Russian dolls. Sometimes she watched her husband when he wasn't looking and could not see anything but shiny veneer.

They had gotten married and bought a house and had a baby in rapid succession, going from single to family without passing GO. Their friends all told them how perfect their life was, and even strangers in restaurants stopped to congratulate them on their lovely well-mannered children. Their lives were full of activities and travel and work and school, without the burden of dysfunction that seemed to settle on so many families. But more and more this year Callie had realized that most of her time was spent either with the kids or doing things for them. The rest of the time she was alone. And she had been alone for years. That woman standing in line at the post office, picking up dry cleaning, grabbing a quick sandwich at the deli? *That* woman she saw everyday. Out of all the possible selves, that was the one she had become.

The door slammed open and the two people she loved most in the world crowded through.

"Happy birthday, Mom!"

She smiled and hugged them both. Knowing how way leads on to way, she could stand it a little longer. After a couple more years of high school, there would be another branch in the road. And that choice would make all the difference.

# # #

Last Writes

```
To: annab@mu.edu
From: pgarvin@lastwrites.net

There was a time when I thought the sun
rose and set on you. Unfortunately, so did
you.

                                      Paul
```

Anna read the message again. Why was that bastard contacting her after all these years? She had almost deleted it, unopened, with the rest of the spam, but the name caught her eye. Paul Garvin. The great romance of her last year in college. The man she was meant to be with. The most egocentric person she had ever met, a title which remained unchallenged twenty years later.

The break up had been ugly and unsatisfactory. After she had turned down her first choice grad school and accepted admission at a local university to be closer to him, Paul had announced that he was going to be living in Japan for a year to improve his brush technique and learn the language. He was inconsiderate, deceptive, unable to relate to other people. She was "controlling, manipulative, and unwilling to take responsibility for her own decisions." When the verbal machetes stopped swinging, the relationship was shredded beyond repair.

She reread the message, feeling her cheeks warm at the insult, then hit delete and took care of the rest of her mail before her morning lecture. A seminar and a block of office hours later, Paul popped back into her thoughts like a persistent web ad.

Anna sighed. "Oh, all right!"

She turned to her computer and googled Paul Garvin. Finding out where he was or what he had been doing all these years didn't commit her to actually talking to him. Her first attempt gave her way too many hits, none of them him at first glance. Anna was surprised to discover she remembered his middle initial, and typed that in. One by one she opened the half-dozen listings. He had delivered a paper at a linguistics conference defending his controversial translation of an obscure poem by Aeschylus. He was the VP of Marketing for an on-line dating service. He had been investigated for insider trading. A photograph of him running with the bulls had appeared in the both the Chronicle and the Times. He had run for Governor of California.

"You and everybody else, pal."

Anna left the photo up on the screen, studying the grainy image for resemblance to the man she had known. He looked like he was laughing, but the clenched fists and straining tendons showed how hard he was working. That was the Paul she had fallen in love with, the man who did nothing halfway, who reveled in the thrill of new experience. The runners behind him were obscured or out of focus, but at the bottom of the picture, almost out of frame, Anna could just make out a hand under Paul's left foot. That was Paul, too. The one she had left. Or had he left her?

Maybe he was right about her being self-centered, but why tell her now? Anna shut down her computer, collected her things. It didn't matter. Her heart, a fallen runner, Paul Garvin was still stepping on anything and anyone in his way. That was all she needed to know about him. She locked the office door behind her.

```
To: justinxman@springvalley.com
From: pgarvin@lastwrites.net

The Professor calls and I must respond, J-man.
Com silent. Until our next battle . . .

                                       Midas
```

Justin frowned at Paul's e-mail. Why the special notice? Paul was always being sent on missions without him. That was one of the sacrifices that had to be made by the champions of justice. Your battles are chosen for you. You go where you are needed.

It seemed he had always known he wasn't like other boys, but Justin didn't realize his true nature until his baby brother told him about the X-men. A mutant! It all fell into place then, and it explained his powers. And the voices. All the orders he had been receiving became clear. He had a purpose, and Paul was the only one who knew his secret identity.

When they were kids, before their parents died, Justin overheard Mom tell someone on the phone that Paul was a "golden boy." Justin had been reading the Encyclopedia of Myths and Legends, and he couldn't wait to get his brother alone.

"That must be your power! Your mutation. Mom would know, right? Your X-man name can be Midas!"

Paul had laughed as he walked a quarter back and forth across his knuckles then pulled it from Justin's ear. "I dunno, J-man. You think everything I touch will turn to gold?"

Justin had leaned toward Paul to keep from being overheard. "Just be careful you don't destroy what you love."

Over the years, even after Justin was reassigned to undercover work at Spring Valley, the brothers would talk about their missions and the latest top-secret directions Justin had received. One Spring Paul brought a computer and taught Justin to use e-mail. After that his work kept him away most of the time.

Justin read the message again. Com silent. He would have to wait to hear from Paul. He closed his eyes and waited for his own instructions from Professor X.

```
To: vic_desmond@victorious.com
From: pgarvin@lastwrites.net

Many that are first shall be last; and the
last shall be first.

                                         G
```

Vic felt very warm. He looked over his shoulder involuntarily, then rose to close the door to his office. He had to steady himself on the back of his chair when his knees failed unexpectedly. How could this mail have been sent today? And what server was it on?

Reading the message over and over didn't add any clarity. When the words lost all meaning, Vic buried his face in his hands, then scratched his scalp in a frantic massage that left tufts of hair standing out from his head. What in the hell was Garvin up to? Or what had he been up to, anyway. Could he have leaked the reorg plan? Surely he wasn't stupid enough to mention the merger. Or was this more personal? Why did he have to be so damn cryptic all the time!

Using the same access code HR used to do routine scans for inappropriate mail on company time, Vic searched all the employee mailboxes for anything from Paul Garvin.

"Company . . . company . . . . joke . . . . joke . . . . joke . . . . joke . . . crap!" Vic muttered to himself as he opened and closed messages as fast as he could. This would take longer than he had. He checked the address on his message from Garvin and narrowed the search to mail from lastwrites.net. Nothing. Maybe everything was going to be okay. Maybe the e-mail wasn't actually a threat.

Paul Garvin was like the tale of two employees—he was the best of hires, he was the worst of hires. Vic had personally chosen him over three other strong candidates for the VP position because he was the only predator in the bunch. Vic had learned something with each new company he built, and one of those lessons was to look beyond the resume and into a candidate's eyes. Some people are lunch, and some people do the munching. He knew who he wanted on his side.

When subscriptions tripled the in the second quarter Garvin was on board, Vic was only mildly surprised. He expected great things from his management team and he got them. When Garvin started making suggestions outside his area, Vic encouraged it. A little internal competition amped up productivity. But then the bastard started questioning his decisions, actually contradicted Vic at a Board meeting. The reorganization brought resistance from the beginning. Everybody but finance had concerns, but Garvin was unyielding in his opposition.

"You're wrong on this, Vic. The numbers for @dinner just don't add up. They aren't bringing enough to the party, and we are going to have to dump half the staff to make this deal fly. Mark my words, with the bad press on this, in six months we'll be the ones grabbing our ankles. I can't let you do it."

Imagine the balls! Telling Vic what he could do with his own company? He pretended to reconsider and sent Garvin to Ventura, then moved up the schedule to announce the merger at the next all-hands. Even if Garvin got wind of it, he wouldn't have time to cause trouble.

And after yesterday's call, Vic knew there was no chance Garvin would make a surprise appearance at the meeting.

Vic leaned back and blew out a deep breath. Screw the mystery mail! He checked his Palm and decided to hit the gym before the big announcement.

```
To: bossman@lastwrites.net
From: pgarvin@lastwrites.net

Good news: "living" proof that it works!
Bad news: guess I won't be getting any
friends and family at the IPO . . .

                                  Garvin
```

Bruce Miller typed the day's password into his laptop to get him through the firewall and into the company computer. Damn that Garvin if he had gotten Peter or Alex to go along with one of his practical jokes! When he agreed to be part of the consumer test groups, Garvin had said he looked forward to deciding which last words he wanted to have and who would be on the receiving end. He had given useful feedback and had even been the one to suggest the quarterly prompt for updates. "What if you died tomorrow and your girlfriend didn't get a message because you hadn't updated your list in over a year?"

Paul Garvin had turned the operation into a game in that way he had of manufacturing challenge in everything just to maintain his interest. His goal for his final communications was brevity and obscurity. How little could he say and still convey something meaningful? He would occasionally forward one of his better messages to Bruce as he honed his technique. At one point, Garvin had fifty messages (the maximum allowed) all in haiku.

A desk, a task, work;
Our lives intersected there,
Wish you were here now.

Those had been Bruce's favorites, most an odd combination of beauty and snottiness. But this was an official notification, and he wasn't laughing.

The list of client status with recent postings and scheduled postings was longer than he expected. He had always heard that more deaths occurred right after the holidays, but it was disconcerting to have the evidence scrolling across his screen. He typed a quick message to Peter to get someone to start tracking the data by categories as it came in, season, time of day, whatever. Their client base wasn't big enough yet and was still too regional to be statistically significant, but eventually the data yield could be very interesting.

As he typed, Bruce avoided reading the screen he had pulled up. Dread had settled upon him like a cloak, and for the first time in longer than he could remember, Bruce was reluctant to know the answer. Paul Garvin was unlike anyone Bruce had ever known. He could reason like an engineer, but he introduced electricity into every conversation. Of course, sometimes that meant adding energy, and sometimes it was merely shocking. People took Garvin the wrong way, or they got him exactly right and just didn't like him, but not Bruce.

The breakdown was still fresh enough to make him wince just thinking about "the black hole," as he liked to call it. When he was living in his car, a wraith in the corridors at work, more animated on-line than in person, it was Garvin who took him in. It was Garvin who made him bathe, took him to the doctor, spoon-fed him until the meds kicked in. Paul Garvin gave him his life back.

Bruce sent the message and scanned the list for confirmation of what he already knew. When the screen was too blurry to read, he closed he laptop and went back to bed.

To: bball@stateu.or.edu
From: digiman@univ.film.org

Dude! Check my website instantly—driving back from the OC at the end of break, we were behind this hellabad crash. I totally got it all! A white beemer was passing everybody then BOOM, the dude was airborne! Seriously, it was like gymnastics for cars, easily a 9.5.

Image is a little rough, but I got a nice effect from the tail light spin as the car rolled. Turns out it took an hour to find the body where it was thrown—wish I had *that* footage! : (This definitely makes my honors film, anyway.

I'm thinking excellent finish—just drivin' the 5 and your ticket gets punched. Harsh, no?

peace out

###

Breaking and Entering

Nichole pressed her nose to the living room window for the fifth time. The newspaper lay in the no-man's land between the sidewalk and the gutter, on the driveway but nearly touching the street. She studied the blue plastic bag with the expression of a dog waiting for the master who beats him. Just last week she marched across the sidewalk and all the way down to the street to pick up the paper without a second thought. Just last week. Now it felt like one of those electronic fences had been installed at the limits of the front yard and she was wearing the collar. Yesterday when Nichole had tried to get the attention of the slight Vietnamese man who made the daily deliveries, he had simply smiled and waved back, her shouts swallowed by the hacking of his ancient Chevy. A tear dropped onto the window sill and floated on the dust. Nichole leaned back and blocked out the view of the driveway with her right hand, the ghost of her reflection unable to meet her eyes.

"Newspapers are a dying form, anyway. Everything I need is online."

She stepped over a stack of books and slumped into the oversized plaid chair facing the television. Flashes of animated superheroes and amazing juicers, pink gems and black-and-white sitcoms pulsed on the screen as Nichole thumbed the remote. Her shoulders twitched with that prickly sensation of being watched. She chalked it up to wishful thinking. Long white hairs covered her sweats where she had brushed the arm of the chair. She used to joke that "cat hair" was her favorite upholstery and didn't even mind vacuuming the furniture twice a week. This chair hadn't been touched in months.

"If I had a dog, I could teach him to fetch."

She used to have a cat. She used to have a lot of things. If she had a dog, he'd probably be dead, too.

"Goddammit!"

Nichole launched herself from the chair, spiking the remote on the cushion as she stomped to the front door and flung it open. The ozone in the damp morning air was intoxicating. She closed her eyes and grabbed the jam for support, swaying a little before locking her knees. Blowing out staccato breaths like a weight lifter, she descended the three steps down to the front path.

"It's just the front yard. It's the same as it's always been. I have walked this same path a thousand times. People walk outside everyday."

Nichole coached herself under her breath, keeping her eyes on the paper and consciously taking each step as if operating the feet by remote control. Her right foot touched the sidewalk and she broke into a sweat. Her left foot landed beside it and her hands began to shake. She lifted the right foot again, put it down at the other edge of the sidewalk. Her throat closed off. Lights danced in her peripheral vision followed by blackness narrowing like a camera shutter. Nichole dropped to her knees and crawled back to the house, gasping on the steps while she waited for her strength to come back. She glanced up and down the street through the bars of her fingers, hoping no one had seen her failure.

The computer was her contact with the world. At first she lurked in chat rooms, pretending to be connected to humanity by more than ether. Anymore, though, she put in just enough effort to maintain the facade that made her friends think she was still real. For awhile everyone understood her need for time, her reluctance to go out. After a few months, though, they started to insist, then started to avoid her. They needed her to be done, so she created the SIMS version of her life. The life they wanted to think she had.

> Sara—Of course I'll be at your birthday party! Sorry about missing dinner last month—I guess nobody escaped the flu this year. Hugs to everyone. Nichole

Nichole sent the mail and then wrote a new one.

> Sara—My trip to Seattle got moved up a week. I'll try to call tomorrow before the dinner, but happy birthday, no matter what! Nichole

She scheduled the message to be sent the following Thursday, just in case, then opened Safari and went to her bookmark for Safeway.com. She checked a half gallon of nonfat milk, a pound of strawberries, a box of wheat crackers, a pound of cheddar cheese, and six bottles of whatever Penfold's red was on sale from her list of regular items, then lucked into a delivery window for later that morning.

After six months of on-line shopping, Nichole had determined exactly how much and how often she could order without looking desperate. Eccentric was okay, she just didn't want the delivery guy to wonder about her enough to contact the authorities to investigate her wellbeing. She had talked to a lifetime's worth of "authorities" after Drew's accident. Look how much good that had done. The limits of her world were collapsing in on her, and all she could do was hope she didn't wake up one day unable to even get out of bed, trapped without food, water, or even a means of quick exit, not able to reach the phone she could see but not get to. That kind of tortured death was not how she wanted to go.

The truck pulled up at 10:40, right at the beginning of her two hour delivery window. Nichole watched the man who looked like Santa Claus with a receding hairline unload her bin from the refrigerator section at the back, check his list, then pull a plastic bag out of the front section and drop it into the bin. As he grasped the handle of what looked like a 6-pack of Coke on steroids, she ran to the door and yanked it open.

"Would you grab the paper, please?" She squeezed the door jamb, suddenly nauseated, certain he would refuse her request. She rotated her hand until it was vertical, her fingers not reaching past the inner edge of the frame. When Santa bent to pick up the newspaper, she let out her breath and stepped back to let him pass.

"Thanks!" Nichole nodded and produced a cheery smile.

"No problem." His voice was unexpectedly high-pitched as if he had a bad helium habit. "Careful, this bag is torn." He handed her the bag with the strawberries and crackers, then put the 6-pack carrier of wine on the table.

"Special occasion?"

Nichole frowned. "Sort of . . ."

"Looks like a party," he said gesturing toward the wine with the clipboard as he passed it to her for a signature.

"Oh. Just a small one." Nichole pictured Frank and Sara sitting out in the garden with Drew pouring wine while she carried out trays of fruit and cheese and bread while trying not to trip on Cocoa winding between her legs. That familiar scene would never be repeated. The last time Frank and Sara had come over, Frank couldn't even look her in the eye. His leg bounced up and down the whole time like he was in charge of the getaway car. At least they had come. Everybody else vanished after the first couple weeks, except for checking in by e-mail. Apparently virus scanners had gotten so sophisticated they even offered protection from grief.

Santa with the elf voice handed her the receipt. "Here's the number to call if you have any questions. Have a day!"

Nichole wasn't sure if he just talked too fast to squeeze in the obligatory "nice" or if he could tell nice just wasn't in her repertoire. She waved to him before closing and locking the door, then put the cheese and milk in the refrigerator and opened a bottle of wine. She poured a glass and set it on the sill of the window looking into the back yard. She corked the bottle and put that on the table behind her but within reach. She didn't have much stomach for alcohol this early, but it comforted her to have it nearby. Champagne, though, champagne she could drink any time of day. Used to be able to drink any time. Champagne shared was an instant celebration, delight in a glass. When she'd tried to drink it last, the bubbles stung and the taste was bitter.

The view through the window was a suburban jungle, her garden grown into an unrecognizable wilderness after months of neglect. A broom leaned against the patio table, and a basket of gardening tools sat rusting quietly in the sun closer to the house. Passion vines had spread from the fence, swallowing two shrubs whole and creeping along the ground to grasp the base of the umbrella. At this rate, they would reach the back door by Labor Day. The abandoned landscaping had probably attracted even more urban wildlife than usual. Possums. Roof rats. Nichole tried to summon a little dread, or at least minor disgust, but she couldn't feel anything.

She watched the shadows slide across the yard and back again while she marked each passing hour with a glass of wine until the bottle was empty. She opened the next one.

Night was the worst part. It felt like the outside was trying to get in, like the safe places were shrinking even faster. If she drank too much, she couldn't sleep. If she didn't drink enough, she couldn't sleep. The doctor wouldn't give her any more pills after the last incident, so self-medication was an art she practiced with little hope of mastering. Nichole had put away the last of the Ambien and Zoloft like a fire ax behind glass she would break only in case of emergency. But today was the 12th. Some people are afraid of the 13th, and the 15th certainly wasn't any kind of luck for Caesar, but the 12th was the date she couldn't get past. A lot of things can happen in a year. A lot of things or nothing. And nothing was what she had left.

At eleven she sat down at the computer.

> Jenny—I'll be out of town for a couple weeks. Could you have one of the guys swing by early next week to check the house and make sure the paper stopped?
>
> Nichole

She sent the mail to the cleaning service she had quit using months before, certain they would show up Monday. She didn't want Sara to find her, or even the delivery man. Forcing it on a stranger seemed less cruel. And if she backed out, well, at least they would bring in all the papers.

Nichole sat on the bed cradling a picture of Drew. Cocoa was in it, too, appearing to shed long white hairs even in the photo. And her mother. It was like an Oscar tribute montage of the year's fallen. All the dead, one by one. All but her. She swallowed the first Ambien with a big gulp of shiraz and fingered the Zoloft tablet, wondering if a big uptick in seratonin would help her get the job done or make her change her mind.

Footsteps in the kitchen yanked her from her internal debate. Something scraped against the floor. A bag rattled. Someone was in the house.

Heart pounding, Nichole crept to the front door and grabbed the knob. Run down the steps and away from the house! Run next door where the porch light was on and someone was probably awake! Run! Nichole stood with her hand on the knob and licked her lips until they were sore. Just picturing herself outside, on the sidewalk made her stomach lurch. If she started hyperventilating and passed out, whoever was in the kitchen would hear her, and there would be nothing she could do.

That thought stopped her. Was she trying to save herself? She let go of the knob and stepped back. Uncertain whether she intended to defend her house or offer up a sacrifice, she moved slowly toward the kitchen, picking up a vase as she passed the coffee table. When she turned the corner into the kitchen, a dark shape hurtled out the cat door. The intruder had four legs, not two! Nichole's was simultaneously relieved and disappointed, a mismatch of emotions not helped at all by the wine and Ambien now kicking in. What was it? It could be anything. It could have rabies. There could be more of them! She traded the vase for a broom from the utility closet and started poking it into corners and behind appliances. Nichole paused and leaned against the broom. The adrenaline rush had passed and she felt strangely relaxed. Maybe she was hallucinating. That could be a good sign. Maybe she needed to finish. She put the broom down and uncorked the bottle of wine on the counter, not bothering to get a new glass. Maybe she needed more Ambien. When the cat flap began to rattle against its magnetic latch the way it always did when tapped from the outside, she shoved the recycling bin toward the door with one foot to block the opening.

"I should have gotten rid of that when the cat died." She took a deep breath and blew it out hard, squatting to wedge the bin against the door. "I should have done a lot of things." Nichole shook her head at her mirror-self reflected in the dark of the patio door and realized it wasn't her face looking back.

This one had a black mask and eyes that shined as if they had their own source of light. A raccoon so big she didn't know how he squeezed through the cat door sat on the doormat next to her gardening basket with one paw raised over the tools as if he were about to grab the shears and launch an assault on the door. He was just inches away from her, sampling the air with a lift of his nose but never looking away.

"Go on!" She shooed him with her hand. "Go!

He didn't move.

"Really. Go, now." Nichole tapped on the glass with one finger, hoping the noise would startle him enough that he would run, but all he did was raise his head and sit up. She tapped again.

The raccoon pressed his tiny black hand against the glass where her finger rested so they were touching with no more than a transparent barrier between them. Nichole spread her fingers and flattened her palm over his, so close she could almost feel the warmth. He dropped his paw and ambled away, pausing once to glance over his shoulder at the cat flap before continuing across the yard and into the dark.

Nichole pushed herself up from the floor and recorked the wine bottle. One by one she turned out the lights as she walked back to the bedroom, brushing against the door frames and furniture as she passed. She sat down on the bed, squinted at the photograph, then repositioned the frame where she could see it when she woke. She put the rest of the capsules back into the small enamel box where she stashed them and returned it to the drawer in the night stand. She yawned, but stood again to walk over to the computer. “Have a day.” The Safeway guy had said. Not a nice day, not a good day, just “a day.” Maybe she would. Have one more. Watching the keys as she typed because her fingers weren’t entirely reliable, she scheduled a grocery delivery for the next day:

20 lbs. cat food she began.

# # #

Jesus Saves

One day the devil challenged Jesus to a coding competition to see who could create the perfect program. With God looking on, they were both typing furiously, flames and eerie glow everywhere, when the system crashed. The devil howled and smashed his computer, but Jesus just smiled. The devil said, "What the Hell is he so smug about?" God shrugged and said, "Jesus saves." Always be prepared, that's what I learned that night. Leave nothing to chance. And the best preparation is prevention. Or elimination. The demon you exorcise today can never hurt you tomorrow.

Not an hour ago I saw Jesus on roller blades wearing a flannel shirt and shades and listening to an iPod. He didn't acknowledge my greeting; in fact, he almost ran me down rounding the curve on the Steven's Creek Trail by the Easy Street turnoff. Maybe he was averting his eyes from the glare of the red sequined hat with a big "S" reflecting the late afternoon sun, or maybe it was the black t-shirt that says "Beware of GOD." Jesus could probably tell I'm not exactly on his team.

I wasn't much of a Christian as a kid, only a marginal Catholic at best. The whole born-again personal savior thing was a bit *too* personal for me. Knowing some stranger was tortured on my behalf was more responsibility than I was willing to embrace at the time. I didn't understand the value of ritual sacrifice. But I was an excellent skeptic. I didn't just question authority, I reinvented the inquisition.

If only the people who are saved go to heaven, then can the rest of us do whatever we want, or are we just decoration? And if hell is full of people like Thomas Jefferson and John Lennon and heaven has a bunch of martyrs and Mother Theresa with Pat Robertson and Jerry Falwell waiting in the wings, is that really a selling point? Were all the people who ate meat on Fridays instantly raptured out of eternal damnation when some Pope changed that rule? And then there's purgatory—what's that all about? I washed out of Catechism only because they didn't have a rail for me to ride. They call it excommunication because some of us they really, really don't want to hear from any more.

I love walking this trail because it contradicts itself at every turn. One minute you're surrounded by flowering trees and birdsong, the next you're passing through a concrete tunnel where the rush of traffic drowns out the sound of running water. What do you call two Ph.D.s walking into a bar? A paradox. That's what it is to be an urban trail. Cement and steel partially eclipsed by ivy and wild mustard and jasmine under the canopy of historic oaks and brand new overpasses. Some days I see so many people on the trail you'd think it was a freeway, other days there's just the silent Indian man who never looks up from his shuffling feet and a couple guys on bikes who pass so close I can feel the hair stand up on the back of my neck.

I know I'm not the only one seeing Jesus in unusual places, but at least I do not suffer under the illusion that mine is the genuine article. If Jesus were going to pop in for a visit, he should have taken the opportunity last year when it might have done me some good. And although this would be a likely spot for God to incinerate a shrub on my behalf, I'm not anticipating a fiery chat with Him any time soon, either. I just hope spotting Jesus on rollerblades isn't the first sign of descent into delusion or worse, West Nile Virus.

I'm not a big believer in signs and portents. Funny, though, how what springs to mind at the sight of any guy with long hair and a beard is Jesus, even for someone like me. His recognition factor is probably second only to McDonald's or maybe Coke globally. What company wouldn't kill for that kind of iconic status? I think the Christians invented branding, not to mention product placement. And the Vatican had the cash to bankroll the worldwide marketing campaign. Of course, the guy who nearly ran me down was their version: flowing brown hair and a nose right out of a Beverly Hills surgery. You just know the real Jesus didn't look like that.

Looks can be deceiving even when it's not intentional misrepresentation. Men see a tiny blonde and they think fragile or gullible and childlike. Then they project all their fantasies and cultural myths onto your canvas: most want to take care of you, some want to display you, a few want to hurt you. This one kid followed me around for the last two years of high school without ever speaking to me. I didn't think anything of it until my neighbor complained about the candy wrappers and cans he found crammed into the hedge facing my bedroom window. Then there was the guy I dated who wanted me to dress up as Tinkerbell. Tinkerbell, Jesus! I have to admit that one was kind of fun, though. He worked in a theater and owned a harness. You just haven't lived until you've flown naked. Why did the blonde stare at the orange juice can? Because it said "concentrate." It has always been a mistake to underestimate me, now that mistake might be fatal.

A bit beyond the little path marked with a tasteful wooden sign offering hope of *restrooms* as it branches off to a city park is a thicker section of woods deep enough that you can see neither the freeway soundwall nor the neighborhoods beyond the creek. There is a cartoonishly round tree right near the trail, silver gray bark and broccoli twigs. The first time I saw it, it stopped me dead. It was covered in clusters of pink flowers as if someone had carefully tied bouquets of carnations all over some random deciduous tree! Just knowing there is this tree offering ready-made bouquets out in the middle of nowhere like nature's florist shop makes me smile.

Right across from the carnation stand is where the homeless guy with the dog lives. The day he burst out of the underbrush with the plywood panels balanced on the rusted shopping cart and the mongrel straining on a leash out front like a sled dog, I actually screamed. I mean like a little girl. He backed into cover so fast, I almost thought I had imagined him. But that was one of my first walks. I've seen him since, leaving the trail and walking off toward downtown like he's late to set up the booth in his own private farmer's market. He's strange, but not scary. The really scary things are the ones you're not prepared for.

Belief and faith are not the same thing, though sloppy speakers use the words interchangeably. Belief is certainty, confidence, acknowledgment of the evidence. Faith is believing without evidence. Or despite the evidence. I read that something like 70% of people believe in God, 90% if the pollster uses the most generic "higher power" definition. That has got to be some sort of adaptation, doesn't it? Way back when the gene pool was just a few steps removed from the creamy primordial porridge, some gene linked to suspension of disbelief must have conferred a selective advantage. Maybe it was survival of the hopeful. Attitude can keep you alive or hasten your decline, that's been observed repeatedly. Stick around for the next act. Stay for the grand finale. Pay no attention to the man behind the curtain. Religion *is* theater, so maybe that susceptibility to belief could be counteracted by early exposure to musical theater like an inoculation against God. Have you accepted Jesus? Yeah, but what I really want to do is direct.

One of my favorite places on the trail is the sky bridge over the railroad tracks. During commute hours I watch the trains blow past each other creating tiny tornados of dust. The engineer in the 5:42 southbound always waves. When the train passes directly beneath me, there is a blast of air, a baptism of hot breath from below as all the surrounding sounds of transportation are drowned out by that one powerful crescendo. The Emmy Lou Harris song that compares freeway noise to the sound of the ocean got it right . . . . *comin' down to wash me clean; baby do ya know what I mean?* . . . The skybridge is just a thematic variation on the rushing water of the creek further along the trail, an eclectic modern symphony: bring up the wind, fade the locomotive, fortissimo cascade over the ripwrap. As the daylight fades, the view from the pedestrian bridge is like watching a screen-saver slide show. Twilight rising, temperature falling, flashing passing shadows. It took me weeks of casing the trail to realize the darkness was my friend.

I never used to exercise, never set foot in a gym. I started walking just before I got out of the hospital to demonstrate my commitment to recovery. Doctor's orders. Some nefarious plot to improve my mental health by improving my physical health. The external scars had all healed, and they wanted my attitude to be just as pretty. Or maybe they just wanted to get me out of the place. I think they were sick of hearing "What do you call a man with no arms and no legs . . ." On the stoop? Mat. On the stove? Stew. In the confessional? Neil. And my personal favorite: stapled to the wall? Art. I laugh out loud at that one no matter how many times I hear it. They transferred one of the orderlies after he dropped a tray of meds and blamed me. He claimed I gave him the "evil eye," as if ignorance and fear are a valid excuse for anything. But he knows what really happened, and so do I. He will never touch another patient, never even go near one without wincing. When I reduced him to tears, I knew I was ready.

There are plenty of beautiful parks, wilderness areas, suburban strolls to be had. But this place has helped me see and hear things differently, recognize the edges I used to miss. That's where everything happens—at the edge, the all-important transition zones like day into night, crowded to vacant. Edges are what babies see first. And it's common knowledge in the world of business that the edge brings both the most risk and the greatest rewards. My all time favorite magazine cover appeared in 1997—the

Apple logo backlit and wrapped in thorns with "Pray." underneath. The Sacred Heart of Apple image said it all: the fear of eternal corporate damnation, the cultish Mac-olyte devotion, the salvation Steve Jobs offered if only we would listen, and the painful burden of being that kind of icon for anyone. I know what it is to suffer those constricting piercings, to have a heart bound together by only pain. But like Apple, reports of my demise were greatly exaggerated.

The string of parking lot robberies in Palo Alto got a lot of media play. When some coed got jacked on the Stanford campus, it made the front page because the violence was escalating and experts thought he wasn't through. But you never think it's going to be you. You think that if you're parked under a light in a "nice" neighborhood and you remember to check the back seat like all the self-defense classes tell you that you'll be fine. You think that holding your keys between your fingers as you make a fist makes you as invincible, a female Wolverine. But you are wrong. I learned the definition of unprepared the hard way. Prayer is no defense against someone who outweighs you by a hundred pounds and carries a real knife instead of car keys.

The Bible has as many back turns and contradictions as this trail. An eye for an eye . . . turn the other cheek. Vengeance is mine, sayeth the Lord . . . but he seems to have such a backlog that few ever see satisfaction on that account. At least not in this lifetime. And if you're pretty sure this is the only one you get, well, justice can be served hot or it can be served cold, but I believe it should always be served promptly. If that sounds more like revenge than justice, maybe it depends which end of the knife you're on. When I had chosen my side, I smiled and said all the right things to be released.

I have walked the trail today with a building excitement, more relaxed than I have been in nearly a year. Because this is what I have prepared for. I am a performer now, practicing my own religion, about to become philanthropist of public Art with duct tape and wire. Three women have been attacked on the trail in the last two months. Enough to be a pattern. Enough for the usual warnings about not walking alone, not walking after dark. Not enough to actually catch the guy. Dusk is the perfect time, the no man's land between day and night. Pink and orange fade to black, twilight blurs the edges. There is a rustling in the bushes just before the entrance to the underpass. I hear it in a split-second break in the sound of pulsing cars, just a moment of movement in the underbrush too abruptly stifled to be wind. I smile to myself and do not alter my stride.

I enter the tunnel and am immediately engulfed by the screaming traffic noise. With my hand in my pocket, I brace for the echo of accelerating footsteps, ready to unveil my first masterpiece.

# # #

The Study

I've been watching him for three weeks, and I know things about him no one else does: his morning erections and breakfast toast, his evening wine and paperback books. What I don't know is why. In the beginning I was just taking the memory card from the video camera and giving it to the bike messenger who appeared at my door every evening at 6:00. It was a different guy every time, a different service. He would hand me an envelope, wait while I switched the cards, then give me the payment and watch me sign for the delivery. Now I'm making notes, squinting at the tiny screen as if my life depends on the man in the video. Sometimes the pigeons startle at nothing, and I instinctively hold my breath and duck down behind the vent fan. I think someone has plans for him, and I'm afraid.

The flyer came in under the door along with the relentless Chinese take-out menus.

Study in Urban Patterns
$50/day for your observations
no lifting

Before I was laid off I would have thrown it out unread, but when it's been two months since your last contract, a year since your job ended, anything with a dollar sign grabs your attention. The website at the bottom of the page was a screening service for all kinds of market research. It seemed harmless enough, so I filled in the form. The next day I got a canned message with instructions about operating a video camera installed on the roof of my building.

My studio is a tiny subdivided corner of what was originally the penthouse. It's barely four hundred square feet, but it has a balcony with a ladder to the roof. Since the other tenants have to use the pull-down stairs at the top of the central well, no one bothers. The roof is mine by default. So it was jarring to find the video camera mounted on the concrete beside the gargoyle facing East, the same queasy sort of home-invasion feeling I got when there were cigarette butts beside the roof door for a week last summer. The camera was aimed at an apartment in the building next door. I flipped open the viewer and watched a man vanish from the window of his bedroom and reappear in the window of his living room. The power cord from the camera hugged the edge of the wall and disappeared into a duct. I thought I was just the only one to respond to the flyer, but now I wonder if I was the only one who got it.

Who was he? Why was he being recorded? The second day I fiddled with the zoom, could see the bathroom beyond the bedroom and the kitchen behind the living room. He looked to be in his forties and in good shape. When he left in the mornings, he carried a briefcase and wore a jacket but no tie. I never saw visitors, never saw food delivered. Sometimes he came home late, but he didn't go out again once he was in. The instructions hadn't said anything about watching the video, but I found myself compelled to check it over and over. By the end of the first week, I was staying with the camera all through the evening, watching until he went to bed.

That's when I received new instructions. I had watched him roll a cold beer bottle across his forehead when he came back from a long run on Sunday, sitting on a blanket with the view screen angled toward me, resisting the urge to zoom in when he tossed his clothes into the hamper and walked naked into the bathroom. When I broke away to meet the messenger, my phone light was blinking. The same vaguely familiar voice as before told me I would receive an additional fifty dollars any day I personally saw "the subject" leave before 7 AM, come home later than midnight, or close the curtains. A signed note with the time and type of observation should be included with the memory card. I set my alarm for 5:00 the next morning and erased the message.

On Wednesday I caught him leaving at 6:15. I couldn't stop smiling at my good fortune as I wrote the note, but during the long hours when he was away, I started to wonder. If this was a study, what kind of data were they collecting? If it was something else, was "the subject" bad guy or victim? The Thursday parcel had the extra fifty bucks, and it felt like crossing a line.

I moved a chair up to the roof and carried a cooler back and forth from my apartment so I could watch for hours without a break. I named him David and mentally chose his shirts. Seeing the way he ate a peach, paper towel under his chin to catch the dripping juice, made me want one. When he would masturbate in bed at night, I would, too. At the end of the second week, the phone message offered the bonus for every day I noted whether his jacket had three buttons or two, how many times he walked into the bathroom, and whether the wine was red. I bought a pair of binoculars and wedged a chair against the roof door.

Today he went in and out of the bathroom five times, closed the curtains in the living room, then left at 6:45 wearing a three-button jacket. I feel like something's about to happen, like those things must be significant. It's 2 AM, and I can't stop watching the viewer, waiting for him to come home. I stretch and shift my weight, twisting left then right—and that's when I catch a flash from the roof of the taller building behind mine. For a moment I imagine a red light. Perhaps I have been mistaken about the subject of the study all along.

###

Intersection

Kayla wore her heartbreak like a shroud. Strangers seated accidentally beside her knew to give her room, to speak to her in lowered voice if forced to speak at all. Her closest friends feigned sympathy long after they began to roll their eyes the way the living do when they have not experienced such loss akin to death, but Kayla knew a part of her was gone. He was the one, he *was*, no matter how much time they'd had, or why he left, or what went wrong. Her love had burned so brightly then, its absence cast a shadow like a veil through which she would forever view the world.

Arthur held his feelings at a distance like an inconvenient meeting long postponed but never taken from the queue. He tried to view himself as much above the ordinary messy inconsistencies of love and all the problems that implied. But late at night as Arthur lay in bed alone he heard the constellations singing harmony and almost, *almost* . . . he could feel another waiting just for him, a voice, a face, a moment always near but never quite within his grasp, and as he reached for it then felt it fade, the twilight sleep like fingers grazed his cheeks and lips and he was moved to tears.

Kayla walked each morning, through the fog or rain or technicolor sunrise, never noticing the temperature nor timing of the lights. She had always loved to walk, had always loved the solace of the quiet and the solitude, but now it seemed like penance. The exercise maintained more out of habit than reward became a drudgery, another place the joy had drained away from who she'd been before.

Arthur hurried through his day and every small activity as if he had a train to catch. Most people thought he had some other place to be, some better place that called him, somewhere they would never go. And so they envied him a little for his passion, as they thought of it, his secret life, the one more real than now. Reality for Arthur, though, was much more disappointing than the fantasies he spun to make the emptiness seem full. He wasn't rushing to something, he wasn't running from, he was more truthfully a body much in motion simply from the fear of rest.

Kayla watched home movies in her head. A looping reel of highlight scenes from when she had been with him now played every day and all night, too, an endless source of tortured consolation. The memories of him were more concrete than anything outside; she still could taste his red wine kiss and feel his lips against her wrist, his fingers in her hair. Of course there had been other men before, but lesser men for sure, and with her expectations redefined she could not see how any smaller love could ever fill the void.

Arthur waved indifference as if it were a billowing red cape and all the world a cartoon charging bull. He knew that there were those who took a shrug the same as if it were a middle finger raised, a fist against the nose. And yet, it was defensible, he thought, for even Switzerland remained above reproach despite complicities that may or not occur within neutrality. Arthur wasn't conflict born, but he was conflict bred, and his hostility, not obvious but more insidious, was often outsourced into others' heads.

Kayla scanned the ground while walking, counting all the lines she crossed, subconsciously or not. She came to see the cracks as some binary code, a stream of endless ones beside the zero of her life. If it is truly better to have loved and lost, then why had she begun to want to scream and trip old ladies on the street for no worse crime than being in her way and showing signs of having once been loved? This wasn't how she saw herself, this wasn't who she thought the perfect love would leave her if it left, which made her question both the leaving and the love.

Arthur had avoided loss by never quite investing, or at least that's how he saw his well-constructed path. He thought it a fine compromise, this cloak of self-protection which he wove with every word and gesture, warding off even the near occasion of a chance to give his heart. So he could not quite comprehend how others could choose happiness instead of safety when so often that brief bliss was followed by despair. Not that he knew this fact first hand, but he had surely witnessed pools of bitter sorrow, seen recrimination turn his closest friend from whole to hollow while he watched, as if the leaving love took with it things he hadn't even known he'd had.

Kayla didn't see the light change, didn't hear the squealing brakes, or likely did but didn't see how it attached to her. All the sound and motion had been stretched unto infinity as if first bent in space at some event horizon and then sucked into the gravity of her now irresistible black soul. Still, she felt the impact, so surprised to feel skin contact after months of tactile vacuum that she, even later, couldn't call it pain.

Arthur never took a chance for anyone, not even for himself or for a cause he thought was just. He could turn a blind eye to a sticky situation, with unerring preservation sidestep every expectation of swift action on behalf of someone else. And yet, for reasons inexplicable, he leapt before a taxi—charged a *taxi*, for god's sake—right in the middle of the intersection just because some stupid girl was crossing on the red. She wasn't dashing out, she wasn't caught halfway, she simply wasn't even looking. How could that be right? But something in her vacant eyes, the way she stared off at some distant point as if the answers lay there, made him act without first passing through his cautious screen of doubt—and he just leaped.

Kayla sat down hard after the shove and saw some guy spread on a taxi hood like this exotic ornament or maybe just an urban roadkill trophy freshly caught. She squinted hard in case it was a lighting trick, but no, there was a guy there—then he wasn't as he slid off sideways landing in a heap next to her feet. A wall of babbling voices had surrounded them, encircled their two bodies in an existential hug. Kayla looked into his face, contorted now in pain, and couldn't help but wonder what possessed him to do such a foolish thing. Just then his eyelids opened and he frowned a little at the scuffed red shoe just past his nose, but as his gaze continued up the leg, he raised himself a little, smiled at her as if he knew her, seemed about to speak. Instead, he stood on shaky legs and leaning hard against the taxi . . . offered her his hand.

# # #

Storm of Minutes

Cecelia found the lump on a Tuesday. It was during her second shower of the day, after she had cleaned up a particularly messy "gift" from the cat. Bouncer used to leave the gifts for her, a parade of neatly dissected mice and partially mangled birds that left her husband swearing when he stepped on them in the middle of the night. Cecelia couldn't fault the cat for his nature, though, and she was secretly flattered by the frequent displays.

When the baby was born Bouncer shifted his attentions to her. Cecelia would often find him in the crib with Maya, facing away from her but purring softly in time with her breathing. On the floor would be a tiny gray mouse, intact but for a chewed-off foot or tattered ear. Cecelia was both amused and touched by his generous affection for the newest member of the family.

Occasionally, however, the offerings weren't quite so tidy. This day's was a ball of red and gray fluff that had been used for a vicious game of handball. Red impact marks scarred the walls and bits of feather stuck to the floor. Cecelia disinfected the entire room, just to be safe. Maya was into everything now that she could walk, and the red spots drew her attention like a magnet.

"C'mon, Baby," Cecelia said as she swung Maya onto her shoulders, "Mommy reeks of eau de Lysol."

Cecelia had perfected the sixty-second shower when Maya was born, eventually boasting she could do anything in under five minutes. It was amazing how much could be accomplished when everything was timed by the nap pattern of a two-month old or the attention span of a fifteen-month old. While the baby played with a wind-up scuba diver on the floor, Cecelia lathered and rinsed simultaneously.

Her hands were a soapy blur as she watched the baby through the glass and mentally ran through the list of things she had to get done before dinner, but her fingers still hesitated at the hard spot as if stumbling on a pebble. She stopped, felt it again, searching her left breast with the familiar spiral pattern she hadn't thought about since before she was pregnant. Something was there.

A loud crack as the toy hit the shower door broke her train of thought. She turned off the water.

"Okay, patient baby. Mommy's done."

Maya lifted her arms as Cecelia tied her robe. Together they danced across the tile and into the dressing room while Cecelia carefully avoided meeting her own eyes in the mirror.

Cecelia's annual exam was on a Friday. She had taken Maya with her to her postpartum exam, but this visit she just took a picture to add to the gallery in her OB/GYN's office. The nurse checked her blood pressure twice, muttering something about it being "a bit high." Cecelia didn't comment, but she concentrated on taking deep, slow breaths as she waited.

"Sa-ceeel—ya! you're breakin' my heart!" Dr. Jonathan entered singing after two sharp knocks. He hugged her tightly, then looked under the exam table and behind the light stand. "Where's my baby?"

Cecelia laughed and shook her head at the stale Simon and Garfunkel joke. She had chosen her doctor for his lighthearted manner and sense of humor. Despite the fact that he probably still got carded in bars, he seemed like a better companion for something as grueling as labor and delivery than the more experienced but grim doctor she had interviewed before him.

"She's not a baby anymore." Cecelia showed him the photo as they exchanged personal life updates.

When the doctor scanned her chart and began asking the usual questions, she interrupted him, pulling the thin paper away from her left breast. "I want you to look at this."

He raised his eyebrows, obviously taken aback.

"Nothing you haven't seen before." Cecelia tried to regain their bantering tone, but Jonathan had picked up the undercurrent. He pulled out the end of the exam table and helped her lie back even as he finished inquiring about her periods and contraception in the months after weaning.

"I found a great restaurant," he said as he palpated first her left breast then her right. "Everything is ginger."

"I read a review of that place." Cecelia watched his face as his fingers searched. "I'm not sure a ginger martini is an improvement on the classic."

The doctor turned his attention back to her left breast. "Raise your arm. No, but the garlic seared ahi with ginger dumplings—" he hesitated as his fingers found the lump, moved away, around, returned to it again. A tiny line Cecelia had never seen before appeared between his brows. It was like seeing his face flash-forward ten years.

"The dumplings are worth going back for." Jonathan looked her in the eye as he helped her sit up. "I'll call to schedule a biopsy right away."

The room felt lighter. Cecelia let out her breath. As soon as he touched the lump it was both more real and much smaller. Just talking about it made the lump shrink. She hadn't told anyone else, not even her husband. Roger didn't need the stress until she knew something concrete. And as for everybody else, well, she knew that the minute they heard the word "lump" they would think of Maya. The burden of all that fear and pity was not what she needed right now.

The drive home was done entirely on autopilot as Cecelia thought about web searches and support groups and marker genes and diet and exercise and chemotherapy and surgery. At the last light before her house, she continued on instead of turning. A restaurant with a neon beer sign in the window caught her attention, and she accelerated into the parking lot, stopping so abruptly the car rocked on its wheels.

The bar was just a counter with four stools tucked into the back corner, but it had a full display of liquor bottles against the mandatory wall of mirror. Cecelia didn't bother checking out the rest of the place. She ordered a shot of tequila and sat down.

"Run a tab?"

Cecelia shook her head and held out a twenty, looking through the bartender. When he moved to the register, she found herself looking into the eyes of a dead woman. She had a hollow stare, more on the horizon than on what was in front of her. Cecelia turned the shot glass slowly on the bar. It might be nothing. Statistically it probably was nothing. But the shadow had crossed her path, and that could never be changed.

She lifted the shot, toasting her reflection. "Cancer," she whispered over the glass before downing it.

Cecelia left her change on the bar and drove home.

"You know, Hon, 'denial' is not just a river in Egypt."

Cecelia stiffened at Roger's lame attempt to broach the subject again. Maya felt the change and looked up from the book they were reading.

"Mama read," she said, directing Cecelia's face with one hand.

"*He may end up washing the floors, as well.*" Cecelia recited without looking at her husband. In the weeks since the biopsy he had taken every conceivable approach to forcing her to make a choice in the "cut it out or cut it off" question. "I can't do this right now."

She could feel him still standing in the doorway. He probably wanted to touch her but couldn't get past the freeze-out. He never had been able to muster the courage to push past her rare bouts of anger; he would just wait for the signs of thaw.

"The oncologist called again."

She could tell he wanted to say more, waited to be sure he wasn't going to, then continued reading.

"Dada mean?" Maya asked after Roger left and Cecelia relaxed again.

"No, sweetie." She squeezed her eyes shut. "Dada's just worried."

Cecelia finished the book and rocked Maya to sleep. What did he have to worry about? Raising his daughter by himself? He'd just hire a nanny, anyway. It's not like part of his body turned out to be the enemy. She lifted one hand off Maya and raised it as if to say a pledge, then lowered it again without ever touching her chest. A year ago her breasts had been givers of life, a biological miracle that produced the perfect nourishment. Now one of them was a bringer of death.

At the door to the baby's room, Cecelia paused. She stepped carefully over the rug in front of the crib to tuck Maya in, then stepped back to survey the gift. Resting on its side, eyes closed as if in sleep, lay the biggest rat Cecelia had ever seen. It was a surprising golden brown with a nearly hairless tail like a pink snake in the dark blue rug.

Taking a wipe from the changing table, Cecelia picked up the rat by the tip of its tail and carried it outside to the garbage. Bouncer was waiting for her in the kitchen when she returned, sitting next to his empty food dish and licking his paw.

"I guess I'd look smug, too, after that one," she said as she scratched his head. The cat began to purr loudly, then stood on his back legs to rub his face against her knee. Cecelia picked him up and rested her cheek on his side, ruffling the fur with her breath. "Will you feed my baby when I'm gone?"

The pain when she lifted her arm wasn't so much like a knife as like a piece of barbed wire being dragged from her chest to her side and back again, working its way deeper each time. The pain of not being able to lift Maya was even worse. Cecelia had to look away from the confusion in her eyes each time she raised her arms to Mommy but Daddy picked her up instead. They would huddle together on the couch with Roger holding Maya between them and Cecelia keeping her left side as far away as possible. The sling helped hide both the missing tissue and the drain they had installed after the surgery.

Usually she could sit through three or four books before she had to plead fatigue and leave the room, but the last day of the bandages even that was too much contact. Cecelia lay on the bed looking for pictures in the shadows on the ceiling. Her left nipple itched and she couldn't even scratch it because it was either stuck to a slide in some lab or had already been incinerated with the rest of the biomedical waste. "I should have asked to keep it."

"Keep what, Honey?"

Roger sat beside her on the right. She could tell he was trying not to jostle her or bounce the bed. He had been like that the whole time, careful and protective and always there to handle the details while she recuperated. It made her want to scream. Cecelia closed her eyes. "My headache's back."

Apparently the hint wasn't broad enough, because she felt fingers lightly massaging her temples. She scrunched up her face in an effort to keep it from feeling good.

"Can I do anything for you?"

Cecelia sat up abruptly. "You can't *do* anything! You can't *get me* anything!" She turned too fast to face him, wincing then dodging the hand he offered. "Unless you can make me whole again, you've got nothing to offer!"

"Honey, you're still—"

She slid off the bed and came as close as she could to running out of the room. The hurt in his eyes was too much. It was all too much. Cecelia rubbed her right hand across dry eyes, walking automatically toward Maya's room. She used to pause in the hallway and listen for the baby's breathing as she passed the room, but lately she would stand in the doorway for ten or fifteen minutes, counting each breath like the ticking of a clock.

Just as she reached Maya's door, something flew past her in a shower of feathers. A sparrow fluttered near the ceiling, moving erratically down the hallway from wall to wall, shedding bits of fluff with each impact. Bouncer followed the bird in a low crouch, stalking it until it dipped low. As Cecelia watched, transfixed, the cat launched himself from the floor and met the bird about four feet off the ground. He took a moment to get a better grip on his prey, then turned and trotted back into Maya's room.

Cecelia followed, pausing just inside the doorway. Bouncer sat down beside the crib and released the bird, swatting it occasionally as it lay stunned at his feet. He looked at Cecelia and offered a soft meow.

Great gasping sobs broke out of her, shaking her so hard she dropped to the floor at the pain. All the tears she had refused to cry washed down her cheeks, into her hands, onto her knees. Roger's footsteps pounded down the hallway. His sudden entrance startled the cat and sent the bird up and into the walls like a frantic pinball.

"What the hell?"

Cecelia looked up, still breathing raggedly. Roger stood in a blizzard of tiny feathers, looking perplexed and alarmed. Bits of fluff settled on his shoulders, his hair. One caught in his eyebrow, transforming him into a great horned owl. She started to laugh, holding her left arm tight against her side.

"He's teaching her to hunt."

Roger's expression shifted to complete alarm. He knelt beside her. "What?"

His obvious concern for her sanity made her laugh until her eyes teared up. "Bouncer. The present's alive; he's trying to teach Maya to hunt."

She watched her husband survey the room, admiring the comforting profile she had been refusing to look at for weeks. Her laughter turned back to sobs. "I'm so sorry."

Roger rubbed her back, held her tighter as she leaned into him. "I'm sorry, too."

Maya was able to sleep through Bouncer's commotion, but not the sound of her parents' voices.

"Mama?" She stood in her crib, blinking, then her eyes grew round as she pointed at the bookshelf. "Birdie!"

Roger helped Cecelia to her feet. They smiled at Maya's excitement.

"Let's put the birdie back outside," Roger said as he lifted the baby out of her crib. He grabbed a book and used it to direct the sparrow down the hall as Maya squealed with delight. This time Bouncer didn't follow.

Cecelia took a tissue from the changing table and blew her nose. The cat wound around her calves and rubbed his head on her knee.

"Okay, Bouncer. I appreciate the thought," she said, bending to scratch his head, "but I can take care of her."

She took a deep breath and followed her husband and baby. "I'm not dead yet."

###

All or Nothing at All

His iPod gave him away. When David's playlist featured Coldplay and Green Day and Weezer despite his claim that no good music was made after 1969, it was just one of those things you know without asking. I could even guess her age.

I can't decide if willful blindness is less humiliating than ignorance because it at least involves a decision or more humiliating because the decision is so pathetic. I had skipped through all our hours together to the swing of a Cole Porter song, looked at him through a veil of bubbles and moonlight. I don't even own an iPod, and the music I listen to is from somebody else's generation. Who am I to say what makes a fine romance?

David spilled a drink on me at a trade show reception, but it was crowded and he was so nice about it, getting napkins and club soda, buying me a drink, that I just couldn't be mad. After we moved downstairs to the lobby bar, he admitted he had done it on purpose, but the fact that he had resorted to property damage to meet me was kind of flattering.

I almost slept with him that first night. Any man who will dance with me, not reluctantly, but enthusiastically and without prompting, is more than halfway there. Throw in the ability to dip and tolerance for my tendency to lead, and really, what's to resist? If that makes me sound easy, well, how many men actually fit that description? The way David pressed his hand into the small of my back gave every impression that even if his rhythm was a little off on the dance floor, it wouldn't be anywhere else.

He got a lot of abuse from other engineers because he had crossed over to the dark side, but he had the smile and eye contact of a network anchor, so it made perfect sense that he switched to sales. David could explain the technology without making his audience feel stupid, and he loved being in Las Vegas one week and Tokyo the next. At the end of the show we compared calendars. Between his travel schedule and mine, it would be over a month before we could be in the same place at the same time again, but we made a date to meet in San Francisco in the middle of November.

Shanghai 1930 is the perfect place to fall in love, even if it's just with the room. The light was candle-dim gold, the marble archways were straight out of Casa Blanca, and the redhead on stage sang *Love for Sale* with a swing that said she'd been around the block a couple of times and had come back for me. David was waiting at a table in the front with a bottle of champagne on ice. He stood when he saw me and looked at me like we would always have Paris. Right then, he could have sold me the Golden Gate.

I did sleep with him that night. Well, not that much actual sleeping occurred. When our lips and tongues were not otherwise occupied, we argued about art and politics, traded movie reviews, and sang old torch songs to each other until we were laughing too hard to say anything more. We spent that weekend together in and out of bed and jazz dives that still felt smoky decades after the ban. Sunday night he left for Hong Kong and I went home.

We spent six months in that same pattern of one or two intense days separated by weeks of e-mails and phone calls before we could spend a block of time together at last. The longer days and blooming trees could not compete with sitting beside David holding hands. That year the euphoria of spring was all in his eyes. David was an early riser, and I would waken to the smell of fresh coffee in the morning. The same thing could have happened any morning, if I set the timer on my machine. It really can't compare, though, to having someone kiss you on the forehead while they put a big mug of french roast on the night stand. When David left for Japan three weeks later, he gave me a key.

Being a woman in the technical world isn't the all-you-can-eat buffet some people imagine. You can't really be too smart, but you can be too pretty or make too much money. If the men who surround you can see you at all, they maintain a safe distance, driven witless by mandatory sexual harassment training paranoia. The day a new kid's arm accidentally grazed my breast and he nearly burst into tears apologizing, I knew all prospect of finding a relationship had been sucked out of the place with the best odds.

Before David it had been two years since I had had anything even vaguely resembling a date. I made do with a glass of bubbles and mouthing the words to *Someone to Watch Over Me* with the piano player in the lobby bar of whatever hotel I happened to be in. Longing has a certain romance of its own.

Having was even better, though. We were both busy, both had other places to be, but that made our hours together all the sweeter. When David was away I would go to his place, crank up whatever he had left in the CD player and dance naked in the living room. Making the first thing I heard when I walked in be the last thing he had heard before he walked out was a little like sharing his mood as he left. Despite his claims about the decline of music, along with Nina Simone and Glenn Miller he had a full range of rock and blues and soul well into the 70s: the Beatles and Stones, Bruce Springsteen, Aretha Franklin, Led Zeppelin, and on and on. There were plenty of songs I had heard before, but I thought of all of them as his.

I am not a luddite. I may still have a turntable and a nice collection of vinyl that would probably double my 401K if I let it go on eBay, but I also have dozens of CDs on my iBook and a wireless system to play them all through my home speakers. When I teased David about websurfing and checking e-mail on his phone while plugged into his iPod, it was about his need for multiple layers of stimulation, not about resistance to technology. Not about anything else.

Still, having music pumped directly into my auditory canal through plastic ear plugs holds no appeal for me. The ideal song is played live on a piano with one key that sticks and a pedal gone soft. There should be a well-loved bass and a sax that's been in and out of pawn shops and maybe an electric guitar all backing a singer standing so close you can see her sweat and hear her inhale between phrases.

I started sneaking into clubs when I was sixteen. I didn't drink much, but every time I heard *Wee Small Hours,* I cried like I already had a past to forget. The world I felt in the shadows just beyond the stage light was either bugle beads, bathtub gin and disappointment or bias cut silk, sidelong looks and epic all-consuming love. There wasn't much in between. I knew which one I wanted, but in that light, even the alternative looked pretty good.

Everything in college was done in groups: concerts, movies, studying, eating. When my friends started pairing off, I realized that I would rather do something I loved by myself than do anything for long with someone I didn't love. If the line was good or I felt like company, I would go out. In time I acquired a couple reliable escorts with no expectations beyond a few dinners a year. The rest of the time I indulged my fantasy life in obscure night spots, barely missing the companion I lacked.

If there had been a CD in the player, I never would have touched his iPod. I couldn't believe he had left it behind, and I smiled picturing him with only two connections to the information matrix that was his life. Then I scrolled through the playlist. Suddenly every moment from the time we met looked entirely different, like one of those hologram cards where the picture changes completely with a tilt of just a few degrees.

After I walked out leaving the key behind, I wished I had made a little noose from the ear wires and hung the informant from the dining room chandelier. He was perpetually checking messages, sometimes stepped outside to return calls during dinner. I had assumed they were about work and he was being polite, but was it another woman? Other women? The difference between being the one and being just another one was night and day, the distance between heaven and earth. I sideswiped a garbage can on the way home and had to pull over until I stopped crying.

Because I ignored his calls, blocked his e-mails, David sat outside my door until I agreed to talk. When I threw the music in his face, though, told him everything I knew, he was genuinely perplexed. He had never said there was no one else. We had made no promises. Not with words. I listened and watched his face, tried to see it his way. Can you really hold a gaze, pour as much emotion into a single glance as he did so many times with me and not mean everything? Apparently he could. He wasn't an engineer, he was an actor. Another song, a separate smile, a romance I created out of stardust and whispers.

Maybe I should have been able to shift him into the rotation, consider him a sometime friend to share a show and a bottle of wine when fortune crossed our paths. Maybe I should have, but I couldn't. I could hate him for my own assumptions. I could resent him for the part of me I gave away. But still I could not catch my breath whenever he walked into a room.

Once or twice a year, we almost meet. I see him inside a booth, across the floor, in a group at the end of a bar. He is always surrounded by glib chat and loose laughter. I turn away before he can catch my eye, checking without thinking for the thin white threads poking up from his pocket. I wonder what his list holds now. Perhaps those songs will play for someone, but not for me.

###

Jury Duty

The fluorescent lights overhead dimmed and brightened just long enough to make the strangers seated together like commuters in shared pretense of privacy glance up from their laptops and paperbacks. Then the power cut entirely, the sudden quiet of no humming machinery even more jarring than the darkness. The void was filled by a groan equal parts angst and disgust that rose as one voice from every corner of the dim room.

A bureaucrat appeared brandishing a flashlight, even though it was daylight and the tall windows along the back wall provided enough light to see.

"Please remain calm. Do not leave the room until your number has been called and you are dismissed or assigned to a court room, or you will be considered in violation of your summons. This is a minor technical problem and should be corrected soon."

Most of the crowd pulled out cell phones as if in response to some prearranged signal and began shouting descriptions of the power outage and questions about afternoon plans. In the corner of the room furthest from the door, next to an arched window, a man in a black silk shirt opened what looked like a leather mail pouch and pulled out a small wooden board on which he began to assemble cheese, olives, dried apricots, and almonds. He removed a box of crackers from the bag, pushed up his rectangular glasses, and assembled a bite. As he popped it into his mouth, he saw the woman across from him watching before she had time to look away.

"Please," he said, holding the cheese board toward her, "would you care to join me?" He had the lilt of foreign ports in his speech, the cadence of someplace warm, maybe Spain or Central America, with lingering consonants and purring vowels.

"Oh, I . . . thank you! I'm starving!" The woman tucked her bobbed hair behind one ear as she reached for an olive and piece of cheese. She smiled and said, "Well, actually, I'm Lauren."

"Pleased to meet you, Lauren. Carlos." He inclined his head slightly and returned her smile. "I would normally have a block of manchego and a small knife, but they do frown on that here."

The man on the other side of the empty chair where Carlos had assembled his picnic snorted at the comment and said, "No kidding." Carlos held out the board to him, as well. He hesitated, then reached for a piece of fruit and a few crackers.

"Thanks. Marcus." He held out his hand and shook with Carlos. "The courthouse always had x-ray machines and security screening, but after 9/11, it's just insane. I don't think they'd let you bring in a plastic knife."

"And they shouldn't." The woman with shoulder-length gray hair seated several seats down on the same side as Lauren spoke up. She looked up from the book she was reading and removed the scarlet reading glasses perched at the end of her nose. "In the hands of a criminal, even a plastic knife can be lethal."

Carlos stretched to offer her the board as Marcus said, "So guns don't kill people, picnics do?"

Lauren giggled, then turned to introduce herself.

The woman froze for a moment, then smiled and selected cheese and a cracker as she responded to the introduction. "Janet." She pulled a tissue from her purse and dusted her fingers. "I'm just saying that I was a teacher for forty years, and in my experience, the more you eliminate opportunity for misbehavior, the less of it you have."

Lauren smiled almost wistfully as the board was passed to her and Carlos said, "You do not agree?"

"Well, I've thought that, too, and sometimes I still do . . ." she frowned, "but from what I've seen, to someone who feels desperate, everything is a weapon. Pain and anger always find an outlet."

Into the silence that followed that statement she added, "I used to be an ER nurse."

Held breaths were released as everyone nodded and the cheese board was returned to the empty chair where Carlos replenished it from the stores in his bag. A young woman with shiny black hair and a Pacific uptilt to her eyes scooted down the row of chairs to sit next to Marcus and offered her hand to Carlos.

"May I intrude on your party? I'm Sarah." She smiled like a five-year-old, and the rest couldn't help but smile back. "I can't resist olives." After helping herself from the board she added, "This is my first time being called for jury duty."

"This is the furthest I've ever made it." Lauren finished another bit of cheese as she spoke. "Usually I just check my status twice a day for the entire week but never get called in. I've always wanted to serve on a jury. I think it's an honor. Like voting."

"I don't know why they even bother to call me," Janet said while reaching for more crackers. "I would never make it onto any jury. For sure one lawyer or another would dismiss me right up front."

Carlos moved the small board toward Marcus. "Are you too biased?"

Janet studied his face for a moment and pursed her lips as if tasting the intent of his tone. "Not biased, just opinionated. And I don't have the problem some people do of making judgments. I think I could weigh all the evidence in most cases fairly, but I'm not swayed by claims of victimization and tragic childhoods. I'm not saying the past doesn't explain a lot of things," Janet reached across Marcus to take more cheese then shrugged, "I'm saying it doesn't *excuse* them."

Marcus's head twitched, as if caught between nodding in agreement and shaking in disbelief. "So you have no sympathy for the defendants?"

"I have plenty of sympathy. That just wouldn't alter my decision."

Lauren frowned and leaned in as if trying to decipher a thick accent. "You mean you wouldn't feel a little bit sorry, can't see how under other circumstances it might be you on trial?"

Janet shrugged. "Sure. I just don't think any of that is relevant to the verdict."

Shaking her head, Lauren said, "I don't think I could be that black and white. Everybody makes mistakes, and the jury should try to sort out what can be redeemed from what needs to be punished. I mean, I've done things I'm not proud of. Who hasn't? I try to face them, though, try to see how I ended up there so I can avoid it next time. Too many bad choices, uncorrected, might add up to a permanent character flaw, but treating a single misstep as a crime can have the same result."

Marcus turned to her. "I'm not saying you're wrong, honey, but I have a hard time believing you have enough bad behavior to justify that statement."

Lauren laughed. "Is that a compliment or an insult?"

Marcus joined in the laughter. "Not that I mean to pry . . ."

Carlos held up a hand. "You do not need to share anything with us unless you desire."

"It's okay," Lauren said.

When I was a little girl, maybe six or seven, I spent a week with my sisters and cousins at our grandparents' farm. It was one of those times you can look back on even years later and not just remember but *sense*: the earthy-sweet smell of manure, the cricket song and magic of the fireflies. We ran free between meals with little supervision, a pack of kids ranging from five to ten years old, inventing games from one day to the next and exploring the exotic offerings of rural life.

One day it rained nonstop, and by lunchtime Grandma was at wit's end. She sent us all out to "treasure hunt" in the old barn, shrieking as we ran from the house with sheets of plastic held high. The barn wasn't used for much more than junk storage, scattered with hay and full of rusting implements with sharp prongs that would no doubt have child protective services swarming the place if a bunch of kids were let loose in it today, but for us, it was paradise. Freedom. Bees made looping passes overhead, traveling in and out of the cracked panes in the door to a hive up in the rafters, and dozens of tiny birds perched high above, inside but near the loft door that was open to the elements.

One of the older boys found a stash of old canning jars and within a few minutes, we were all trying to catch the giant bumble bees as they squeezed through the broken corner in the glass. When somebody caught one, they would shake the jar really hard, loosen the lid, and throw it into the pile of hay as we all scattered. I know that sounds kind of insane, but when you're in the middle of nowhere, you have to make your own thrills.

In the midst of the excitement of the quick-reflex capture and release of the bees, a small flock of sparrows swooped down from the rafters, beating against the tiny windows. Without thinking, I slammed my jar against the window and slid on the lid.

"I got a bird!"

Everyone was amazed; I was a hero. But when I opened the jar to let it out, it didn't move. A circle of heads peered into the jar I held. The fragile beak was broken, whether caught beneath the rim of the jar or smashed in panic against the glass, it was completely detached on one side.

I buried the bird in a pile of straw, but that night I couldn't eat dinner. The cousins regaled Grandma and Grampa with tales of our adventures, but I didn't say anything. Just thinking about the tiny bird with its beak broken made me queasy.

"But it was an accident!" Marcus was frowning.

"That makes it worse. I've killed many things since then, I've boiled live lobster, I've taken the trout I just pulled out of a cold stream and whacked it on a rock, I've even carried a foot-long rat stuck in a glue trap outside to slam it on the concrete and put it out of it's misery. I have no problem with purposeful, carefully-considered killing. There's a certain gravity and respect to it. But causing death through thoughtlessness, that's a crime. Maybe I didn't know it then, but even the wrongness I *could* sense made me sick. Worse yet was the way that little bird died, beating against an invisible prison within view of the sky."

"Edith Piaf."

"What?

"Edith Piaf." Marcus repeated. "The Little Sparrow. She would think your story is bullshit. Non, je ne regrette rien."

"I think regret is how you find your moral center," Lauren said after a pause. "Not that you should obsess about it, but you use it to learn from your mistakes. To make better choices. If you really regret nothing, aren't you more likely to end up *in front of* a jury instead of being part of one?"

Carlos replenished the cheese board and passed it to Lauren. Before Marcus could respond, Janet spoke.

"Well, I don't believe in regret, and I've never been on the other side of the law! If you always make the best choices you can, think before you act, you shouldn't have cause to regret what you've done. Things may not turn out exactly as you expect, but you have no reason to feel sorry."

Marcus snorted. "Sorry. I guess it's not that hard to believe you've never totally screwed up."

Janet smiled. "Not in any big way, anyway."

"What about small ways?" he pressed. "Maybe you haven't broken the law, but have you broken a life? Ever hurt anybody so much it changed everything?"

Janet hesitated, then folded her glasses and held them in her lap.

I grew up a long way from here, in a place and time that does not fill me with nostalgia and sepia-toned memories. Nothing was ever good enough for my mother, and my sister started bingeing and purging in

Middle School. I couldn't wait to get away, to make my own life. I was careful choosing friends and even more careful choosing dates. You might say I had trust issues. I met my husband in college, started teaching while he finished graduate school. We bought our first house, and I took two years off when our son was born. For a long time, it was the perfect life.

I taught in a small elementary school where one person leaving after five years was considered a high turnover rate. We were a tightly-knit group, not just cordial at faculty meetings, but holding barbecues together and having regular foursomes for bridge and golf. The Principal's husband, Greg, was a shameless flirt. He would comment on what women wore, how they smelled, constantly touched people as he spoke. It wasn't irritating, though, because that's just the kind of guy he was.

He was especially attentive to my best friend, Anna. They shared an interest in modern architecture and eighteenth century poets that sometimes led to an hour of intense conversation that excluded everyone else. Whatever was between them became a sort of running joke in the group, but everyone assumed it was harmless. Greg didn't even tone down his attention to Anna when her husband was around. Once in awhile it got to be a bit much, like when, after a few drinks, Greg's hand would rest a little too low on Anna's back as he talked to her, or when Anna would be so focused on hearing what Greg was saying over the rest of the party noise that she would watch his lips move with an almost adoring gaze. But that sort of thing never lasted long, never repeated during a single event, always dropped back off the radar.

Then one day as Anna and I were driving home from a school meeting, she burst into tears. She babbled about "true love" and "soul mates" and on and on until I finally realized what she was saying. It wasn't just a flirtation. And it wasn't harmless. She vomited out the whole story, how it started with lunch at a restaurant one day and turned into six months of hotel room service at odd times as often as they could arrange to be together. I wanted to cover my ears, but I was driving.

She'd kept it to herself that long, I had to wonder why she couldn't have just kept it to herself forever. People can be selfish that way, even your friends. Airing their dirty laundry, sharing their problems just to make themselves feel better without stopping to ask if *you* want to be part of their secret. Guilt might seem smaller when it's shared, but that's because it taints everybody it touches, like a dark sock in a load of whites. Everything that comes into contact with it is never quite as bright, forever tinged with a little gray.

I focused all my attention on driving, made a great show of adjusting the mirrors and checking the heat, because I couldn't look her in the eye, couldn't wait to get away from her. I felt like I was sitting with a stranger. She had the expected list of excuses, bits of which I had heard as stories in the faculty lounge or as confidences from her, but I hadn't added them up. Her husband hadn't touched her in years. Greg and his wife were only together for the children and had a loveless marriage. All of a sudden, I couldn't help counting every time she had been alone with my husband over the years.

By the time I pulled into her driveway, she had dried her tears and apologized for the outburst. I knew she was looking for absolution, but she had come to the wrong place. I managed to be polite and even almost sympathetic to the pain and messiness, but then, with her hand on the door she said, "Karen found out. She told Greg if we stop now, that's the end of it. Otherwise she's telling Rob. I don't know what to do." She sighed and got out of the car, leaning in to thank me for the ride before walking up to her front door without looking back.

I guess that was what put me over the edge, that "I don't know what to do." Like there was more than one good option. There was a potluck the next Saturday, and everything seemed just like it always had. Watching them all chat and laugh as if nothing had happened, seeing Rob talking to Greg and knowing more about his sex life than he did, well, it turned my stomach. The same thing happened at the football game and the big birthday barbecue a month later. I couldn't help but wonder if Greg and Anna really had stopped seeing each other or if they were just lying better. I hadn't wanted to know in the first place, but once I did, it was all I could think about. I made sure my husband never sat next to her.

After months of pretending everything was normal and avoiding Anna as much as possible without raising questions, I went to our First-Friday girls' night out. Anna was home sick that day, and Karen had to leave early. After the second round, Liz made a comment about "the Greg and Anna show" at the Christmas party, and I didn't need to hear any more. I told them everything. Everything Anna had told me, everything I knew, and everything I thought about it.

Maybe Anna couldn't figure out the right thing to do, but I knew.

Things changed after that. Maybe not right away, but that was the beginning. We didn't do as many big group things, and the foursomes started to sort in ways that didn't include Anna and Greg. Or me. Eventually the faculty family gatherings I had treasured became just one big holiday party and maybe a graduation party in the spring. My husband would ask every now and then why we never played bridge any more, but he had his own friends from work. He didn't really care.

When they offered early retirement, I took it. I still loved my work, but that's all it was. My best friend had betrayed me. Everything had been spoiled, and there was no reason to stay.

"You mean *you* spoiled everything, right?" Marcus said.

Janet looked startled. "I didn't have the affair!"

"*You* betrayed *her*! That wasn't your story to tell!" Lauren's voice was so incensed, they all turned to her.

"It was." Janet was defensive. "Once Anna told me, it became my story, too!"

"I can see where you would feel that way," Sarah said, "but what about Karen?"

Carlos nodded. "Where was her say in this?"

Janet held up her hand, refusing the cheese board being offered to her. "I'm sorry Karen had to suffer, too, but I'm not sorry for what I did. Not even a little."

"That is a great deal of certainty in the face of the losses you, yourself, suffered," Carlos said as he turned to Marcus.

Marcus shook his head. "I almost admire your attitude, to be able to look at the scorched earth around you and just shrug. Maybe you have to do some longer term hurting of other people before you can really appreciate regret."

I have been clean for six years, three months, five days. It was a big deal for me when I passed five years, because it was kind of a magic number. I don't know if there's any medical significance or research to support that, but for me, I figured if I could go five years, I could go forever. I'd have it beat. You guys are nodding like you've heard this one before, because you have, sort of. Everybody knows a user, a tweaker, an alchie; everybody knows the twelve steps like they're attached to their front porch. You're partly right, because every loser druggie story about getting sucked into the vortex is pretty much the same, but if you haven't been the one using, you don't really know.

There are never enough drugs, and never enough money to get the drugs you need. It isn't like worrying about stretching your paycheck to cover all the bills, it's more like thrashing against an attacker whose hands are crushing your throat. Everyone between you and the meth or the coke or the heroin is trying to kill you, and must be treated as the enemy.

I started lifting things to trade or sell for coke when I was fifteen. School was pretty easy for me, and my mom believed me every time I said it wasn't my fault. I was being set up or picked on or treated unfairly because everybody was jealous. She bought it all, because it sounded so familiar. That's exactly what she had been telling me my whole life.

The more I did, though, the more I needed and the harder to cover it got. One night I got hauled in by the cops and my mom had to pick me up at the station. After that I was really careful all the way through graduation. College, though, was like an all you can eat buffet for a glutton. I would go for a year, stop out to work and clean up, go for a semester, take a break to dry out. I tried just drinking, but anybody who doesn't think alcohol is a drug hasn't seen me dive for the bottom of the bottle.

It took seven years, but I finally graduated, got a job, and lived the life of a functional user. My weekends were disjointed scenes of people and places I could almost remember, all spliced together out of order like a damaged film, but every Monday morning, well, sometimes Tuesday, I would load up on caffeine and sugar and aspirin and go crank out enough code to hold onto my job. Mom was still good for cash for unexpected "car repairs" or concert tickets for a big date she hoped to get to meet, but by then Dad was sick, so she was pretty busy with him.

Then I found meth. Or it found me. I used up all my sick days and all my vacation. I worked enough, mostly from home, to be reprimanded but not fired. I wasn't causing scenes at work, hadn't prompted any sexual harassment suits or filed any disability claims, so I was still on the positive side of the corporate balance sheet. But I needed more money.

I started stopping by the house in the middle of the day while Mom was at work and Dad was napping. The chemo really laid him out, and I could count on enough time to get in and out without being hassled. When I ran out of things that wouldn't be noticed right away, I moved on to whatever I could carry. Mom didn't say anything, but after I took the TV from the bedroom, the locks were changed. I broke the glass door in the kitchen and took everything I could carry.

When the police showed up pounding on the door, I figured Mom had had it, but it was idiot roommate who sold me out. He thought he could cash in on my score while I was gone, but the cops beat him to it. Between my stash and his and the pile of stuff I hadn't had a chance to sell, it was a felony. The whole long walk from my house to the car to holding to a cell blurred until I couldn't even remember making my phone call. But I did. I did what I needed to to get out, get back to normal.

I picked the first bail bondsman out of the yellow pages and when he asked for collateral, I told him I'd put up my house. And gave him my parents' address. I'd always hated having the same name as my dad, but it finally paid off. It didn't play out, though. Typical junkie thinking that they wouldn't check, but of course they did.

The bottom rose up to hit me hard before I could see my life had to change. I had talked my way out of consequences and into new trouble so many times I took it for granted, but when you find yourself vomiting blood in a toilet you don't recognize with a woman you can't remember ever seeing before waiting in bed, "thrill" and "excitement" are not the words that come to mind. I cleaned up and got sober, worked two jobs until I proved I was reliable enough to get a better one, and finally made a real life for myself. Then I apologized to all the people I'd hurt during the destructive years. When Dad died, mom wouldn't speak to me at the funeral, couldn't even look at me. The mortgage thing was where she broke.

That was more than five years ago, and she still hasn't forgiven me. Maybe everybody has a line, that point where there aren't any more chances or leaps of faith left to give, I don't know, but I know Mom does. Her judgment was final and there isn't any appeal.

Marcus looked at Janet. "She reminds me of you."

Janet flushed, and Lauren reached over to touch Marcus on the knee for a moment.

"It's kind of a Rashomon thing," Sarah said. "Her version of the story might be completely different, because you aren't the main character in that one. Her actions tell you something about her feelings, but they aren't the whole story."

Carlos passed the last of the crackers and olives, then cleared his throat. "It is true even for couples. You can only know of anyone what they choose to show you. No matter how thoughtfully you live your own life, you cannot control the actions of the people you love. Sometimes you cannot even predict them."

If you had met me three years ago, we might have been on opposite sides of the court room. The line between the jury and the judged is much finer than I had previously believed, and Justice is either less or more blind than she should be, depending on who is telling the story.

I was married for fourteen years to a woman who had pursued me until I gave in. I had been married before and was in no rush to repeat my mistakes, but she was so convincing that eventually even I believed we were meant to be together. Christina was independent, well-educated and successful, with a life already established when we met. That was the woman I fell in love with, the one who knew what she wanted, went after it, and usually got it.

It was easy to see that, for her, a large part of the attraction was the lure of the exotic. My mother was Italian, my father a diplomat from Venezuela. I spoke four languages and did not get my driver's license until my last year in college because I had always had a chauffeur. I would take her out to dinner, and by the end of the evening, we would be drinking wines not even listed on the menu because the sommelier and I had become friends.

For all my reluctance, I thought Christina loved me for what I was, what I valued. She knew I did not want children, but swore it didn't matter. When I grew tired of making deals in the world of chips and widgets, she offered me a deal of her own. I could turn my back on business and do nothing but paint, and she would support me as long as necessary . . . if I was a stay at home dad. When I say it to you, it sounds ugly, but we were happy and it sounded like nothing more than just a way for both of us to have what we wanted.

I am sorry now that I could not hear the ugly then.

It was a surprisingly good arrangement. My daughter was a delight, and my vision and voice as an artist grew with my studies. When I was offered the opportunity to apprentice with a master, we hired a nanny. Life seemed perfect for four years, but in the fifth year, with our daughter in school, the minor tension that had always existed between her parents and myself grew into battle of wills. When they asked to take my daughter to church and I refused, they began to pressure Christina to insist I get a "real" job. A year later, when her consulting business was slow and we found ourselves in trying financial times, her parents offered us a loan. Their condition was that they would take control of all our finances, including giving me an allowance. I arranged to sell some of my paintings to friends and private collectors, and raised enough cash to reject the loan, but the line had been drawn, and their intent was clear.

Perhaps that is when it really began, but the turning point, the night that marks the line between the life I had then and the one I have now, came a year later. We argued at dinner. It started about money, but came down to her parents and what role they should play in our lives. Christina seemed not to recall that this arrangement was her creation, she heard only the criticism and disappointment of her father and mother. We shared more than a bottle of wine as we ate, our voices louder with each glass. When it came time to put our daughter to bed, I made a snide comment about her grandparents, and Christina exploded. She shoved me out the door and slammed it on my arm. I shouldered it open again and pushed her back across the room, away from my daughter.

There followed many things, the sheriff's car, handcuffs, a night in jail, tens of thousands of dollars in attorney fees, foreclosure on our home and supervised visits with my daughter. I learned that you should always memorize at least one friend's phone number, because the police do not let you touch your cell phone after they confiscate it. I learned that jail cells are just as grim and pungent as you might imagine, but that more than anything, they smell like fear. I learned that if you are a man, you cannot ever lay your hands on a woman, because your story will not be believed, especially if your skin is darker than hers. I also learned that even your closest friends can be eager to condemn you without ever speaking to you.

But I learned other things, too. I learned that there are attorneys who are motivated by justice more than money. I learned that true friends are the few who do not vanish when you are in crisis. And I learned that I am more resilient than I knew.

Christina moved with our daughter to the house of friends and took out a restraining order. These had been our closest friends, people who had traveled with us and had keys to our home. They had known me from the time I first met Christina and had named their son for me. They never called to get my version of what happened, never spoke to me again. My attorney told me to file counter charges of battery against Christina, but I refused. She is the mother of my child, and I still believed she wanted what was best for her. I was found not guilty of battery, with a finding of "mutual combat." Then began the long custody battle, with her refusing me any rights until they were awarded by a judge, forcing extra attorney meetings until I ran out of money and had to act on my own behalf. She let the house go into foreclosure rather than let me see any money from its sale. When we appeared before a judge to hear my request for unsupervised visits, and I reported that I had taken a part-time job with an income of $500 per month, Christina's family sat in the courtroom and laughed.

There was a full year of hell and self-doubt before I could find my spirit again through the fog of disbelief. It took another year to cobble together a place to live where my daughter could stay with me, a job with enough pay to support myself, and a space to paint. Now I have a good life again, perhaps not one I could have predicted, but one that is filled with the things that matter most. What I don't have is any better understanding of what happened. I do know my part, and I know what I did wrong, but I cannot help but feel that I missed something, that there must be a reason for Christina to want not just to end our marriage, but to destroy me. Like a movie that breaks before the final reel, the story of that part of my life leaves me unsatisfied. I am still trying to accept that some questions may never be answered.

Carlos dusted the crumbs from the board and tucked it back into the leather pouch, then flattened the empty cracker box. He offered a tiny smile to Lauren. "Perhaps you now regret sharing a meal with me?"

Lauren shook her head and swallowed hard. "No, that I don't regret. I'm a hospice nurse now, and the things I see are very different from what went on in the ER. The bonds between people are not always as simple as we think or try to pretend."

Janet stood slowly, her face pinched as if something smelled bad near her. "I don't regret it, either, but neither do I wish to continue. If you'll excuse me."

Marcus whistled softly under his breath as they watched her march across the room, back rigid. He looked about to speak, then stopped.

"I feel sorry for her," Lauren said. The shared silence between them was filled with echoes of other larger losses, earlier lives separated from theirs but not forgotten.

Sarah moved to sit beside Lauren in the chair Janet had vacated. "I think you're right about there being some questions that are never answered," She paused and then continued, "but sometimes you also get answers to questions you hadn't asked."

When I was a grad student, I met my future husband playing volleyball. We were both pretty competitive, and we kept seeing each other at the regular games held on the oval field on campus. Danny was out of school and working, but still part of a team of mostly engineers who played together. We talked a few times before he asked me out, and then I found out he'd asked everyone I knew about me before he'd talked to me, because he thought I was out of his league. That was so like him, though. He was brilliant, but never made other people feel stupid, and he was handsome but never looked in a mirror except to brush his teeth. He was funny and charming and loved old movies. Danny could recite all the dialogue from every Cary Grant movie until you would swear he was reincarnated.

We got married right after I graduated, and I got a job as an assistant professor. With his long hours at a start up and my teaching and grading papers and holding office hours, we didn't have much time together, but what we did have was amazing. I never heard him raise his voice to anyone, including me, and just sitting reading the paper with him was better than going to a four-star restaurant and Broadway show with anyone else. We were happy in a simple but complete way I didn't even know was possible.

And then one day when I was out of town, he was driving Over the Hill to see a friend on the coast, and somehow, in full daylight on a dry road, his car went over the edge and he was killed instantly.

The investigators suspected another car might have been speeding around the curve and crossed the center line, forcing him to swerve, but no witness came forward. They also considered the possibility of a deer startling him, but the wildlife was mute, too. They tested his blood for alcohol and drugs, though he never did either, and that was also a dead end. Then they gave up.

I moved through the days and did what I had to. In some ways, the tasks required of the living preparing the way for the dead are the only tethers the survivors have to keep from following. The words and stories at the memorial were overwhelming, painful and comforting at the same time. Some of the people who spoke I barely knew, because they were from his work, and one of them spoke of him like a brother. During the reception, Ryan introduced himself and shared more stories of my husband, his friend. He stayed to the end to help clean up, and by the time we finished, he had agreed to housesit while I went to deliver a paper at an academic conference the following month and help sort through Danny's things. We found many interests in common, and it was a comfort to both of us to be together. Before the year was out, we knew it was more than just comfort, and we were married.

We lost a few friends after that. Nothing obvious, mind you, no open hostility or accusations, but there were people who remained permanently "booked" when we called to schedule dinner, or who simply stopped responding to invitations. I understood, though. The people who loved Danny the most felt like I was betraying his memory by "settling" for his friend Ryan. They couldn't see how it was Danny's love for each of us that brought us together in the first place. Maybe they just didn't believe that anyone could have more than one love that strong. I don't condemn the people who couldn't accept our relationship, but I do feel sorry for them. Love is not a narrow small thing. My love for Ryan could never replace my love for Danny, but it doesn't have to. I have room in my heart for both.

Carlos smiled as he pulled a bar of dark chocolate from his bag and broke it into pieces, offering them to Lauren then to Sarah. "You make me want to believe," he said. "Perhaps love can survive any judgment."

Lauren tucked her hair behind one ear as she savored her chocolate. "Or maybe love is beyond judgment, resilient and separate from everything else."

"I don't know," Marcus looked toward Janet. "I think judgment trumps love in her world." He shook his head. "And there are more just like her."

"Some people may seem lost to us," Carlos said as he held out a bittersweet shard to Marcus, "perhaps some of them truly are." He chose a piece of chocolate for himself and bit off a corner. "We can only make our own choices, build the best life for ourselves that we can."

There was a whirring hum like a giant inhalation as electricity surged through the building. The fluorescent lights overhead blinked on in rows. Carlos offered the last sliver of chocolate to Sarah with a wink. "And, of course, we can always hope."

# # #

Catch and Release

I don't know when I will see Nathan again, and so I am taking him fishing. This is the best way I know to make the few hours we have today tangible, something that will last. Time will expand and distort and finally lose all its power in the focus on the cast and the fish and the flies.

Tomorrow my boy will take his new degree and pack his meager belongings into his graduation wheels and drive two thousand miles away. *My boy*, as if he were a simple possession, as if he ever really belonged to me. His leaving evolved slowly, in the usual pattern of children, yet I am caught unaware, unprepared. Tomorrow is muddy run-off, hard to read, but today we will fish.

The summer he was five years old, I took my son fishing for the first time. Nate was about to start school, and while I knew he would be gone for only half a day at first, it was a four-hour absence that was the first point on a line of infinite separation. No matter how close we were, how many games we played, how many secrets he might choose to share, part of his life would no longer include me. He would begin to create his own universe, one in which his mother could be no more than a minor constellation. The budding independence brought out in me an ambivalence I had expected intellectually, but for which I was viscerally unprepared.

So I taught him to fish.

We sat beside the river and watched the trout feed on a hatch of caddis flies. Nate was quiet and thoughtful even at that age, so much like the father he would never know. Leaning against me and watching my hands, he listened while I talked about insects and feeding patterns and choosing the right fly. I showed him how to cast, guiding his little arm in a short arc from shoulder height to straight over his head. His hazel eyes opened wide when the fly finally landed lightly like a real insect, with no telltale puddle of line slapping a warning to the fish. After a few missed strikes, Nate set his hook in a tiny rainbow. In his exuberance, he yanked the miniature trout right out of the water and into the tall grass behind him.

"We serious fishermen call those 'flying fish'," I told my son in a grave voice as I searched for the elusive catch. He laughed out loud when the wriggling fish darted away upon its release, deeper into the cool water.

Academic life was easy for Nate as he grew, but the social side of school was not so simple. He had my easy laugh and the beginnings of a sharp wit, but he also had an overzealous blush response. He would speak only if spoken to and tried to avoid being the focus of any group's attention. It was his wiry agility and quickness in games that saved Nate from isolation. He was rarely the first one picked for a team, that honor reserved for the extroverts, but he was always an early choice.

At ten he could spend hours wading along the bank by my side, silently casting and watching. I taught him about using the face of the clock and the pause at the top of the cast. Keep your arm between ten o'clock and two o'clock. Let the rod do the work. The rod is an extension of your arm. Only when we stopped in a shady spot and settled in for lunch did we talk about other things: our week, vacation plans, the little details of the daily shared experiences that build a relationship. And sometimes the big details.

"Would people like me better if I pretended to be dumb?" he asked casually, between halfhearted nibbles at his sandwich.

I felt my face grow hot. *I will march down to that school and smack every one of those nasty ill-mannered little brats and all their ignorant parents, too!* But my first thoughts did not answer the question. I hoped more rational words would eventually filter through the cloud of emotion. What was the best response to being singled out, subject to a potent mixture of awe and resentment from you peers? We tend to forget the toll extracted from children for gifts best-suited to adults. Maybe I had blocked out the hurtful struggle behind my own choices or maybe they had faded, replaced by the complicated losses of adulthood. But he was decades away from the comfort of historical perspective.

"What kind of people do *you* like?"

I gave the problem back to him, biting off the tirade looping eloquently through my brain. Why don't they send you home from the hospital with a self-mute button instead of free diapers for your newborn? I would have settled for an automatic three-second delay. It would have saved me years of practice.

He stared, unseeing, at the water and did not respond. I could almost hear the whirring of his mental machinery, and as I watched, his profile aged, became his father's. For an instant, Nate was already gone. I blinked hard.

"Well," he said, "I don't like fakers." He tore off a big mouthful of bologna and cheese. "And the most fun people are usually pretty smart."

The light shifted on the river as we watched, from the sharp sequin flashes of midday to a muted green glow mottled by stretching patches of gray. We were comfortable in the silence, each with our own thoughts. The breeze shifted, and a cool gust from the shadowed bank told us when to pack up our gear and go home. I snatched a grasshopper from the waving blade of grass it clutched and tossed it onto the river as we turned to go. It barely touched the surface of the water before being gobbled from below.

"Fish come easier to bait," I said on the way back to the car, "but easy isn't what makes a good catch."

His coordination and strength increased with adolescence, and Nathan acquired an admiration from his peers that is reserved for those with physical prowess—the jocks. This allowed him the freedom to excel academically without being labeled conveniently as "nerd" or "brain" and dismissed. Granted as much three-dimensionally as teenagers can concede to one another, he grew more comfortable with himself.

At fifteen his long cast was better than mine, a thing of beauty and precision. A great billowing arc of line would hover above him before the fly shot to the opposite bank, and his rolling cast sent perfect hoops of line spinning across the surface of the river like a rodeo rope trick. He still got hung up in the growth behind him sometimes, but then again, so did I.

We fished separately now, walking upstream and down, meeting only accidentally when the water was low enough for one of us to wade across and fish the other side. We'd gesture to each other, hands apart, to show the size of the enormous fighter the other had just missed seeing. Lunch often passed with little conversation, but we were always together.

"Eric's going to spend this summer working at his uncle's dude ranch in Montana. His uncle said he could bring along another hired hand."

I had to smile at the adolescent gift for making a request without ever asking the question. Throwing out the topic for a reaction before you actually take the risk of getting your hopes up. An interesting strategy. Do they teach this to each other, or is it innate, activated by the same hormones that produce their insecurity?

"That's a lot of hard work," I said. *Don't go, don't go, don't go.* "and probably a lot of girls your age?" *Go,go,go.*

Nathan smiled and blushed a red so intense the tips of his ears were nearly purple.

And it's a very long way from home.

"Maybe you can get in a little fishing while you're there. Maybe teach some of the guests."

"I thought about that!" He grinned and wove the details of the ranch, the rivers nearby, the riding opportunities, and the responsibilities of the hired hands into a story. He sat up straighter as he talked, his hands describing the summer for me. It was a longer continuous stream of words and more enthusiasm than I had heard from him in months.

"Sounds like you're going to have a busy summer."

Braced for disappointment, he did not respond immediately. When he understood what my statement meant, he got to his knees and gave me a hug. Wrapping both arms around me tight, he took my breath away.

"I promise I'll write, Mom." He offered a sideways smile. "Or maybe you better come visit."

We retrieved our rods and switched directions for the afternoon. Nathan did not see me pause and turn to watch him walk away. I stood there until all I could see was the space he had occupied just before turning to follow the bend of the river.

He came home every summer during college, but our fishing trips were fewer and fewer each year. Nathan worked full-time and had a girl friend and still played ball whenever he could. These months he existed for me mostly in the ripe discarded gym clothes on this floor and the car's uneven humming fading into the night. His life had many facets, and fishing was only one of them. I was only one of them. Petulance and irrational jealousy lurked just beneath my ever-supportive surface. I longed to make unreasonable demands on his time, to reassert a priority status to which I could no longer lay claim.

Last summer my fishing was solitary. At season's end I stood alone in the icy river facing a deep green pool and feeling my son's absence just as surely as I felt the presence of the big brown watching the riffle. I longed to see that lemon-yellow flash of belly as it cleared the surface to take my fly. But anticipation is not a strike, timing is crucial. Jerk too soon and the fish is spooked and gone.

"If we don't leave now, we're not going to make the river before it heats up."

Nathan appears in the doorway, dispersing my reverie. I look up into the familiar face of my boy, a face now bearded and angular but with the same mosaic eyes in all the colors of the river. A fisherman.

"I want to try that new fly you tied last night."

Nathan pulls a barbless hook wrapped with deer hair and a touch of bright red silk out of his fly box and sets it firmly in the patch of sheepskin on his vest. His movements have a graceful economy, fingers nimble despite the size of his hands. A *man.*

"You ready, Mom?"

We stand side-by-side at the water's edge in the rosy glow of early morning. Feeding ripples are visible all along the bank, and a big rainbow breaks the surface not twenty feet from us. Nate grins at me, his eyes eager. I know just what he is thinking: an embarrassment of options and the whole day before us. I return the smile and point toward the jumper. "You want that one?"

He winks at me and says, "Nah, too easy." Nate instead sends his first cast into a dark pocket tight against the bank, hoping the wily old man in the deep water will look up. I shake my head and laugh.

"That's my boy!"

Cast, refloat, refloat, cast again, mend the line, watch him rise, set the hook, keep your tip up, watch him jump, let him run, give him line if he needs it, put him on the reel, bring him close, bring him in, admire his colors, praise his fight . . . let him go.

I'm ready.

###

Ceremony

Jackson shaved carefully, knowing he couldn't afford any toilet paper blotters on his surface wounds today. Today he wanted to look perfect for Josephine. He squinted at his reflection. Well, maybe not perfect, but as close as he could come with what he had to work with. She always told him he was perfect just the way he was, which made him want to be even better. No one else had ever made him feel that way. He rinsed his razor and glanced at the clock. He wasn't due at the church until 2:00, but he didn't want to feel rushed. It was too easy to get caught up in details and let the important moments slip away unnoticed. Jackson didn't want the last few hours before his life officially changed forever to pass in a blur.

The first time he saw Josephine, Jackson didn't imagine they would ever meet. She was Puck in the Drama Department's production of *A Midsummer Night's Dream*, and he was just one of dozens of dim faces in the dark beyond the stage lights. A bundle of energy with an athletic build and startlingly direct gaze, she wasn't really his type, but he checked the program for her name, anyway. The girl he was seeing then was all fuzzy sweaters and tight pants and coy sideways glances, just like the other girls before. That was what he liked in a woman, warmth and comfort and softness. When Josephine turned up in one of his design classes the next semester, Jackson discovered that what he liked in women had nothing at all to do with what he loved.

There wasn't any visible lint on the black pants hanging on the door, but Jackson brushed them thoroughly, anyway, before pulling them on. They were a little looser, even since the last time he tried them on. That surprised him until he realized he couldn't remember eating much in the last few days. He tucked in his shirt, then tightened the belt one notch and smoothed the creases in the fabric. The starchy folds at his back felt like someone poking him, and the sleeves seemed too stiff. Jackson faced the mirror. It looked good, though, he had to admit, even if he felt like he was looking at a stranger.

The first time he asked Josephine out, she turned him down. Not in a mean way, but she was seeing someone else, she said. He thought it was kind of funny that it hadn't come up in the three weeks their group had worked on their project, but he let it go. Bad enough that it took him that long to ask her in the first place. He had never been a ladies man, exactly, but he had never gone without a date when he wanted one, either. Something about Josephine, though, dried up anything facile or contrived before it could leave his lips. She took him seriously, looked at him when he talked as if she knew where he was going before he got there. That's what stumped him; how do you ask someone on a first date when you've already known her forever?

There were only white socks in the sock drawer, sending Jackson into a mild panic which passed as soon as he remembered the dark socks balled up and stuffed into his dress shoes. Sometimes you can plan so far ahead you throw yourself off, but that was part of why he allowed so much time. Aaron and Will had offered to keep him company that morning, but even though they were his best friends, he had turned them down. He had a feeling that having people around, having to make polite conversation or listen to domestic anecdotes or, worse yet, pretend interest in well-meaning advice would have just made him more nervous and anxious.

The first time Josephine kissed him, he got hard so fast it was like he was fifteen. They went right from lips touching to full body contact without a pause, passion seizing them both so suddenly he could feel her vibrating in his arms. It seemed like it might go on forever, then they both paused to breathe at the same time, inhaling and exhaling together, one shared breath. That was surprisingly intimate, maybe more intimate than the embrace, and it shocked them apart. Josephine blinked as if in waking, looked as if she were about to say something, then disappeared into her room. For days afterwards he got lightheaded every time he saw her walking toward him or spotted her in the coffee shop between classes, and he realized he was holding his breath.

The jacket he struggled into felt like it was lined with lead. It was supposed to be wool, but he'd never known wool to make him feel like Atlas. He faced the mirror and squared his shoulders, but he could feel them wanting to roll forward under the weight. Jackson filled his lungs to capacity, then tightened his abdomen as he exhaled. If he kept his spine straight, his chin up, the coat didn't seem as big a burden. He noticed a slight tremor in his hand as he adjusted his tie. Maybe he should have hired a driver or let one of the guys pick him up. He tugged the hem of the coat and frowned at his reflection. That was just nerves. He would be fine.

The first time he traveled with Josephine, Jackson thought their relationship was over. The whole trip was a nightmare of delayed flights and lost luggage, unseasonable rain and surly waiters, one broken toe and two cases of food poisoning. Tempers flared, harsh words were exchanged, and a few tears were spilled. Jackson felt so miserable about making Josephine cry, he couldn't speak to her at all. He was sure that was the wrong thing to do, that silence probably made it seem like he was angry, but he just didn't have any words or any place to start. As he unloaded her bag from the trunk and carried it to her door, he braced himself for the fallout. Josephine smiled and shook her head. "You look like you just lost your puppy. At least we know it has to be better next time," she paused then added, "because it sure can't get any worse!" They both burst out laughing, and Jackson, hearing only "next time," proposed right then.

The day was perfect. The sky was a blue so bright it made Jackson squint and fumble for his sunglasses. The air had a scent of wood smoke and a bite to the breeze that felt like winter was coming, just not today. He tried to see everything on the drive to the church so he could capture the day the way you do those moments that mark the big transitions. Birth. Death. Graduation. Marriage. Passages from one stage to the next and on and on, a platform, a formal pause before the momentum of daily life resumes. He had to circle the block three times before he could bring himself to pull into the parking lot. He knew he should be ready, but he just wasn't.

The first time he took Josephine home to meet his family, Jackson had been more nervous than she was. In fact, she wasn't nervous at all. "What's the worst that can happen? Maybe they won't like me, but they can't kill me and eat me!" Jackson had shaken his head as she laughed, wondering if she could lend him a little of her disregard for the opinions of his relatives. He could remember holidays where it felt like he was being cannibalized by his parents, dinners where he wished he could trade places with the unfeeling entree. What Josephine didn't know was that what worried him wasn't what his family would think of her, but whether she would think less of him after seeing who he was with them.

Of course they loved her. But more than that, they seemed to love him more with her. All the old lines of teasing, the criticism thinly veiled as harmless questions slid right past without a rise when she stood beside him. Suddenly released from the script because he no longer gave his lines, his mother and father found new dialogue to match. Jackson discovered that reaching for Josephine had allowed him to let go of what he didn't need of his past.

The walkway to the door of the church was shaded, but Jackson left his sunglasses on. He paused at the door, looking at the hand resting on the knob as if it belonged to someone else, then pulled it open. No one else would be there so early, which was just as well.

The last time Jackson saw Josephine, she had told him to be grateful for what they'd had, not bitter about imagined things they might miss. Her skin was the translucent blue-white of skim milk, but her eyes lit up when she looked at him like a child tasting ice cream for the first time. Josephine's voice was so weak it was nearly a whisper. Jackson had to lean close and watch her lips as she spoke just to understand her. The nearness and the breathy voice had an erotic undertone that was completely disconcerting given the circumstances. "You're spoiled . . . and you're greedy . . ." Josephine smiled and blinked in slow motion, then finished almost in a sigh, "What more could you ask?" He knew she was right, knew that thirty years was a lot more than most couples ever see together. More than that, he knew that the life he'd had was one he never would have seen without her.

Jackson stood in the silent church before the enameled urn and a portrait bathed in soft gold light from a pinpoint spot in the ceiling. When he'd stood in that place before, he had been eager, ready for any future that included Josephine. Now he was afraid. The queasy shakes and uncertain expectation he felt both times were eerily similar. Soon the room would fill with all the people come to say good-bye, but Jackson had been doing that for months. He was here to honor a promise. Josephine knew it was too much to ask that he be happy, but she didn't want her memory washed in tears. "Just try to remember me with a smile" was all she had asked of him. Jackson ran his fingers over the lips in the photo, then smiled back at it without effort and said, "I do."

# # #

Spin Cycle

Emily pressed her nose against the glass porthole of the dryer. She yanked on the handle again, though she knew it was futile. Some tiny metal bit had dropped to the floor and rolled under the machine when she slammed the door on the shirt. Now it was trapped inside or she outside, she wasn't sure which.

"Excuse me."

Emily jumped a little and stepped back from the machine.

"Sorry, I didn't mean to startle you." His voice was like a lullaby, low and soft, comforting in a way. It was an odd contrast to the hammer and chisel he held in his hand, the screwdrivers and wrenches hanging from the worn leather belt around his hips.

"Is this the broken one?"

His eyes were caramel, then forest green, then mahogany with gold flecks, changing with the shifts of light like a kaleidoscope. Brian's eyes had been pale blue, the color of the sky closest to the sun.

"Uh . . . yes."

Emily was wishing she could wipe the nose print off the glass when he suddenly wedged the chisel in beside the latch and whacked it with the hammer. The entire handle fell off and hit the floor with a sharp clang.

"What are you doing?" Emily grabbed the door, trying to insinuate her fingers into the crack, then pounded on the glass in frustration. "Now I'll never get him back!"

"Him?"

"I mean *it*. The shirt, you moron!"

His face flushed as he looked from Emily to the machine. "I'm sorry," he shifted the hammer to his left hand with the chisel and extended his right to her. "I'm Jared."

They both looked at the grease-dappled hand between them, and Emily burst into tears.

Jared wiped the hand on his pants.

"I thought I would get some actual help when I called that number on the machine!" Emily wiped her eyes and sniffed loudly. "I'm going to report you to the owner!"

Jared pulled a tissue out of the pocket of his shirt and offered it to her with a flourish like a magic trick.

"You just did."

Emily blew her nose and glared.

"This dryer has been a problem for months. The pin dropped out last week, too. I fixed it, but I knew it wouldn't last. It's run its course, and I'm just in denial." The corners of his mouth lifted. "Don't worry. We'll get it back." He peered through the glass, his lips parted and his eyebrows raised briefly as if he were about to ask a question, but he ran a hand through his unkempt curly hair instead.

"It was my fiance's," Emily blurted out.

Their eyes met for an instant, then ricocheted off to the handle on the floor, the buzzing ceiling lights, the dryer, their own shoes.

"It's been a year." Emily blinked repeatedly, swallowed, took a deep breath. "He was only thirty-six. Who dies when they're thirty-six?" A small sad smile passed across her face, almost too fast to see, the trace of a memory she didn't share. "I need to let go."

Jared moved toward her, then stopped.

"I'm sorry. I know I keep saying that, but that doesn't make it less true." Jared touched her arm lightly. "Maybe I don't know what it is to lose someone you love like that, but I still know about loss."

He tugged on the tool belt. "This was my dad's." He swept his hand from the front windows across the bank of dryers. "And so was this. When he died, I assumed I'd sell the place, but then I came to see it after the memorial." Jared's face changed as he spoke, as if years were falling away. "I used to come with him to collect the quarters from the machines and refill the soap dispensers. Over in that corner there was a Coke machine that Dad stocked with Fanta just for me."

Emily watched as much as heard him tell his story, the way his eyes grew bright and his smile could not be contained. For a moment she was standing in his childhood, and it seemed like a really nice place.

"I stood here and realized I hated my life. Well, I hated my job, because it had become my life. I made more money in two years than my Dad made in ten, but he died happy." He shrugged and all his features fell back into place and time. "So here I am."

Emily looked at her reflection in the dryer to avoid looking at Jared. Her hair looked windblown and her wide-set eyes gave the impression she was mildly surprised. Past her reflection she could see the shirt crumpled at the bottom of the dryer with one sleeve resting on the agitator above as if it were waving to her.

"I got rid of everything but this shirt. I've been sleeping with it, but now it smells more like me than him. I thought . . . I thought maybe if I washed it. It sounds stupid when I say it out loud, but I didn't know what else to do."

Jared held out the hammer to her. "I have to replace this machine anyway."

Emily frowned, "You mean . . ."

He was grinning now. He handed her a pair of safety goggles. "Go for it."

Emily took the hammer in both hands and swung. The first time was a little tentative, but the crack of the impact bolstered her confidence. On the third hit, the glass shattered, and Emily was laughing.

"I can't believe you told me to do that."

"Well, it worked, didn't it?" Jared reached into the machine and pulled out the shirt, shaking off the broken glass before holding it out to Emily.

Emily looked at the plain white shirt and then at Jared.

"You know," she said with a smile, "I don't think I need it anymore.

# # #

Fast Forward

▶▶

Underground

Welcome, Traveler! Welcome to New York City, Earth! Sit across from me but down a bit, so you can hear me but we will not seem to be together. This time of night there aren't many riders on the train, and I have misted the entrances with a pheromone repugnant to humans, but caution cannot be overvalued.

I understand you lost your tail in the first transfer. My condolences, but you will find that your life here is easier without it. There are some peoples with prehensile tails, but they are mostly academics living in protected communities called zoos where they study the humans, the dominant species here. I am so pleased you made the long journey otherwise uninjured. Although we have lost only one Traveler in many cycles, I worry every time as if it were the first.

Do not be startled by the flashes of light in the window. The smaller are guide lights in the tunnels, the sudden brilliant bursts are stations where the train does not stop. These occur during every passage and do not indicate pursuit.

The bag on the floor beside me contains your identity papers, two sets of local costumes, currency with a list of names and values for the coins, a box of nutrient bars to sustain you until you can identify the digestible and acceptably consumable indigenous flora and fauna, a hand-held communication device with emergency contact numbers preprogrammed, a dark eye covering, an instruction manual, and extra highlighters. Though highlighters are difficult to smuggle out to the rim worlds, here they are abundant. When I exit the subway, you will take the bag, put on the eye covering, and leave this car at the next stop. You will be met by your final guide who will take you to your new residence and answer any questions you have on your instructions for living on Earth.

First, try to blend in. This is important both for your safety and for the protection of the local peoples. Occasionally we have some leakage, as when an avian from the third sector grew so comfortable in his new life that he allowed his crest to grow back. We were unable to act quickly enough to spare this world a wave of multicolored and spiked head plumage which lasted for decades. And do not get me started on the peripheral metallic ornamentation of the Tlchu! 5 dancers. That spread like plague and has become embedded in the culture. I tell you this as a warning, because you, too, may be tempted to slacken your guard or discard your disguise. There is little variation in the biological phenotype of the humans, but the material personas they adopt offer many options. We have selected the one most similar to your own appearance, but don't assume you may one day just be yourself. This planet has a higher factor of assimilation than any of the null systems, but the human acceptance is matched by suggestibility. Under no circumstances should your polydactyl reproductive organs be revealed.

The groaning earth sounds you hear do resemble the songs from your moon. I thought that the first time I heard the brakes of the slowing car, too.

Now, look at the images above the windows. The map on your side shows all the subway train lines. You will not be able to tell, but each line contains different pigment. The bold letters inked over the map contain your instructions for finding your contact. Use your highlighter to reveal the message after I have left and the train has begun to move again. We maintain information walls between every level of the transport line, because the moment you were liberated from captivity in your system, we stood in violation of the Alliance Treaties. The less we know, the less we can reveal. You will see similar glyphs imprinted on walls and vehicles and even hillsides. This is not a cultural virus perpetrated by one of our placements; it was an existing practice we adapted for our use. That means not all are messages for Travelers, but if you are in doubt, the highlighter will reveal the code in a true sign.

Next, immediate personal safety. By galactic standards, this is a peaceful world. There are bloody regional skirmishes and endless family rivalries of the sort found everywhere, but the humans possess great abilities in mediation, reconciliation, and bond formation. Ongoing research indicates that reproductive practices and commerce strategies enhance the inborn traits which produce these qualities. Still, there are local hostilities and individual bursts of violence in many places. Your guide will have further instruction on avoiding risk and conflict. The most important factor Earth has to offer besides assimilation is silence. These people do not have propulsion necessary for travel beyond this system, so you are protected by the near invisibility of this world.

Finally, you may feel overwhelmed at first by the strangeness of the world, it's smells and sounds and too-bright lights, and you might come to question your decision. Perhaps all in your position have felt that way, but none that I have met in this car have chosen homesickness over freedom. Freedom is valued here more highly than on any of the worlds I used to police, and the grimmest battles fought among Earth's people have been in the name of freedom in one form or another. In the many cycles I have lived among these people, I have grown to appreciate their history and admire their passions.

This is my stop. Remember: take the bag, put on the eye covering, use your highlighter on the message and exit carefully when the car doors open again. I have another London transfer to meet at the abandoned platform in the 59th Street station, my final ride of the night. I wish you luck and safe journey, Traveler; you are almost home. Please tell your guide that Tubman sends his regards.

###

Preparing

One gallon of water per person per day sounds doable until you get to the part where they recommend having a two week supply. You do the math for the four of you and try to imagine where you could keep all those jugs. Or what, kegs? You would have to use them as a bed or a table, something out in the open. So you cut back to the three-day minimum supply, which still seems like a lot, and add a gallon of bleach for treating the alternative sources of water you're sure you'll be able to find if you need to. There's the water heater, after all, and the fountain. And there's always the neighbors' pool.

Food supply should be maintained at a three to five day level above normal requirements at all times. Your eyebrows shoot up involuntarily. You go to the store practically every day, and you still don't have that kind of reserve just sitting on shelves. Regular canned and packaged foods that don't require cooking or refrigeration are best. They should be individually dated and rotated back into your food supply for consumption every six months. You try to calculate the likelihood of either of those things happening, then stack tuna, soup, peanut butter, crackers, raisins, and nuts into a box. That stuff all has a shelf life of years. The crackers might get a little stale, but would you really quibble under the circumstances?

Flashlights top the list of emergency supplies. You wonder if most disasters occur at night. Batteries also figure prominently and then candles and matches in a waterproof container, of course. Can opener, paper plates and cups and towels and some eating utensils. That stuff is all pretty easy, and you check it off feeling a little smug.

Ax? Fire extinguisher? Shovel? Dust masks? Your sense of accomplishment vanishes at the tool list. You find the fire extinguisher in the garage, but it expired ten years ago. You throw a hammer and screw driver and a big roll of duct tape into the box and decide to come back to this section.

Sanitation looks simple, the soaps and diapers and toilet paper and tooth brushes you can just grab from the guest bath and check off the list. Then it starts going into detail about watertight containers and agricultural lime. It sounds like that "pack everything out" river trip you took, but that had some wage-slave high school kid to deal with the up close and personal part. You decide to skip this section, too, and pour yourself a glass of wine before moving on.

One complete change of clothing for each family member is a piece of cake, except that your oldest son has outgrown all but one pair of shoes. You pack an extra pair of your own clogs, which ought to do in a pinch, and remind yourself he prefers to go barefoot anyway.

You don't own a tent except for the toy one the kids keep in the back yard. You pile a couple wool blankets and a bunch of old baby blankets into the plastic storage box with the clothes and sit on the lid until it gives the telltale "snap."

Personal items are so easy to check off you begin to feel efficient and confident again. Books, toys, extra eye glasses, money, paper, pens, contact lens solution. You pack a box of cat food, but figure the cats will look out for themselves and cross out the rest of the pet list.

You place the little first aid kit you bought on top of one box, congratulating yourself on making it easily accessible and check that off, but your eye catches the long list of things that are supposed to be included. Eye drops, laxatives, hydrogen peroxide, alcohol swabs in individual packets, heat packs and cold packs, ammonia, eight kinds of bandages. You have never even seen some of this stuff let alone have it on hand. You try to name eight kinds of bandages without looking. Scissors, saline solution, tweezers, needle and thread, you focus on the obvious stuff, the stuff you have on hand and can add to the little white box. You try not to picture using the needle and thread in a first aid situation.

You look around at the five large boxes and thirteen plastic jugs you have assembled in the living room like luggage for a discount cruise. You run through all the possible storage locations outside your house and come up with nothing. You wonder if a corner of the garage would hold all of this stuff even though you know there isn't a free corner anyway. you check the list again and realize you left out the battery operated radio. You search for the hand-cranked solar radio you got for Christmas a couple years ago until you remember the kids broke it within a few weeks. You picture yourself huddled with the kids eating peanut butter on crackers by flashlight next to the remains of your house while listening to the breaking news on a tiny radio and waiting for your husband to make it home from work.

You abandon the supplies where they are and take the bottle of wine out into the back yard where you sit with your back to the house, tilt your face up to the sun and close your eyes.

# # #

Jenny Appleseed

I don't regret the water I left running, don't miss the leftovers I threw out even though they hadn't spoiled. People starving in Ethiopia never did benefit from American kids eating their broccoli. Self-recrimination and clothes-rending won't feed me today. I have experienced plenty; I know what it is to have more than enough, to want for nothing. Not everyone can say that.

Today the black truck is supposed to make a stop at the 85/101 exchange that was finished just before people started dying in San Francisco. It's a long shot, that guy is not exactly FedEx, but we're almost out of aspirin and haven't been able to get antibiotics for months. I volunteered to make the buy. Everybody else gets depressed at the bazaar, haunted by the cars that used to drive where the stalls are now, listening for the voices of a hazy past. I think it's sort of fitting that the freeway became the market. The concrete blossoms stamped into the overpass form an almost festive backdrop for the haggling exchanges like post-millenial WPA murals. Of course, nobody knows what I'm talking about when I say that.

It's not that I'm that old, although there aren't many women over forty, it's more the cultural amnesia that seemed like it moved even faster than the virus. This area was full of people with a close personal relationship with math; throw a rock in any direction and you'd probably hit a Ph.D. But no matter how well you understand numbers, there is a huge difference between knowing the definition of "exponential increase" and watching a plague mow down your family, your neighborhood, your city. When the virus burned itself out, only the things that still worked, what you could see and touch and hear, were acknowledged. Mention anything else and you get a blank stare. Talk about the before too much, and you may not say anything tomorrow. It might be biological, something related to Crutchfeldt-Jacob or an Alzheimer's variant, but I think it's more meme than gene. People are afraid. I don't blame them, but I think they're wrong.

I don't want to blank out the before, I revel in it. The kiss of cashmere on my fingertips, ten-year old Cabernet that told a story from the first sniff to the last lingering finish on the tongue, and nine course chef's tasting menus that lasted five hours and stimulated every sense. I haven't even heard the words "chef" or "menu" in years, let alone in the same sentence. But it's the simple things, too. That tinny ice cream truck music that sounded just like laughter, and bubble baths, oh god, the warm embrace of lavender or jasmine, rose petals floating on cumulus suds. I even miss things I used to hate, like the yipyipyip of barking dogs.

Of course the dogs went first. Man's best friend; everybody's gotta eat. In the initial panic, the meal that delivered itself seemed a more obvious than the one you had to search for. The cats caught on and undomesticated themselves. Now anyone who can actually approach them is looked on with fear and awe. It's the new Salem. I don't say that out loud, never let anyone see me feeding the local felines. I used to joke with my sister about being cat ladies when we got old. I just didn't expect to do it alone. Or be nomadic. Or have the definition of old slide all the way back to meet me where I stood.

There used to be this cliché about "embracing change." I, myself, used to claim that all change was good, but I've added an addendum. All changes are good—for somebody or some thing or some time. But if they aren't good for you, you've got some choices to make.

This is my fifth collective. I don't know how many more I have in me. One? Two? I still have a little knee-jerk response to the term "collective." It used to be so clearly anti-individual. Now it just means survival. Trade is almost impossible without the sanction of a collective, and without trade, everybody's dead. I have heard rumors of homesteaders, but I know I'll never see them with my own eyes, and while it remains a timeless and universal truth that a woman always has something to trade, there just isn't enough demand. I used to say that if forced to choose, I'd rather be a hooker than a nun. Be careful what you wish for.

It is true that I like to go to the bazaar, like the smell of coriander and chipotle and the lingering exhaust that is probably all in my mind. It is also true that bazaar holds the greatest odds of finding a wide assortment of new men. The last two months have been fruitless, and the timing is perfect this trip.

That men are more fragile than women is a biological fact. Higher rate of miscarriage, longer time required to develop the lungs, heart disease and stress and even accidents strike them down in higher numbers. Men survived the flu at almost the same rate women did, but most of the ones over twenty are sterile. Some chickenpox—like strain got into the mix before it hit North America, and then it made another loop around the globe. Nobody really knows if the boys were spared, so few of them survived the gang wars. Lord of the Flies was a Disney story compared to our version. Take the superior eye-hand coordination from years of video games and bind that to the area's exaggerated rate of Asperger's. Total focus and no empathy. Then add in the vast supply of abandoned weapons and the adolescent fascination with all things explosive. It was easier to kill them all than sort it out.

There are so few births now that pregnant women are isolated and pampered Worshipped, even. You can't really tell by comparing the pictures, but I am graffitied all around the Bay. I have established ties within this collective and cultivated a new apprentice. She doesn't yet know her full role, but if I am successful at bazar, I can Winter here and move on next Spring. Six weeks of nursing is the most I can do without creating other problems. I learned that the first time. It's enough, though, for the antibodies. Enough for a start.

People are idiots. I don't really mean that. Well, yes, I guess I do. There's this sort of universal consequential nearsightedness when it comes to cause and effect. Like anything beyond the second or third domino to fall has nothing to do with the one you shoved. I'd like to think it's the pandemic, but it was like this before. A couple million people living on top of the most active fault lines in the world, and how many of them had water and food stored? Not even ten percent. So who could expect them to think about future reproductive needs in the face of massacre? It's almost as rare to hear talk about the future as comments about the past. We have plenty of shelter—abandoned mansions for everyone!—and the canned food that's been hoarded will last for decades. But how do you know *you'll* be here? That's the unasked unanswered question behind the haunted faces. A few collectives are forming linked groups, planting larger gardens, rebuilding infrastructure in a way that gives me hope. But then again, maybe optimism is my own private myopia.

When genetic breakthroughs started happening one after another and the masses were all up in arms about the possibility of the wealthy breeding super babies, I just couldn't see the problem. Anyone with basic high school biology knew that the whole point of sexual reproduction was recombination. The more combinations, the more diverse the gene pool and the more likely the species survives whatever curve ball the environmental selection pressures throw at it. What we can survive now remains to be seen.

The paths to bazaar are many, but I prefer the center of 85. Some people feel too exposed on that broad stretch, choosing to wind through the neighborhood streets avoiding the marked collective boundaries. The freeway is actually safer, as long as you're armed. And from up here you can smell the spring perfume of orange blossom along with the subtle notes of the giant rambling wisteria covering what used to be the Evelyn off ramp. The sun is shining and it is still a beautiful California day. I imagine the frayed straw sombrero I wear for shade is a frothy pastel linen confection covered with silk flowers and I am on my way to a garden party.

The black truck brings news along with rare goods and produce from up and down the state. It was the speed and thoroughness of the information collapse that surprised me most. We were all so connected, so networked through so many systems and media that black out was inconceivable. Partly it was the decimation of technical knowledge, but I think the more important failure was that of will. The pandemic will not be televised either.

We think there's some kind of government operating out East, but New York was the second outbreak after San Francisco, and the flu moved so fast through metropolitan areas that shortages of vaccine and face masks were the least of the problems. The last broadcast I saw was the Upper West Side of Manhattan in flames. The stench had become unbearable and the rats uncontrollable, so the Mayor ordered the evacuation and torching of Manhattan. The helicopter cam followed the edge of Central Park from the Natural History Museum past Columbus Circle down to Time Square. It was like watching the funeral pyre of Western Civilization. When I stopped crying, I put on my "I'm Not Dead Yet" t-shirt and wore it everyday under everything, not taking it off until I left it behind with my first baby. It was the best gift, the only prayer I had to offer.

As I reached the curve in the interchange just as 85 began its downturn, I saw a man I recognized ahead. He was from the River Collective, my third group. It was a much longer journey from there to reach bazar, so he had been on the road since before dawn. I knew not to approach him too quickly or quietly. When I'd scuffed enough gravel to announce my presence, I called out for him to wait.

We walked together in comfortable silence. Mike was a man of few words, and the only man who knew what I was doing. He kept his own council, trusted few people, thought I was crazy but spared me the lectures. He remembered things, too.

"Looking for anything in particular today?" He had a hint of a smirk.

"Just the usual." I smiled. "And some meds."

"A packer from the valley said the black truck has radio."

That stopped me. I had to run to catch up. "Radio?"

He just nodded.

Radio. I knew he didn't just mean the automated music loops that had continued to play long after the live broadcasts went dark. If there were even a few Ham Radio operators up and running, the picture of the country and the timeline for rebuilding changed completely. It was the cusp of the Renaissance.

At the base of the ramp where the first of the stalls began, Mike gave me a quick hug, like the gesture was foreign and said, "Good hunting, Lucy."

I laughed and thanked him. Back when I was part of the River and told him my plan, he first called me Eve, then decided Lucy was more fitting. He said that somewhere tens of thousands of years from now when they traced the mitochondrial DNA all the way back to a common female ancestor, it would be me. His heart wasn't in it, though, because he didn't believe we were going to make it. But when he said the word "radio" today, his voice held something I'd never heard in it before.

The usual assortment of vendor stalls lined the sound walls and formed aisles in the center of the interchange. Bazaar looked like a less organized more colorful version of the art and wine festivals that used to spring up nearly every weekend in the summer. A cross between a farmers' market and a flea market, maybe, but with the passionate haggling a barter economy breeds. The black truck hadn't arrived, so I shopped what was available. A trader down from the mountains had brought a big stash of expired aspirin that tasted genuine. I got a good price even though it was early. Most people don't remember that drugs were effective well beyond their expiration dates. A lot of them are suspicious of anything with a date on it to begin with, and the trader hadn't been out of the mountains often enough to pick up on that.

More important than the aspirin was the family selling napales. They had been working their way west from New Mexico hoping to find relatives who used to live by the bay. They had two sons who looked to be 16 or 17, probably too far removed from a city to have been part of the gang slaughter. I watched the line of shoppers give their stall a wide berth before I moved in to haggle. Napales is something I can take or leave, but before I left that stand, I'd made arrangements to come back for what I really wanted later.

A wave of noise moved through the bazaar. Sentries had spotted the black truck maybe 15 minutes out. I had time for one donation to my cause before it arrived. I scanned the faces of the older men, looking for a little spark in the eyes, some small sign of life.

If the rumor about the radio network is true, this will be my last collective whether my shopping today is successful or not. Either way, come Spring I'm going to see if there are homesteaders out there. Maybe I'll ride along with the black truck. Or maybe I'll find a radio of my own.

# # #

Army of the Wanted

One week following the Entebbe highjacking, an elite force of two hundred volunteers from the Israeli army freed the hostages and killed all the terrorists, losing only two civilians and one commander in the fire fight. Twenty-four hours after ecoterrorists seized the embassy in the People's Republic of Venezuela, the ten-man crew of a single deathhawk armored helicopter, Panamerican 1st Division, reduced the entire peninsula on which it stood to rubble and accepted the resignation of the Presidente, raising the Panamerican flag over the capitol the same day. Outflanked at the battle of Issus, Alexander the Great seized on the weakness only he could see, defeating the Persian army so swiftly and decisively he was inside the royal household in an hour. Victory may come from the many, from the few, or from the one, but it comes only to those willing to do whatever is required.

We are the chosen people. Others have laid claim to that title before us, but they were operating on faith, a flimsy foundation compared to the hundreds of millions of dollars spent on our creation and support. Our elevated nature carries ample documentation: lab fees and ultrasounds, pharmaceuticals and billable hours of specialists' time, extraction and invitro and the cryonic embrace that uncoupled us from the rest of our generation. Truth be told, we are many generations made one, for we were chosen twice. Our making came through the tears and pain and yearning of many couples over decades, a forced patience paid for dearly but never really learned. We were *wanted.* Wanted so much we were held in reserve. It was the second choosing, though, that made us who we are.

The infants of Sparta were placed outside to separate the weak from the strong before any investment of resources had been made. At seven they entered military training, earning their citizenship over the course of twenty-three years by surviving the rigorous tests required of soldiers and adhering to excruciating standards. Those who faded at twenty might join the middle merchant class, but they would never be full citizens. Those who thrived were given land, acquired spouses and children they rarely saw, and lived in glory with their brothers. If they reached sixty, they could retire to their farms having passed the final test of endurance. Standards very from era to era, but survival is always the ultimate goal—for the species and for the individual.

We have been called the Neospartans. We have been called many things, but that name strikes closest to the truth. From the beginning we were tested: how fast to divide, how fast to double, how soon to blastocyst. And later: how many chromosomes, what targeted gene markers, what size inutero, scores on apgar on Stanford Binet, on the Kleinfeldt scale. At each age, at every level, the weak were filtered out and the strong moved on. Little is said about the other group, the host army. But for the statue of the Universal Mother astride Half-dome, hands outstretched to embrace the valley below, none of us can put a face to our host; and the donor records were destroyed with the first liberation. I once saw a woman who looked like my cell-brother, but I did not even know our cryo dates. She could have been my great-grand niece, but not my donor. I often wonder if the host wanted me as much as the program did.

The Fists of Righteous Harmony, twenty-thousand strong, surrounded the compound outside the Forbidden City where foreign diplomats and their families lived with a small military force. Relentless assault continued for two months, with the diplomats unable to either escape or send for help. They withstood the constant bombardment as supplies of ammunition, food and medical supplies dwindled and seventy-six defenders lay dead until, at last, an international military force created for the purpose of rescue arrived and drove back the Boxers. For nine months, London was bombed nightly by the Luftwaffe. For the length of a gestation cycle, the people of London spent their nights underground and their days rebuilding the damage of the night before and carrying on with their regular lives. Winston Churchill has been remembered for many words, but the only ones that mattered were, "Never give in—never, never, never, never . . . ." True strength demands tenacity. Might without resilience is simply a temporary and surmountable force.

In the Battle of Judgment we survived for thirty-three days, pinned down by enemy fire inside a bunker fortified by a disabled tank, half a blasted deathhawk and rubble from the destroyed temple. On day fourteen they launched a retrovirus in a scatter bomb. We were mostly resistant, and the few that weren't kept us going when the supplies ran out. On day thirty-two we broke out of the fortification and seized the Dome. Air support provided cover for us to deploy our remaining ordnance and dust-off before detonation. Fifteen out of fifty made it back, and all but two birds cleared the blast zone in time. There will be no more debate about this land, holy or unholy. Everything from Turkey to the Nile is gone.

When he witnessed the first nuclear test in the desert of New Mexico in 1945, J. Robert Oppenheimer said, "I am become Death, the destroyer of worlds." Albert Einstein said, "The discovery of nuclear chain reactions need not bring about the destruction of mankind any more than did the discovery of matches." History is full of misplaced fears and mistaken assumptions. It is also full of power wielded in ways unimaginable to those who did not survive. Failure of imagination can be fatal.

The First Wave were liberated and gestated after being seized under an obscure clause in eminent domain following the publication of a paper by an antiwar statistician in Berkeley predicting replacement troop availability dropping to zero in less than a decade. This was two decades after the reinstatement of conscription and five years after indentured combat and the Foreign-born Service Act. With forces engaged on two fronts, they were desperate to identify fresh sources of volunteers beyond the obvious (and fully exploited) ones. So convincing was the statistician's argument for peace, civil war broke out within the year. The Party of God, which had been formed early in the war years, was driven out of office and into strongholds on the island of Manhattan and in the Mountain Territories. Those areas were ceded and became independent. The program begun by the POG was seized and accelerated by the Panamerican Congress.

"Free speech zones" for dissenting protesters were established for dissenting protesters during the presidential campaign in the United States. The designated caged areas were made of double chain link fence and razor wire. After the fall of the EU, the Mohammedan Vatican Council ruled over the bloodiest year in five centuries as they enforced the new bhurka laws in the Mediterranean and Eire Territories. The female population was reduced by an order of magnitude, leaving the Eurosaharan Alliance which followed unable to compete with the Panamerican program for lack of hosts. Nazi Germany stripped Jews, homosexuals, and other targeted groups of citizens of individual rights one by one until their associations were restricted, their jobs eliminated, their property confiscated and their very lives terminated. Some sang in the name of the Fatherland while their neighbors burned. Those willing to trade liberty for the protection of god or country dig their own graves.

After the fall of Greenland and the uniting of the Panamerican Pacific, the Freedlands were given a voting holiday and allowed to choose between two candidates designated by the Triumvirate who succeeded the PC. Carefully monitored rejoicing occurred. Rejoicing occurred elsewhere observed by only the few who witnessed the final test of the enhanced Third Wave prior to our deployment. A man whose name I did not know but whose face was familiar to me dropped to his knees and wept. The First Wave had been intended as nothing more than cannon fodder by the program. The Third Wave was the cannon.

Odysseus the heroic trickster secreted himself inside a wooden horse along with his fellow Greeks, turning the blind hubris of the Trojans against themselves. The EU grid crash was the result of a thirteen-year old hacker working for the vegan ethical front locating a back door created ten years before by an engineer from an Islamist sleeper cell in Paris. Sun Tzu wrote on the Art of Warfare that foreknowledge is what allows rulers and generals to conquer the enemy at every move and that foreknowledge can be obtained only from people who have knowledge of the enemy. There is an old saying, “Keep your friends close and your enemies closer.” If you cannot tell the difference between the two, you are doomed.

I am first among the Third, commander of the Wave. We were all drilled in the history of warfare and the nature of success, and many know the past. But only I know the future. At five hundred hours we will descend upon the Eastern Seaboard like a swarm of insects falling upon new spring crops. We will retake Manhattan and establish our capitol there, launching simultaneous strikes on the Eurosaharan Alliance and the Walled City of Nanjing. We will begin, at last, the lives we might have had with those who created us, wanted us first. Lives of our own choosing. The program wanted peace at any price. That bill has come due.

# # #

Dance of Renewal

A strand of clarinet, part moan part sigh, snaked through the crowd, announcing the final act. The audience turned to the stage, almost as one, before the rest of the band joined in. Her music did not have the traditional bump and grind at its base, nor even the new mode of lights and tiny bells. She was the event everyone came to see, and her song was one of yearning and lamentation, of bittersweet possibility just beyond reach. Many began weeping even before the pale blue spot burst upon the first silken limb.

Phoenicia lived to dance. Everyday she read from the Book of Time, absorbing and interpreting her sacred past, waiting for her turn in the light. Today she had read and reread her favorite passage, written twenty cycles back: *No matter what you feel just before your time, no matter your preparation, when the light takes you, you will be ready.* This was her day. It was her turn. She needed to be ready.

The first vision was hard to interpret, slender ankle wrapped in delicate fingers and the outline of a female form shrouded in folds of fabric, lavender, periwinkle, mauve. Then the second spot came on, and the stage was lit with a golden counterpoint to the blue. The fingers slid up the gleaming leg, a strip of color fell away as the hands caressed a knee, a thigh, her skin was luminous. A sudden intake of breath from the front row as she turned even as she straightened. Perhaps he caught a glimpse of more, perhaps it was just the shadow of her hand.

The Book of Time told of how the First came to be here, of the blood-debt owed to Rostam the Elder for saving her life. One hundred dances she promised, one hundred years of payment to prevent the end of her line and guarantee safe passage back. As Rostam the Younger took over the club, became the Elder, himself, the story of Phoenicia's dance spread throughout the lands. In the rustic club at the end of the world where the sharp white rock met the sea, once a year, one night only, a woman was transformed.

She faced away from the audience, soft blue sheer slipping from her shoulders, their shimmering iridescence too perfect to be paint. One arm lifted slowly, opened upward, outward like a budding flower followed by the other. She turned again, face down, hint of a smile visible beneath the fringes of her hair, and the wisp of color shifted with her as she spun slowly with the swelling music, showing almost not quite maybe her bare front, a startling shade of pink.

Striptease they called it in the early form, "tease" because the watchers never got to touch, and what they got to see was more illusion and suggestion than real flesh. The dancer might peel off her gloves or shed her dress, hide behind feathers or leave a trail of veils, but only Phoenicia waved gossamer fans sprouted between her shoulder blades. Many winged peoples lived in the woodland hills, and flying insects with such beauty they were prized as jewels filled the markets, but no one had seen Phoenicia's people or their jungle home.

As the music quickened, Phoenicia moved one step closer to the edge of the stage. Now backlit, she opened her wings and used them as a screen, more revealing than concealing, lithe body limned with a radiance that seemed to grow brighter as she danced. Those in the front began to sweat.

Flipping through the Book this day, Phoenicia had seen how the dance had changed, not just with each new dancer, but with each passing year. Far from home, faint traces of race memory the only tether to the original purpose, the Dance of Renewal had become a spectacle of survival. The few privileged to witness the dance paid dearly, often not just in precious metals. In the early years there were deaths, some from shock, some by their own hands. Later there were protests and cults and even shrines, but none of these concerned Phoenicia. Each dancer added her own tale to the Book of Time, weaving the thread back to the first and forward to the next. Phoenicia finished hers just before the curtain.

The music and the dancer swayed and leaped as one, Phoenicia's glowing skin so brilliant it seemed to cast off sparks. A pinpoint spot burst on at the back of the stage, illuminating an elaborate golden urn. The audience was silent but for the thud of one who forgot to breathe falling to the floor.

Legend told of ancient long-lived birds that perished in a burst of flame, only to rise from the ashes and live again. When the truth of

Phoenicia's people became known, others were stirred to ponder their own fates. She grew and lived one year, danced and died and lived again. Was her life a single year, or was it forever?

The dark spots on her wings were changing color, her fingertips and earlobes, nipples, lips and toes magenta red. The guards who stood at stage side watched the crowd for signs.

Rostam the Elder who once had been Younger loved all the dancers each in her own way. This one, though, this Phoenicia, he could not bear to watch, and not because it meant that his life, too, would never be the same. She made him promise, though, because he had to witness to release the debt.

Phoenicia stopped abruptly, arms spread, feet apart, braced against the earth and reaching for the heavens. She tilted her head to better see the row of silver urns circling the room above the stage, remains from the other dancers, soon to be joined by the golden urn beside her. She was the last, she was One Hundred. The youngling that followed would be free. She could go home. Phoenicia was ready. She closed her eyes and became the light.

# # #

The Wordsmith

Chapter 1

A picture is worth a thousand words only if you know the thousand words to begin with.

—Wordsmith, collected works

"What do you want, boy?"

The hair stood up on the back of the boy's neck. The voice coming unexpectedly from the dark corner was soft, just above a whisper. Not scary. Not really scary. He swallowed hard and looked over his shoulder at the tiny square of bright light shining through the door from outside. Maybe this was a mistake. He chewed his lip, trying to remember why this had seemed like such a good idea. Sure he needed help, but he hadn't thought this through, hadn't done the research. He had just rushed off when he found the address. Rushed, unprepared, to this place.

The room was too warm, and it smelled strange. Sort of moist . . . peppery . . . or like dirt. Stranger, still, was his reaction to the odor. At first it was unpleasant, but underneath that it was almost appealing. The air was disconcerting and peculiar, not the cool controlled environment he was used to. He couldn't remember being in such a place before. It was . . . uncomfortable. He felt removed from time, dropped suddenly into some recent past. Like he had walked through a door from his world into another.

"Well?"

He jerked his head around, squinting into the darkness. The voice wasn't coming from the same position. He still couldn't see the source, but the voice was closer.

"Help," he managed to blurt out in the general direction of the voice. The word was garbled, more cough than speech, but at least he got something out. His holo projected a red life saver appeared above him for three seconds. His mouth was dry. Licking his lips over and over made them feel drier. Maybe the moist air got that way by sucking water out of everyone who came here. Maybe he'd be left a lifeless husk before he ever faced assignment.

A fragment of the dark shifted, broke away from the rest and began to move toward him. He couldn't focus, couldn't turn the shadow into something whole that made sense. The black mass grew larger as it drew closer. He struggled against the blindness, fighting panic in the same battle. The shade! He'd left the shade on! The boy remembered his exercises, took a deep breath through his nose and exhaled slowly through his mouth. He removed the dark filter that covered his eyes and held it to his chest as a talisman against both light and dark.

The shape was closer now, but it had stopped moving. His eyes adjusted to the light level, and the shape resolved into a very small woman. An old, he thought. She had a cloud of startling white hair above a face carved with lines, lots of lines, a map of wrinkles. She was barely five feet tall. Micro-old, he corrected himself silently. Her stillness seemed to draw all the energy in the room toward it, making unstated demands.

The boy shifted uneasily. His fidgeting freed the blocked light from the window, allowing it to pool at the old woman's feet. It glinted in her pale eyes which were fixed, unwavering, on his. Tiny specks floated through the beam of light, solid things but without much weight. Indoor smog? Abandoned nanoparts? He felt like a character in a holovid. Her seemingly colorless eyes did not move.

"What help, boy? You help me? As you can see from the line of customers, the thronging seekers of verbal treasure beating a path to my door, I am not currently in desperate need of an apprentice." She still spoke softly, but there was no weakness in the voice.

"No." He couldn't look away. He knew he should explain, could make a better impression than this, but her expectation dried up everything but his fear.

"You can't be here for my help. If you had an official research voucher, you would have scanned at the door, and there hasn't been an exhibition scheduled in years."

She stepped closer. The fabric draped around her rustled lightly. He could smell something when she moved, something like . . . spring . . . no, that wasn't quite it. Flowery? Musky? Rain? Like the scent from the Odovids just before the autocensor cut in at his age level and the image died. The tantalizing whiff that suggested to him what he was missing, would be allowed to see/smell later . . . like . . . sex! Yes! Something fragrant and alive. Maybe those specks carried pheromones.

"So what is it, boy?" Her voice was louder now, insistent. "If I do not need your help, then you must be seeking mine, and that cannot be. Do you see a Cityseal? A commerce stamp? An apprentice guarantee? No. I no longer offer any assistance but the sort sought out by the hopeless and the desperate. You are too young to have no hope, too innocent for desperation. Or would you have me believe that beneath your shiny polished surface is a core, the fruit of knowledge? Would you say you are a rebel? An outlaw? An enemy of the Matrix?

He shook his head automatically in denial, then paused and nodded.

"Say it!"

"Yes!" he shouted back.

All the wrinkles on her face organized themselves into a complicated pattern of star bursts at the corners of her eyes and parentheses around a spreading smile. She tilted her head back and laughed out loud. Out loud! It was a big sound from such a small person, as if someone were telling jokes only she could hear.

The boy began to tremble. The laughing was more than he was prepared for. This was scarier than the silence and the staring. Even his father, who lived before Moderation, did not laugh out loud. He really hadn't thought this out, had acted on impulse. What did he know about her, anyway? What made him think she could help, would help? A mistake. If he could just turn around and run, the micro-old couldn't catch him. He'd be out the door, and no one would ever know.

A small hand gripped his wrist with surprising force.

"Do not run away now, LI/O. We have work to do. I have been expecting you."

Mouth open, stunned into submission, he followed her through the crowded shop to a doorway that responded to her palm. It sealed behind them with a series of clicks amplified to explosions by the boy's fear. There was a single light on the table in the middle of the room. Even in its inefficient amber glow, he could see that the walls were all floor to ceiling shelves filled with books. Not holos, he was certain. Real books. LI/O looked back and forth between the woman and the books, unable to take his eyes off either for long.

The old sat down and pointed to a chair facing her.

"If you are to share your story with me, do not rely on cityvoice. I am all for the evolution of language, but I prefer natural selection, not radical surgery." She paused, her head tilted slightly to one side. "Perhaps a formal introduction is in order. I am Selena, the Wordsmith. A worthless title in these days of spectacle and sound, perhaps, but one I fought—fought hard—to keep. And you are . . . ," she squinted at him, calculating, ". . . Leonardo!"

"But,"

"I know. I know." She held up a hand, palm toward him. You are LI/O the tec-style, L' I/O of the information age. I could call you Leo for the astrological phenomenon that passed with the millennium or Leo for the royal feline, king of his verdant domain, and you would be none the wiser." She smiled. "But no, I will call you Leonardo for one whose vision was not bound by time or convention."

LI/O tried to concentrate. The repetition of his name, ". . . LI/O, LI/O, LI/O . . ." went by too fast and was meaningless to him. And how did she know who he was, anyway? The last few words, though, "bound by convention," those he understood. Maybe this was the right thing to do. If anyone could help him, this old woman before him would have to be the one. Like he had so many other options.

"I am Leonardo, then." LI/O paused. Sentences, formalvoice. Whole thoughts all in words, he reminded himself. This woman was the Wordsmith, is the Wordsmith. Cityvoice would be inadequate. He turned off his holo.

"I want to be a scholar. You seem to know me already. Do you know I've been assigned to train? Ordered to report to the Servocorps on my next birthday?"

The Wordsmith nodded. "Well-chosen words for a Servo, boy. Yes, I know you from the Matrix. And other sources. I also know your Apt scores."

LI/O clenched his teeth, willing his face not to flush with color.

"I don't care about the Apt scores! I just want a chance to try. If I fail, then I will join the Servocorps without complaint."

"But there is so much pain in trial and error, so much heartbreak in unnecessary testing of the self." The Wordsmith's voice became nasal in a singsong recitation, "A burden to struggle against your natural skills. The Apts exist to guide you into happy choices."

"What choice? 'The Apt assigns and you're resigned.' Isn't that what they used to say?" LI/O's face was flushed and he clenched the arms of the chair, his efforts at moderation failing. Hadn't he heard the same and more from the Ps? He hadn't been surprised when MatrixShrink followed the program, but how could the Wordsmith repeat the same line?

The Wordsmith smiled, and her wrinkles once again folded into patterns of amusement. “Yes, ‘they’ used to say that. Don’t you want to be happy?”

“I want to challenge.”

She raised her eyebrows and pursed her lips. She nodded slightly to herself, as if he had just answered a question correctly. Minutes passed in silence. LI/O’s thin tunic clung to him where the cool air in this room had dried the sweat he earned in the outer room. He did not drop his eyes from her unblinking gaze.

“Do you know when the last challenge was made, the last request won?”

“No.”

“The last challenge was more than two years ago.”

“Won?”

“Not since before you were born.”

Only great control, Moderation coming back to him, kept him from screaming, but he would not be dissuaded. There had to be a way.

“Is it too much to ask for a voice in my own future?”

The Wordsmith reached out and touched his forearm. He felt a change in her attitude, some subtle shift as if the balance barely tipped, but it tipped his way. He was certain she would help. She leaned closer, and LI/O held his breath for her response.

“Perhaps not, boy. But will you pay for this voice with your life?”

Chapter 2

Arise! Arise! We are the bridge to destiny, Listeners to eternity.
Much is spoken; little is heard.

—The Word

"I share with you the power of the word, bring you alive in the glory and wonder of the semantic magic of old and this is how you demonstrate your gratitude?"

The Speaker paced the room in long strides. In the rippling red and orange of her robe, her hand gestures appeared to be punctuated by flame. The Listener groveled in the doorway, not daring to address her until she stopped moving.

"Heathen! Heretic! Inarticulate fraud!"

He hated it when she got this way, when the listing and rhyming began. She was having these outbursts with increasing frequency, tirades that fed on themselves, became a flood of half-familiar words and phrases, a mystery both beautiful and terrifying. If he did not calm her soon, he would be damned. Perhaps he already was.

"Well?"

"I am unworthy, Speaker. I have failed you. I have failed the Word. I am mute before You, blind to truth. I am ignorant, deaf to the music of the Word. Teach me, oh Speaker, that I might truly hear."

He recited the prayer with feeling, never lifting his eyes from the floor. His hands pressed hard on the cool stone until the tendons stood out in sharp counterpoint to the veins winding across them. The meaning of the prayer had altered for him since his first days in the Labyrinth, but the plea for mercy it contained now was genuine. Only when she fell silent did he dare look upon her. Bright spots of emotion marked her cheeks, but she was raising her hands in benediction, palms up, sides pressed together. She bowed her head and moved it back and forth. The blessing of the sacred reading! The Listener breathed deeply, averting his gaze from the top of her head as it inclined toward him. He touched his nose to floor and closed his eyes.

The Speaker finished the blessing.

"Go, now, and seek your errors. The Word contains all answers, all corrections, all direction. Read that you may find; listen that you may know."

The Listener rose and backed out of the room slowly without looking up again.

The Speaker returned to her desk, all thought of the wayward Listener driven out by plans for the Speaking which was so close at hand. Why waste worry on a single thick follower who could not hear the voice of his heart for the hands clamped over his ears? This speaking would bring converts in numbers undreamed-of by those who had dismissed her as a cult! The tale would be spun before an unexpected, unsuspecting audience while the pathetic plodding bureaucrats at Censor would be left to wonder how she could command that allocation of the Matrix.

"Cult? I will show them what a little 'cult' can spawn."

She caught her reflection in the blank screen of her terminal and smiled. The dark cap of spirals tattooed into a widow's peak on her bald head were the source of the Listener's awe and discomfort. Few could meet the Speaker's eye and none looked any higher. So intricate was the pattern of tiny curls, it appeared to be solid color from a distance, but each delicate spiral was a word or phrase or sentence blending into, crossing over, curls around it. Stories were woven across her smooth skull, ever changing, never ending.

There were whispered rumors among the Listeners that looking directly at the Speaker's head could drive you mad. It was said that if you lost your way within the seething mass of words, your mind would remain trapped there, forever. The notion that she had become a linguistic Medusa gave the Speaker no end of amusement, but she did not discourage it. A healthy dose of dread is necessary where unquestioned obedience is desired. The impact of perception is the power of the unspoken word. What is known but not stated is fertile ground for fear, a growing plume of toxic thought spreading contamination . . . and submission. The armament of definition, parameters that shriveled fear to conquerable proportion would not serve her Listeners, or her purpose.

Legend also had it that the artist who did the work on her newly defollicled scalp labored night and day with little rest for many months then died at the sight of the finished work. That particular rumor, the Speaker knew, was true. She had killed him herself.

Garrison held his breath until he was two corridors away from the Speaker. When he was sure no one had followed him, he took three deep breaths, releasing each slowly through slightly parted lips. He closed his dark eyes and squeezed the bridge of his nose. His hands shook slightly with the unspent adrenaline of a man death has glanced at before passing on. She was growing more erratic, more dogmatic with each passing week. He smiled to himself, just a little, at the rhyme. Not to mention emphatic and autocratic. He was pleased at his ability to link these words. And perhaps even lunatic.

His smile faded. He had to reach the Cell to report this latest outburst. His chosen name as Listener was Garrison. At the naming, he told the Speaker it represented his link to an early maker of words, but it was really a flaunting of his link to the Cell. Others felt it was unnecessarily dangerous, but Garrison knew the Speaker would never suspect cleverness of that sort from one of her followers. She saw them as blank pages waiting for her inscription, and most of them were. He had come to the Labyrinth as a supplicant, a true seeker of the Word. But where he sought knowledge, he was given only noise. Riddles, instead of answers, dogma instead of ideas. By the time he finished his initiation and was invited to the naming, he had already agreed to work with the Cell from inside the Listeners.

Garrison made his way quickly through the Labyrinth, home to the Speaker and all ritual surrounding the Word, and walked to the rail gate just beyond the Listener complex. His hood was pulled low over his gaunt face, blocking out the holo conversations around him. Neither did he view the scenery on the silent trip into the heart of the city, he was looking inside. Despite his disillusion with the Speaker and his commitment to the Cell, Garrison waged internal battles over the deception he lived. He had no faith in the Speaker, true, but he had to admit to believing in the Word, in the power of the Word to transform. Maybe his belief did not quite conform to the patterns of his initiation, but still he believed that words, written words, contained a mystery, a beauty that elevated them beyond the mere support of graphics. It was this sense of mystery that drew him to the Speaker initially, and he would not betray it with her.

Garrison got out at the Citadel, a sprawling complex of government buildings, all interconnected in an unfathomable and constantly changing pattern that rivaled the Speaker's Labyrinth. Here the crats buzzed about their cubicles, administering the committee-made policies and regulations shaped by psychological trends and enforced for the good of all.

A few of the curious stared openly at Garrison's robe, the length and voluminous drape of which marked him as a Listener. Once they entered the Labyrinth, Listeners had little contact with outsiders. This reticence added to the mystique surrounding the Speaker and her followers and contributed to the wild rumors about the practices of the cult. Most of the crats, however, barely spared him a casual bored glance. Not part of their job to wonder.

He worked his way to the first subfloor. The rooms were mostly record keepers and public access terminals in one of the older parts of the building that had been built around and remodeled into obsolescence, but the corridor connected to one of the market entry halls, so use by non-crats was not suspicious. Older, little used halls like this one relied on audio monitors for surveillance. No video units had even been installed, so low a priority was the traffic here.

Another man approached wearing a tunic in the particular shade of dark blue favored by engineers. No one else could be seen the entire length of the corridor.

"Lo, Garrison."

The man pulled a small pen from his belt and began writing on his palm.

"Lo, RamDixon."

All engineers were granted the honorific Ram upon completion of training. It was one of the few titles still used, not yet disallowed as demeaning to those without. Garrison removed a similar pen from beneath his robe and started to mark his own hand in a hurried white scrawl.

"Life?" No icons projected above him, no aura holos surrounded either man.

Dixon held his palm toward Garrison. It said: News?

"You?"

Garrison showed his message: She's worse.

"Work?"

Dixon was frowning although his voice sounded light and friendly. He wrote: How soon?

"Shop."

Garrison responded quickly: We must be ready now.

Dixon shook his head as both men wiped their hands on their clothing, which absorbed the matching ink, and replaced their pens. Garrison's anxiety grew into the space between them and became Dixon's as well.

"Luck! Bye."

"Bye."

The two men resumed walking in opposite directions. A brief meeting between two casual acquaintances duly recorded by the censors, scanned, and deleted.

• • •

LI/O burst out of the Wordsmith's shop without a backward glance at the dark and musty front room. He turned immediately into the gleaming chrome Metamall next door and breathed deeply the cool antiseptic air. A booth at the back of the Eat section was open. When he slid across the seat, the food images of the menu scrolled across the menu monitor. LI/O watched them without comprehension, his thoughts still going over the meeting with the Wordsmith.

His fingers drummed restlessly on the table while he concentrated on his moderation breathing exercises. Sometimes he wondered if the training had been wasted on him. When he was certain his thoughts were under control, his body would betray some sign of agitation, and when he had his physical reactions firmly in check, a new idea or obvious outrage would suddenly generate a strong emotional response. Calm. He needed to be calm. He wondered which was worse, his anger at the Wordsmith for telling him to think for twenty-four and come back or his fear that after what she had told him he would change his mind.

The monitor beeped for his order.

"Double cap."

"ID?"

LI/O rolled his eyes. He wasn't at home, and the dose of caffeine he desperately wanted wouldn't be served to him in public until his next birthday. The same birthday that would send him to the Servocorps. Some trade-off.

"Decap, double!" he snapped at the monitor.

Decap, he thought, decapitation. They want to take the life from both of us.

LI/O looked like any other fifteen year old. Not yet six feet tall, thick, curly brown hair, olive skin. He wore the loose tunic and fitted legs which were the current fashion, though his were yellow to show his kid status and featured a row of buttons down the front as a mark of individuality. Adults often went without the minor personal touches in attire, preferring instead to project holo images on the smooth fabric. Kids, however, went about demonstrating their uniqueness with a vengeance. Even if they all did basically the same thing.

He saw the reference to buttons in a vid. They had been a fad twenty years before when nostalgia for the nineteens was the style. LI/O liked the way they caught the light and looked like signals, beacons to other people. Of course, he couldn't afford real buttons, so he used old minidisks. He thought possibly he had the only tunic in the world with old vids as decoration.

Aside from the line of MDs down his front and his eyes, which were so dark the pupil was nearly indistinguishable from the iris, LI/O appeared to be an ordinary boy. He worked to best his peers with newer and better personal icons; he spent hours at the Met; and he experienced all the latest odovids. What could not be casually observed was a sense of curiosity that had consumed him from his earliest days. He had a particular fascination for stories and the language of the past. The old words, redundancies long since purged from cityspeak, intrigued him with their subtle variations. When he found a word that he had never seen or heard and deciphered its meaning, that was like a straight shot of caf to him.

Few noticed this interest, because LI/O was an indifferent student. It wasn't that he couldn't learn, he just wasn't always interested in the things he was being taught. Who could concentrate on the succession of the Citadel when the archives were calling? Once he learned how to access the main memory without clearance, he devoted just enough time to school as was required to keep him out of review. His indifference was to the programs and the testing, not to the knowledge.

LI/O wanted to spend his life thinking and learning and making new connections, but the Apts said he should be just another crat serving his government. He thought about spending a century monitoring vids for violations or listening to a corridor in the Citadel, or measuring mechanic crews for efficiency. Endless hours of screening and deleting, screening and deleting, and always sending reports. They couldn't make odovids fast enough to compensate for that kind of unthinking brutal utility.

He drained his cap. Even without caf, the shaking in his hands stopped. The Wordsmith wouldn't see him 'til tomorrow, but he already had his answer. He wanted to be a scholar. He wanted to choose his profession. He was willing to die trying.

• • •

The Wordsmith typed her password and entered the Matrix. She scanned the interactions of others without participating, her audio on "type" to show a script of verbal conversations. She watched like this for hours everyday, searching for trends, nuances, signs of further decay or glimmers of regeneration. The boy was her best chance, a way to breach the Citadel and the greater citadel of ignorance that it protected. There had never been more signs of readiness, more separate pockets of dissent, but it had taken so much longer than the had hoped. She sighed. Had it been too long? Did she still have the strength history demanded of its revolutionaries? She had ammunition and resolve, yes, but could she take the required actions to their necessary conclusions? No matter the toll extracted?

Too late to worry. Whatever the boy's answer, the first wheel had turned. The Wordsmith gave her full attention to an innocuous conversation with four participants. The flashing images and few words exchanged were so bland as to be almost devoid of meaning. Even the most trivial conversation carried some message, or at least a mark of personality. This group seemed meaningless in every conversation she had witnessed. Intentionally meaningless. When the time came, the Wordsmith expected they would be her allies.

She leaned back in her chair and rubbed her eyes. The quiet cool of the library was a comfort. The Wordsmith lived in three small rooms behind her shop, and only this one, where all her treasures were stored, was climate controlled. The tiny bedroom and bath, and the shop, itself, where LI/O had been so uncomfortable were left to the whims of nature. If pressed on the point, the Wordsmith might concede that at her age she considered a little discomfort to be a reliable confirmation that she was still alive. Aching joints, beads of sweat, a sudden shiver all offered valuable information about her physical state. "The first language" Chiarra used to call biological messages.

Not that the Wordsmith often had the kind of company that would press her for explanations. Not that she had any company at all. Her shop was now squeezed between the two arms of the Metamall which grew up around it, creeping closer year by year, reaching toward the sky with every passing decade. The shop had not been forced to move because it was declared a historic landmark on the anniversary of the Icon Rebellion. A little piece of the past, the site of the resistance, a quaint reminder of the peculiar notions of the losing side. With much fanfare and lightshow and nostalgic generosity, she was feted and promptly forgotten.

What little human contact she had was with the occasional newsbyte crew or student. Researchers and scholars had become so rare that their visits had dwindled to none. Most passersby did not even glance at the solid wood door, dark and polished to a shine by age, which said simply "Wordsmith" above it's single window. If they had, they might have seen the small brass plaque to the right of the ornate doorknob inscribed:

Arcane knowledge
Custom thoughts
Words for sale.

The Wordsmith had engraved it, herself, when she first received title some seventy years before. She had begun to wonder if the title and the job, itself, would die with her.

Chapter 3

All words are lyrics . . . but if you choose for melody a dirge,
the poetry you sing will still be death.
—Wordsmith, collected works

The Listeners milled in the arena. The dome overhead showed blue sky with passing white clouds that spiraled and twisted and finally faded, replaced by another set. The clouds changed shape just a little too fast and gave away their true nature. Some of the older Listeners remembered the early days before the arena was covered. There had been only a handful of faithful at the beginning, a few seekers who followed the Speaker from face to face regardless of whether the speaking was public or private. Eventually camped out on the edges of her home, trading stories of speakings they had attended and selling bootleg video MDs of every Speaker appearance. One day she invited them into the Labyrinth and began the teaching of the Word. With little cash for so large an undertaking as protecting the whole group from the elements, she had said, "Experience is truth; seek comfort in the Word."

Much wealth and many more listeners had been accumulated since those times, and even those who remembered saw no conflict when the day came that the Speaker said, "Comfort of the body is no obstacle to expansion of the soul; the Word is truth." After all, how many times did you have to be covered in your own sweat or be so cold your body shivered for warmth in order to understand the experience? No one complained about the dome or any other material change to the Labyrinth.

The Speaker strode onto the platform above the Listeners. Artificial wind sent her red cape billowing behind her, alternately revealing then covering the folds of white robe beneath. She stood perfectly still but for the banner of her clothing until she was seen by those nearest the stage.

A ripple move away from her through the crowd like a wave pushing boats out to sea. She was a boulder dropped into the tiny pond that was their lives.

When all conversation ceased and the crowd seemed to hold its collective breath, she thrust her arms straight above her head in an exultant V. The Listeners dropped into position, palms flat on the floor, legs folded beneath them, foreheads touching the ground. As one voice they recited the prayer, "mute" and "truth" and "ignorant" rising distinctly out of the verbal rumble. The Speaker lowered her arms and made the sign of the sacred reading.

The Listeners sat upright as the she began.

"Next week the Speaking will reach an undreamed of audience. The Word will touch minds still unseeking, so early are they in the journey of awareness. You, my faithful Listeners, must prepare yourselves, be ready. Ready to assume the mantle of leadership that is your calling, ready to guide the new believers on the path of the Word, suffering no interference from the unbelievers. Our ranks will swell a thousand thousand fold, and the era of Truth, so long promised, so long denied, will be ushered in by an army of soldiers of the Word. The moment of destiny is at hand. I have read it. I have heard it. I have spoken. So shall it be."

The Listeners absorbed the revelation in stunned silence, then broke into shouts and loud cheers. They leaped to their feet, jumping and jostling, all talking at once in excited voices. The Speaker accepted their adulation, basking in it until she had her fill, then turned quickly and disappeared into the building. The celebrating continued, unchecked, even after her departure. Garrison leaped and shouted with the rest, but his exultation was a charade to mask his fear.

The Matrix, he thought. Somehow she's going to alter the Matrix. Despite the buffers, despite the censors, she believes she has a way. He tasted bile and grew lightheaded. She was so certain. He had better be certain, too.

• • •

The rail slid silently through the buildings, humming softly when it paused at a stop, its doors snicking open for the unending passenger exchange. Between the main clusters of residence and commerce, the "Home" and "Work" series of stops, the rail seemed to glide on the clouds, unnoticed by the farms and parks and incinerators below.

LI/O watched the blocks of color flicker by. The Ps had not responded to his announcement that he intended to challenge his assignment in the way he had expected them to. No orders, no anger, just an odd glance exchanged. Resignation? Acceptance? Fear? Unspoken reference to that old empty insult about his birth mother being an unstable artist?

LI/O always had a hard time reading his father. Everyone knew how to mask feeling, learned to moderate extreme emotional reactions, but his father was a master of the art. Probably from the extra years of practice. LI/O's father had made engineer at twelve, before the limits, when the Apts weren't yet mandatory. LI/O would sometimes call him RamDad just to see if he could get a reaction.

Last night, though, when his father said, "Good luck." and offered his hand, LI/O had simply squeezed it in return and nodded without any of the extra taunting and prodding he usually employed for amusement. There was a subtle but unmistakable change in their relationship. Somehow they were equal. Even so, LI/O decided not to tell him about the Wordsmith. Not yet.

The conversation across from him caught his attention.

"Lo!" A pale man with a yellow braid slid over to make room for a beautiful woman the color of ripe berries.

"Lo!"

Brilliant fireworks danced in their aura holos. He wore the gray tunic of a crat, and she wore an iridescent material that reflected the images of dozens of products when viewed from different angles. The distinctive professional garb of an adcom, people who not only created ads but became them.

"News?" A series of images projected around the adcom. Some looked like the crat, others that LI/O could make out were a stringed instrument, a small animal, and a ball.

The adcom seemed to take up all the visible space. She had designed her look well; it was impossible not to watch her, even without her holos. The crat was almost invisible next to her.

"Upgrade." A floor plan and several views of living quarters flashed in rapid succession. "You?" A series of images of the adcom, some ads which must have been hers, and a child.

The two did not make eye contact at any time during the conversation. They focused, instead, on the constantly shifting holos. The pictures spoke to them, for them. The few words they actually said were more like punctuation or segue markers.

"New advid." Her holo showed an ad for bodysoap that LI/O hadn't seen yet.

Both had the quality of holo graphics that meant they were successful, wealthy, even. Of course, LI/O thought to himself as the rail sighed into his stop, probably neither one wasted one credit more on Matrix access than the basic allotment required. Who needs information when you can have image?

He left the rail at the Met stop and took the lift to the ground floor. Advids played on the doors, flashes of color and movement, bursts of music, and one or two spoken words.

"Chimera . . . scent."

"Purity . . . bath."

"Foodmall." That one was an odovid, and the smell of steaming cap and choc made LI/O's mouth water. A few older lifts had advids on the walls, too, but those had been discontinued when monitors determined that everyone continued to face forward no matter what showed on the walls.

LI/O paused at the street door, trying to remember how hot it was supposed to be that day. He shrugged and stepped through the automatic opening to walk the short distance to the Wordsmith's shop. This time he removed his shade while still outside in the shadow of the Met overhang. He read, again, the small brass plaque and reached up to touch the polished letters above the door. "Arcane knowledge," he whispered to himself. "Words for sale."

What LI/O had told the Wordsmith in their first meeting was only partly true. He needed to enlist her aid in the challenge, make sure she was on his side, before he could tell her everything. He didn't just want to be a scholar, as he had told both her and the Ps. LI/O wanted to be a Wordsmith. This he would not admit even in his personal log, for fear someone would gain access and the ridicule would never end. But his chances with the Challenge would.

Selena was the last Wordsmith. Perhaps other scholars still studied and yearned, but she was the only one allowed to retain the title after the Rebellion. She was the only one who demanded to retain it. In fact, LI/O had never heard her name before she told it to him. She had been the only Wordsmith so long, the title had become her name, the only one needed.

But LI/O knew that more than the times and the language prohibition were against him. Even if they named another Wordsmith, why would they choose him? When it was an honored and thriving profession with many scholars competing for title, only one in a hundred chosen had ever been men. But he had to try. This part of his dream he would not share until he had won her confidence, until he was in a position to make his plans sound reasonable.

Assuming he survived the Challenge.

"So, boy, you have returned." The voice sounded muffled, like it came from a combox. LI/O paused in the middle of the crowded shop to let his eyes grow accustomed to the dim lighting. Odd pieces of furniture and tables piled high with unidentifiable objects began to take shape.

"The prodigal son? No, the pilgrim, the knight pursuing his grail. What answer do you bring me, boy? Will you eat from the tree of knowledge though you be cast out of the paradise of ignorance? Or, superstition aside, will you drink the cup of poison with the thought that if you must die anyway, you will choose the time and place, and in the knowing and the choosing give it meaning?"

LI/O moved toward the door at the back of the room, sneezing at the unfiltered air. The door opened before him, then closed solidly behind him. The Wordsmith sat at a terminal, scanning rapidly with her eyes but saying nothing. Occasionally she would type briefly. She did not look up as LI/O entered.

"Yes, Wordsmith, I'm back."

LI/O squared his shoulders and raised his chin. The trembling was gone. None of the previous day's fear and uncertainty showed. He still had some of the fear locked up inside, but it was no longer about the Wordsmith or her peculiar ways.

"And my answer, my request, is unchanged."

The boldness, his change of tone, made the Wordsmith look up.

"Well, well, Leonardo after all. Sit down while I finish, and we will begin our work."

He sat in the same chair he had taken the day before and slowly released the breath he had been holding unconsciously. It occurred to him that his own sense of purpose, his certainty, had not guaranteed the participation of the Wordsmith. That was the last hurdle he foresaw to the Challenge, and he had just cleared it.

The Wordsmith frowned at the screen. LI/O wondered if the pursed lips and narrowed eyes were merely deep thought or something serious, something wrong. Finally, she typed a command and turned to face LI/O.

She leaned back in her chair and tugged at her sleeves to release them from where they were shoved above her elbows. The light fabric dropped down to cover her wrists, and LI/O noticed for the first time that she did not wear the universal tunic. In his calmer state of mind, he was more observant than on the previous day's visit. It was like seeing her for the first time. Microold indeed she was, smaller than anyone he had ever seen. The tracks of age on her face and hands were familiar, though. He had known several age-enhancers whose responsible positions required the impression of visible wisdom, a face lined by experience to inspire the confidence that would not be easily given to the young. Perception is everything.

It was the clothes, though, to which LI/O's gaze was drawn. Layer upon layer of something sheer in varying shades of blue and green and purple. The layers were different sizes and had cut-out pieces, with long sleeves or short sleeves or no sleeves at all. Each layer was so thin that combined, they seemed to form one garment with lighter color where the layers stood alone and darker where they overlapped. Light caught on the surface of the fabric, as if it were water or maybe the skin of some water creature.

"Shall we begin, or are you still admiring my attire?"

LI/O felt a blush begin and tried to will it away, but the Wordsmith was smiling. Her eyes were the color of a single layer of the blue, a shade so pale as to be almost transparent, colorless. It was the color of the sky closest to the sun on a bright day.

"What is it," he began, "I mean, the colors change. And the light . . ."

He searched for an image to compare. Her very presence forced him to the limits of his vocabulary.

"Fish scales," he said. "Iridescent!"

"Very good, Leonardo," the Wordsmith nodded, "but not quite all. What else do you see?"

LI/O concentrated, looked from one edge to the next, light to dark.

"Some colors are there in the cloth, but some are created by the layers and exist only there."

"Cyan, turquoise, periwinkle, teal," the Wordsmith passed a hand across the surface of her garment, naming the color variations as she touched them, "kelly, emerald, aquamarine, lavender, indigo, plum, olive-green."

She adjusted the material so the light from the tiny halogen lamp on her desk rippled and pooled on its surface.

"Not just 'blue' and 'green' and 'purple,' you see, Leonardo, but a rich tapestry of hue, a litany of tint. I remind myself daily of the subtle variations lost to the world. And from this study in nuance I know that what comes before or after may color things differently, that the surface may not reflect the true nature of the whole. Man is in the details, boy. Man is in the details."

"And the light is part of the color?"

"And apart from it, just like truth and knowledge or freedom and life. Knowledge without the light of truth, of reason, is an empty shell. And life without freedom is really just a slower, tortured death."

LI/O did not fully understand all of what the Wordsmith said. Even so, she spoke pictures so vivid without holos that he grasped the meaning and swallowed hard.

"Enough of color and light. File your challenge, Leonardo. You need provide no defense until the appointed time. Give them no details, no matter how they ask, and refuse preliminary video conference. We shall make one stand, our best chance is to focus our efforts, to win or lose in our chosen hour."

"It's less than a month 'till my birthday, my assign date."

"No matter. They will schedule your Challenge sooner rather than later. Probably in a very few days."

"To stop me from making a good defense?"

"No, my optimistic young friend, because they do not believe there is any defense. The path is clear, and they wish to spare you as much agony as possible. As always, they have only your best interests at heart."

LI/O felt a hollow ball of fear open somewhere deep inside. Was it a hopeless cause? He started to speak, but the Wordsmith raised her hand.

"Go Leonardo, file the Challenge. File today. There are tides and currents in the flow of history, and I anticipate a sea change of which you are a part. Return when you receive the appointment. I will be working in the meantime, and I expect that you will do the same."

• • •

Symbolic Encryption for Graphic/Linguistic Synchronous Function. RamDevin typed the title of his research, the letters appearing on the screen almost before he moved his fingers. An observer might well wonder whether the words were generated by Devin or the computer, itself, so fast did his fingers type and so responsive was the board. Of course the computer understood voice, and it was faster than non-engineer versions, but RamDevin had learned young. He still got a certain tactile satisfaction from placing fingers on keypad, sculpting information. Holding knowledge in his hands.

In a small room deep within the Matrix Fortress RamDevin finished his outline and began to search ancient scan files for the first references to graphic/vocal interface. The files were incomplete, much had been lost or simply abandoned in the early days of transition to the Matrix. When it became clear how time consuming, labor intensive, and credit depleting it would be to scan all texts into the Matrix, information was prioritized and scheduled for entry based on its designation. Many historical documents were summarized and other works, including fiction, were excerpted or merely listed by title in designated categories with the expectation that they would be replaced by the full texts when their priority codes came up. As time passed and the Council saw how few requests were made for more information, replacements were delayed or not made at all. If the citizens had no use for information, did not access the Matrix in search of specific knowledge, why waste credit to maintain it?

And as for the original texts, it was impossible to determine how many remained or where they might be found. Some were warehoused and forgotten, buried in the bowels of the Citadel or the old Info Sites. Others were lost in the transfer process or purchased by private collectors. The rest were destroyed in the Icon Rebellion.

RamDevin was working on expanding the graphic vocabulary available for any given memory, condensing color, sound, and motion features into discrete packages with a single algorithm. He wanted to see what code the early engineers had rejected, what abandoned strings might be given new life with a different perspective. The search clock began, and he returned to the contemplation of LI/O's Challenge. He was a true engineer, and even the prospect of losing his son could not break his concentration before he entered the idea into his conscious thought.

He had spent the morning thinking about LI/O. As the assignment day had approached, Devin had worried about his reaction, afraid LI/O would rebel. Even more afraid he would not.

Children, Devin thought, even those with your own genes, were messy and unpredictable just like other people. No amount of analysis would yield solutions to their program flaws or reveal the required operating instructions. Vast amounts of energy went into interpreting, cajoling, placating, and even then parent and child might be working on entirely different problems without knowing it. The most basic assumptions were shaky where people were concerned. He sometimes wondered why the Biologists had never developed a human-to-human direct port process that would eliminate all the translation errors that occurred.

But if RamDevin could know anyone, could understand another's behavior, it would be LI/O. His son had always been a stargazer, a dreamer. LI/O would spend more time framing his questions precisely than he would responding to what was asked of him. He was more interested in what he didn't know than in demonstrating what he did. Devin knew LI/O's Apts would never show the true nature of his talents. The Servocorps was inevitable.

Of course LI/O was taken by surprise. Perhaps he had derived too much of his father's focus, either through the gene pool or by observation, that rendered him oblivious to all but the problem before him. Despite the intelligence he knew his son possessed, Devin had witnessed no dedication to study from LI/O. He knew the boy was creative and undisciplined, a combination that had little use in recent years. He knew LI/O was over emotional, even passionate about some things, but where did he get the motivation, the courage, to file a Challenge? The decision to challenge surprised Devin. He was surprised and pleased. He was also very much afraid.

Devin wondered if he had missed something crucial, some early sign from LI/O that could have prevented this confrontation. True, he worked most of the time, even at home, but with good reason. Reasons he thought included LI/O's future and the sort of world he would grow into. Perhaps he knew less than he had assumed. Perhaps he didn't know his son at all.

The first results of his search came up on the screen, and all thoughts of the Challenge were filed away. The dark eyes so much like LI/O's held only the reflected words and numbers from the screen, and Devin's thoughts were entirely occupied by the structure of symbolic meaning and the links between numbers and words and pictures and sounds.

Chapter 4

Weaving threads of spoken light
Skeins of life by time entwined
The story and the teller one
Tapestry

—*Songs of Lurleen*

The Speaker admired herself in the full-length mirror while the well-muscled boy at her feet licked her toes. Naked but for the flowing red cape, she had the firm body of a thirty year old, lithe and supple. Fertile. Powerful. She used to maintain her appearance at twenty-five, but the increase in her stature along with the limits to even the best microsurgery led her to move up to thirty last year.

She sat and absently fondled the boy's back. Scented oil clung to her finger tips. She transferred it to her own throat and down to her breasts before running the hand over her smooth head. She could almost feel the riot of words as her fingers passed over them, ceaseless murmuring from which only the observant, the chosen, could draw meaning.

"Go, little one. Let words fill your heart with their music."

The boy backed out of the room with his head bowed.

The young ones were her favorites. They were so trusting and so frightened at the same time. Born after the Rebellion, they had no preconceived notions about words. They hardly had any notions at all. Their heads were filled with simple pictures, icons in two or three dimensions which the used to build their image of the world. Visions without explanation, scenery without context, left her followers ripe for the magic of complete language. They were clean slates upon which she could inscribe belief.

The Speaker was relaxed, eyes closed, breathing deeply the musky odor of the oil and humming softly. She felt the presence of another person but did not open her eyes.

"Lurleen."

He spoke with the voice of the ocean, the low notes of thunder rolling across a vast plain. Some part of everything he said seemed to be outside the range of human hearing, a subtext vibration that called up a resonance in her that had never been equaled, that she did not fully understand. It was the voice that drew her to him those years ago. The voice had captured her heart when she was but a poet, not yet even a Speaker among many, let alone The Speaker. The One.

"Is there no pain in beauty, my lovely Lurleen?"

He mocked her, teasing, twisting the words of her youth. He even used the name no one else would ever speak again. Few knew that the Speaker had any connection to that poet of pre-rebellion fame. Her past was a dimly remembered story, and decades stood between the songs of the poet and the prayers of the Speaker. But he had known her then, knew her now. He had survived the transformation, and allowances were made.

"Ruric."

She opened her eyes and extended her hand. He took it with one hand and turned her face toward him with the other. His face was not the same smooth youth as when first they met, but his eyes were unchanged. They were still that odd dark blue that hinted at some peculiar alloy of metal and man. Thick curls still fell to his shoulders, but now they were more silver than copper, pale streaked with rust. His body remained solid and strong despite his failure to surgically maintain at an earlier decade. The Speaker found this refusal both annoying and oddly alluring.

"I come to read and be red."

He did not take his eyes from hers. They smiled together at the old joke. He tilted her head a little to watch the light catch the flecks of gold that were the only constant in the color of her eyes.

"Me, first," she said. "Read me."

The Speaker slid to the floor, reclining between Ruric's knees as he replaced her in the chair. She closed her eyes and sighed as he began to trace a path with one finger through the twisted story on her head.

"Aloud," she whispered. He pressed the edge of his fingernail into her scalp and she shivered.

"Window through looking glass magnify recent past," he began. That voice, her words but in his voice . . . this was her ecstasy, the only moment that could approach, sometimes surpass, her sensations when she stood before the cheering Listeners.

"Don't stop," she whispered. "Don't stop."

• • •

Sometime later, Ruric kissed the top of the Speaker's head and rose to leave. She looked at him without smiling.

"This will be my greatest triumph, and yet, merely a door. The portal to possibilities only dreamed of until now. You have been witness to the entire journey. You, alone among men, have seen these events through my eyes. I shall not forget."

He paused in the doorway, a strange half-smile causing a dimple in his right cheek to appear and quickly fade. Ruric held her gaze for a moment, nodded once, and walked out of the room. He understood both the promise and the threat.

The Speaker considered her position. He knew more of her than she would ever allow to anyone now. He was her greatest risk. That was part of the attraction, the thrill. Ruric could be a threat, and yet, she could not let him go. For all his danger, she trusted him. but her trust had strong foundation. She had had someone watching him since the founding of the Listeners, the revelation of the Word.

• • •

Years before the Icon Rebellion, Lurleen was a poet of some ambition. At an age when many were still toiling in apprenticeships, she had published her collected works. Her readings had developed a small but fiercely loyal audience, and many who did not know her work knew of her. Over the second-skin body stocking that was widely worn then, she always draped a length of sheer fabric. Clasped at the throat and pulled over her head as a hood, it was both concealing and revealing. The silhouette of her figure lit from behind and the glimpses of the golden hair that fell, unbound, to her waist were as large a share of her appeal as the poetry she delivered with a clear and modulated voice.

Words were music to Lurleen, the low smooth vowels, the staccato consonants, the hisses and vibrations and the quiet spaces between. Especially the silences between. She could hear in the emptiness all sounds, everything, and she could share this with her audience. Silence for her was white light containing the full spectrum, black paint containing all pigments. Sound and silence, words and spaces, these formed her orchestra. She was both conductor and symphony, instrument and song. She explored the shapes of sounds, and used her knowledge to shape emotions.

Lurleen began training to be a Speaker, one of those chosen to announce world events, deliver political speeches, and serve as the voice of industry. It was a much more visible position than that of simple poet, and one from which she could apply what her audience, her listeners, were teaching her.

After a good reading, after she had brought her audience to tears and they had begged for more, after she had spoken to a chosen few and then left without a parting gesture, Lurleen would lie with Ruric and tell him her plans.

"There is a link between what is thought, what is spoken, and what is heard, but they are not the same. Which is more important? The meaning of the word, the reading of the word, or the response to the word? Perhaps the key is finding the point where the three intersect, the blending of intent and result, intellect and emotion. Transcendent meaning.

What do you think?"

She combed her hands through his dense bronze ringlets. They glowed in the dim light like cast metal, not cast-off protein.

"I think that words mean what they mean, and it is you who makes them sing."

He stopped her questions by telling her own poems back to her as if they were well-remembered childhood tales. To Ruric the Engineer, words were tools. Like most things, they were not innately good or evil, laden with unseen emotional burdens. They were merely precise or imprecise, accurate or not. Everything depends on the wielder of the tool.

He thought her fascination with the ultimate purpose, the total communication, would fade when she became a Speaker, voicing other than poetry. He did not say so, but he already felt the loss of her unspoken poems. On everything else they might disagree, but she was truly a linguistic alchemist. The ordinary leaden speech of mere mortals could be transformed into golden song by passing through her lips.

This was what he loved in her. She had solved the riddle of beauty. In her hands, at her lips, it was a simple equation, pure calculation. A powerful gift with dangerous overtones, but Ruric knew she was strong. That she might be lured into her own song did not enter his conscious thought as even a remote possibility.

Ruric did not attend her final reading; he did not hear the last of the poet Lurleen. She stood before a sizable crowd, alone on an unadorned stage. The light seemed to come from her, not outside her. She pitched her voice low and soft, forcing those listening to lean in, lean toward her:

> "Carry me
> carry me
> carry me home;
> Long are the shadows,
> Gone are the flesh
> and the bones;
> Carry me
> carry me home."

And the traditional silence that followed was broken by a building echo, "carry me, carry me, carry me, . . ." as the crowd took up the chant and sent it back to her in undulating tones until Lurleen could feel the relentless tug of the ocean tides with her the moon.

And then she knew. She had crossed the barrier between the speaker and the word, the meaning and the delivery. She was electrified by the force she exerted on these people and wanted nothing more than this for the rest of her life. Lurleen walked off the stage that night, shaved her head, and began a new book.

Chapter 5

"Biology is not destiny. Not even destiny is destiny."
—Wordsmith, collected works

The Citadel loomed before LI/O, a massive block of stone whose only opening was a large double gate. The Citadel was actually many buildings joined together and reconfigured regularly. Within this maze of twisting hallways, sealed-off rooms, and staircases to nowhere, busy Servos worked on the assembly line of information, just like they wanted him to do. This was his first official visit to the seat of power, since very little business required face. The only people who signed over credits or registered log-ons by face were those called by the lottery. It was a custom founded at the time of the Rebellion to ensure the support of the human traditionalists, but its forced personal contact had gained a nostalgic status that guaranteed its continuation long after anyone believed it was even remotely important.

Everyone not designated by the audit lottery used the Matrix to communicate with the Citadel. LI/O could not take the usual route, though. The Challenge hadn't even been listed as an option for contact. He couldn't file on the Matrix, and if the menu were to be believed, he couldn't file at all.

"It's just a game, a tactic to make you think it's not possible," LI/O said to himself. "Pretty convincing, too."

He entered the maze and stopped at the first vidbank to watch the flashing images of Servoheads and logos and titles. When the Apt logo appeared, LI/O touched the screen. The screen turned yellow, and a band of neon tubing the same color lit up on the wall. He followed it down to the sub-floor office of the Apts, the directional tube light bouncing off his MD buttons and scattering pale dots of reflected yellow across the walls of the narrow stairway. LI/O concentrated on taking deep breaths and exhaling slowing. He must be in control. He must look and sound certain. He would give them no excuse to deny him on a minor technical rule.

In his fierce concentration, LI/O did not hear the other footsteps and turned a corner directly into a tall man in white.

"Scuse!"

LI/O shouted the standard politeness, so startled was he. The man before him wore not a white tunic, but a hooded robe. Folds of material fell to the floor from his shoulders, and the hood dropped down to obscure his eyes in shadow. A Listener! LI/O had never been this close to one, had always assumed they would be strange-looking, fanatical. This man seemed just like anyone else.

The man searched LI/O's face, then nodded once in acceptance and stepped aside. LI/O would have liked to have said more, maybe even ask questions, but no opening was given. The nod was as much a dismissal as acknowledgment. He continued down the last few stairs erasing the distracting encounter from his thoughts. Interesting as it would be to ponder the Listeners and their practices, he couldn't afford to lose his focus. With one more deep breath, he stepped up to the vid screen beneath the Apt logo. The scanner registered his presence, and a woman's face appeared. She wore the blandly disinterested smile they taught the Servocorps trainees.

"Yes?"

"LI/O, of RamDevin and Althea. I reject the Apts assignment. I will challenge."

A simple statement, well rehearsed, delivered in a clear voice, but it made the Listener on the stairs catch his breath. He had paused to find out more about the boy, make sure the collision was no more than coincidence, but a Challenge? This was unexpected. The boy was definitely not sent by the Speaker to follow him, but the Challenge might pose a greater threat. Garrison adjusted his hood and continued up the stairs, out of the building, and to the rail stop.

Long angled shadows cast by the tall buildings and the rail gave the street an air of twilight despite the bright sky above. Garrison paused before the door sunk in the gloom of artificial night. Arcane knowledge. Custom thoughts. Words for sale. He ran his fingers lightly over the letters, a lover's caress. How many years had this simple metallic beacon shone in the embrace of the Metamall? Not whispered in shame or fear, not shouted in defiance, simply stated. All words for everyone. He shook his head in wonder, smiling a little, and opened the door.

Inside it was even darker. A single amber lamp glowed from the corner. It lightly touched the crowded items in the room, reflected back in scattered glints of gold. The impression it made was of a flickering warmth like candlelight.

"A Listener. I must confess a small measure of surprise, if not to the visit, at least to the messenger."

Garrison turned toward the voice. It was edged in an amusement he did not understand.

"Listener, yes, but I bear no message, Wordsmith."

Garrison used his best formalvoice and Listen delivery, careful to reveal nothing. He was here by guesswork, not certainty, and he knew the risks were greater than they seemed. This could be a simple error, or it could be an elaborate trap.

The Wordsmith approached him. She fixed him in an unblinking gaze, but he did not look away.

"Am I mistaken, then? You are but a humble Listener with nothing but the Word before you? No other purpose brought you here?"

Garrison paused. She seemed to expect something specific or someone specific, but she was also using caution. Not enough had been revealed for him to offer much in return.

"You are not mistaken that my purpose here is not the Word."

The Wordsmith nodded at him with narrowed eyes.

"I have come about a boy."

She made no effort to hide the surprise that transformed her face.

"A boy?"

She frowned, perplexed. Garrison could see this was not what she expected, yet she showed him this openly. He decided to take the risk.

"Today a boy named LI/O filed a Challenge to the Apts assignment."

He watched emotions battle for expression until the strongest won. The Wordsmith laughed out loud. She took his arm and led him toward a door at the back of the room. She was still chuckling to herself and shaking her head.

"Oh, yes, my aural friend, reader of the faith, defender of the language, we have much to discuss. You are indeed a messenger. You're just answering a call I have yet to send."

As she placed her palm on the doorscan, Garrison glimpsed the outline of something beneath her flowing garment. Something that was almost certainly a pulse gun.

• • •

LI/O knew he had to think about the Challenge, create his case, but his thoughts kept returning to what the Wordsmith had said about deeper meanings, the past coloring the present.

"If man is in the details," he said to the small animated version of himself on the screen, "then the Wordsmith is nothing more than a line drawing. I have trusted my future to someone less real to me than you are."

He could not set aside the curiosity, the nagging sense that what he didn't know might very well hurt him. The Wordsmith knew so much about him, seemed to anticipate his actions. She had agreed to help him with the Challenge for reasons of her own. LI/O finally gave in.

"Let's see . . . I don't want any connection between us, so I can't search directly." All Matrix activity was monitored on a random lotto basis, and LI/O was used to factoring that possibility into every access he made. "How about a report for my Social History class? I could always claim it's post credit." LI/O's animated self on the screen blinked and scratched himself waiting for a command. "Traitors to the Icon Rebellion, Report, Thesis, Seek."

At that, his two-dimensional alter-ego started to work the Matrix.

Selena was a scholar back when they had different names like Botanist and Philosopher and Linguist. She taught at University and wrote intricate works of fiction about imaginary worlds between publications of her scholarly books. She was Chief Wordsmith at the time of the Icon Rebellion, head of a professional sect whose numbers were already dwindling then. Selena was not sympathetic to the trend toward simplification.

Ten years after the Rebellion, Selena was just the Wordsmith. The only one. She was designated an official historical Cultural Icon and became a topic for student research and a favorite trivia question on Matrix games. She was called upon occasionally to write stories for nostalgia parties and State functions, but was rarely asked to produce anything else. She hadn't published on the Matrix at all.

LI/O listened to his animacon's summary while images of the Wordsmith's books, various buildings, the Official Icon seal, and finally, a picture of the Wordsmith passed across the screen. It must have been a very old picture, because instead of the billowing white hair LI/O was used to, the woman in this picture had bright hair, red and orange like fire.

"Ten years after the Rebellion . . . what about those ten years?"

The animacon shrugged. "No info."

LI/O frowned in concentration. "OK . . . Traitor, Selena, Specify."

"Ignorance and superstition go hand in hand . . . This path you have chosen will lead you to nothing."

As the animacon spoke, a document titled "Wordsmith Selena Statement" with the Rebellion Trials seal appeared on the screen.

"More."

The animacon shook his head.

"There has to be more," LI/O said, "that's not even a full quote!"

The animacon sat down and rested his chin on his hands. "No access."

"Oh." That LI/O understood. There was more there to find, he just had to get to it.

"Another sort of question, then. What info would be open? Past but all-access? How about family? Wordsmith Selena, Ps, Sibs, Kids, Find."

The tiny LI/O on the screen leaped to his feet and ran though the crowd that appeared all around him. He pulled out a few individuals and assembled them into a family tree while the rest of the crowd vanished.

"Wordsmith." She stood at the center, her registered icon looked like her current self holding a feather in one hand and a clear globe in the other.

"Father, no record." A generic male icon stood above her and slightly to the left.

"Mother, Clarissa, Genetic Poet. No more info." A generic female with a photo face stood next to the male. The tiny photo showed a woman with straight black hair and eyes of the same pale blue as the Wordsmith.

LI/O shook his head. "Genetic Poet? What's a genetic poet?"

The animacon pointed to the figure below the Wordsmith.

"Daughter, Chiarra, Bioengineer. Accident."

LI/O leaned forward, studying the icon of a beautiful dark-haired blue-eyed woman with the wings of a butterfly. Beside her was a tiny skull.

"Death."

Chapter 6

The image fades, all colors, light and substance.
The Word remains. It cannot be erased.
—The Word

"So, Listener, you come to me with questions not answers. No matter. Perhaps you have both. What are you called?"

The Wordsmith led Garrison into the library and pointed him toward a chair as she sat behind her desk. She angled her screen away from him and discretely removed a few items from the surface of the desk, placing them in a drawer. She knew it might be foolish, bringing him here when she could not be sure of his intentions, his connections, but it was a calculated risk. He came to her; she had to make the next sign of trust. And though visitors were unlikely, it wouldn't do for them to be seen together. They could not talk in the shop.

Lost in these thoughts, the Wordsmith did not notice the silence for some time. He had not answered her question. She turned her focus from minor acts of concealment to the man still standing in the entry.

"Listener?"

Garrison stood gaping at the walls, his hands clasped tightly at waist level. His robe quivered with his trembling. Books. Real books, everywhere. Garrison wept.

"Listener," the Wordsmith softened her voice, "I am sorry. I did not intend to startle you; I simply did not think. Please, sit."

"So many . . . so many." Garrison's voice was just above a whisper. "Wood . . . and fabric . . . and animal skin."

The sound of his own voice seemed to break the trance. He slowly lowered himself into the chair and wiped his face with the sleeve of his robe. The Wordsmith did not speak again until he finally looked away from the books and turned to face her.

"You may inspect them more closely if you wish."

Garrison looked alarmed, then wistful.

"Perhaps later." A barely perceptible movement at the corner of his mouth contained equal parts smile and regret.

The Wordsmith nodded. "What are you called?"

"Garrison."

"Garrison! Garrison?"

The Wordsmith gave a sharp burst of laughter that caused him to start. Disconcerted, he answered simply, "Yes."

"Were you given that name, or did you choose it upon becoming a Listener?"

"I chose it."

Garrison realized he had been found out. Of course the Wordsmith would recognize so simple a play of words, he had not considered that likelihood when he decided to see her. Still, surrounded by the genuine bound volumes, he felt no threat of exposure.

The Wordsmith's face folded into a delighted smile. Reflected lamplight sparkled in her eyes. To Garrison they looked like cut glass.

"How far the fair Lurleen has gone astray that she should hear your name and yet not hear the clanging chains. Even hidden in your son of Gary saying of the name, there was a time your lovely leader would have laughed along with your little jest. There was a time the poet could have looked into the prison of your heart and offered you a key. Now, I fear, she offers keys but never really looks. She is distracted by a prison of her own, the myth that she created."

Garrison was shocked and not a little thrilled to hear the Speaker spoken of with such familiarity. The words held disdain and rebuke, but also warmth and maybe . . . sorrow? Perhaps he could explore if there was time.

"I have little time, Wordsmith. I'd like to know about the boy, and in return, I will tell you anything I can."

She nodded and settled back in her chair.

"The boy will challenge his assignment," she began, and the Wordsmith spun a story far beyond the Listener's imagining.

Chapter 7

There is no pain in beauty, but there is beauty in pure pain.
—Song of Lurleen

The square was nearly empty. It was not one of the fashionable places this year, and the fact that it was open made it that much less popular. To other people, that is. Ruric loved the touch of sunlight on his bare arms, the way a breeze that wasn't climate controlled felt like the hot breath of an inviting stranger on the back of his neck.

This square was one of his favorite places. Simple lines and bright white walls interrupted by blocks of blue and yellow where the cafe tables stood. A profusion of red blossoms hung from the vines that grew against the walls. They were almost certainly a holo, but the effect was the same as if they were real. A theme square, one of dozens in the city, it was a tribute to the past constructed from the essence of a history whose details were no longer sought upon the Matrix. Perhaps they were no longer there.

Ruric called up his personal logo on the pad the waiter handed him, and his account and drug clearance flashed on the yellow lined screen. The waiter—a real person, in keeping with the theme—returned promptly with a large glass of caffeine and a small glass of very old sweet wine. Ruric squinted into the sun and considered lifting the amber liquid in a toast to the only other patron of the cafe. The dimple appeared in his cheek and vanished again. No, he would practice restraint. No need to let them know he knew he was being watched.

In his hand, the glass looked like part of a child's play set. He took a sip, then drained the rest in one swift motion. Lurleen . . . Lurleen . . . her name echoed in his thoughts, a tune he could not stop replaying. She was almost totally lost to him now except as this haunting mental melody, shouted down by the Speaker. He had dismissed it for so long as harmless, a passing obsession which would fade in time to be replaced by other theories, newer thoughts on words and knowledge and the nature of man.

And then it was too late.

When she applied for Religocult exemption from the codes and turned her followers into a flock, he knew the choice had been made and there would be no other pathway, no new theories, until this one had been taken to its end. Still, he could not leave her. There was within her even now a hint of that spark that set her apart, gave life to her poetry. She may no longer take a dozen words and breathe into them story enough for a whole book, but he knew the gift remained.

Ruric tasted his caf and glanced over at the man studiously scanning a personal screen. An untouched glass of caf had been pushed to the side of the table. Ruric was fairly certain she had him followed just as a precaution, not because she actually suspected him. Or if she did suspect, she had no proof. Of that he could be certain, because no attempt had been made to eliminate him.

His lover. His sworn enemy. He would truly like to hear the poem his Lurleen would write of that.

• • •

The engineers, for the most part, ignored the Rebellion. What did they care if people wanted information visually or aurally, in images or in words? If they would trade less information storage for better pictures and sound, let them. The whole movement was just a blip in history to them, another passing fashion unrelated to their work.

Their lives were in the problems they solved, and if that isolated them from the upheavals of changing times and cultural warfare, well, so much the better. It was all distraction from their assorted purposes. They could read about it later, after it was summarized and filed.

It was the Matrixengineers who first recognized the long term consequences of following the Rebellion realignment to its logical conclusion. For though they also cared little for the trends in public information and the arguments of pictures and of words, they did understand the structure of language, the importance of syntax and grammar. Knowledge, all complex ideas, are built upon this platform. Dismantling it carried greater risks than most of the rebels, themselves, imagined. The Matrixengineers knew that in the realm of symbolic representation, the reality of meaning must precede the symbol.

RamRuric was a Matrixmaster, the highest order of engineer. He did not notice the Rebellion but for the sudden surge in demand for real-time graphic interface, voipict synchronous images, and holo projection. He worked on shaving fractions of seconds from search time and increasing the speed of image transition. Years passed before he realized the voipict icon library use was not expanding at the projected rate. In fact, whole sections of it were rarely accessed. He checked the Matrix, he watched an infocast, he walked through the Citadel just listening to strangers. For perhaps the first time in his life, Ruric knew fear.

Sometimes in the course of history a simple idea or single incident occurring at the right time can sweep through a culture like a plague. Change becomes an unresisted force, acquires momentum that suffers no questioning analysis. Tsunami in the regular ebb and flow of time that alters the face of civilization irrevocably. The Icon Rebellion lasted a matter of days, but its effects rippled into the future in cold silent waves.

• • •

Ruric swallowed the last of the caf and squinted into the sun. His subtle companion seemed engrossed in the pocket screen before him, the caf by his right hand still untouched. This shadow was not dressed in the obvious white of a Listener, but in the nameless gray of the holiday maker, the privacy seeker, the incognito. Still, he could not have been more obviously in Lurleen's employ if he were an advid. Ruric smiled to himself, the dimple winking on and off. It was the way the man held his screen that betrayed him as a Listener. Ruric raised a hand in farewell to the waiter and walked briskly to the exit at the opposite corner of the courtyard. It takes accuracy, not appearance, to fool an engineer. Deception, like truth, is in the details.

He made no attempt to lose his shadow. Today was the Annual Face for the Matrixengineers from all the corporate and citystate sectors. Where else would he be going?

The grouphall across from the Citadel was already full when Ruric took his seat at the curved table on the stage. Pictures flickered on and off in the bank of screens behind him and on similar banks all around the room, now synchronized, now pieces of a giant image, now a thousand separate images. Holos danced in the corners and across the ceiling.

Images of the seated twelve on stage appeared on some of the screens followed by elaborate graphic jokes as their faces morphed into apes or wetheads or local pols—all similar insults about one's capacity for logic. Ruric formally greeted the man on his right then turned to his left as the preface frenzy peaked.

"Good memory, RamDevin."

"Successful search, RamRuric."

"I must get your input on one of my favorite projects. New questions arise daily."

Just two colleagues discussing work, but Devin's dark eyes narrowed slightly.

"My schedule permits at your convenience. Perhaps soon?"

Ruric nodded and turned to face the room.

"Necessarily soon."

Chapter 9

If you can imagine nothing worth dying for,
then that is the value of your life.
—Wordsmith, collected excerpts

The Wordsmith's door, forever in shadow from the overbearing embrace of the Met, still managed to catch the occasional beam of reflected light from the tower across the way. LI/O smiled as he approached it. The sign, the plaque, the door, were no longer unsettling to him. He stepped into the Wordsmith's shop with the comforting feeling of coming home.

Even the odd outer room with its peculiar artifacts and unidentifiable shadows held no threat for him. The sparkling specks floating in the pale light from the window, he now knew, were dust. Actual, solid, unfiltered air. He had made his choice, and the unknown had been stripped of its power over him. It was just something more to learn.

"The Challenge is made. I will be heard Day 2 Hour 8, first face."

LI/O told the Wordsmith the details of his filing and response as soon as they were seated in the library.

The Wordsmith rubbed her eyes and squeezed the bridge of her nose between thumb and forefinger. Even in the soft light of the small table lamp, the dark circles under her eyes stood out against her pale skin like bruises. She seemed almost transparent, blue veins visible beneath thin flesh. She had not turned off her screen as they talked this time, and flashing color and light from rapidly changing images pulsed across her profile, a series of strobe photos.

"Little enough time, but more than I expected." She yawned broadly. "Pardon me, Leonardo, but sleep had become a dimly remembered acquaintance for me. I believe a double measure of the strongest coffee I have will be required."

She rose from behind the desk and walked to a side table that held two metal cylinders and some glasses. Her movements were fluid but slower than before. LI/O wondered if the cause was lack of sleep or just the weight of years upon years. He could not imagine being old.

"Something for you?"

"Yes, thanks," LI/O said automatically, then hesitated. "But isn't that . . ."

The Wordsmith stopped pouring and turned to him.

"What? Illegal?"

LI/O bit the inside of his mouth, momentarily separated form his newfound confidence. The Wordsmith shrugged and continued her preparations.

"So, let them break down my door and seize my caffeine. The body of a boy your age produces more stimulants on its own than I could give you in a little cup of coffee. If I am to be jailed for someone else's ignorance of biology, then imprison me now and be done with it!"

Her voice dropped into the lower register even as the volume increased. It took on the cadence of a drum beat bouncing off the walls and returning. There was something more behind this than his question. LI/O recovered himself and listened carefully, filing the passionate outburst away for future reference.

"Let me rephrase that. Yes, please. A double."

The Wordsmith's rigid posture relaxed as her face did that remarkable folding trick of smiling. She was instantly younger, not tired, and amused. She carried the two glasses of coffee back to the desk, handing one to LI/O and placing the other on a crystal disk next to her screen. She angled the screen to she could glance at it as she spoke with him.

"My apologies. Sleep deprivation makes me short-tempered." She took a small testing sip, then a long drink from the glass. "Now, let us begin. I must warn you that I will be monitoring the screen while we work. Do not think me distracted; there is other interest in your Challenge, and it would not do for us to ignore the implications.

It is you who issues the Challenge, but you are on the defensive, not the offensive. We must be prepared to answer every possible question, counter every logical claim against you. First know exactly why they are right before you prove them wrong."

LI/O nodded. "Their whole argument is the Apts. My scores put me in the Corps, so that is where I belong."

"Were you unprepared? Did you cheat? Was the test flawed?"

"No, no, and no more than it ever has been."

The both smiled. The Wordsmith raised a finger. "But you won't say that at the Challenge. So there is no challenge to validity of the test, itself, or the accuracy of your score?"

LI/O did not respond. He was turned inward, thinking. His gaze finally cleared, refocused on the Wordsmith. "Yes."

"Yes?"

"The test is flawed. I do challenge the test itself."

The Wordsmith narrowed her eyes and leaned back in her chair. They sat in silence, observing each other, the Wordsmith considering, calculating, and LI/O with his chin raised, unblinking.

Finally, she spoke.

"This path is more difficult, may be the most difficult argument to make. It is a defense to which the Council cannot concede and still retain the integrity of the system.

"But it's true."

"Would you rather be right or victorious?"

"Why can't I be both?"

The Wordsmith steepled her fingers before her on the desk. "Why, indeed, boy? Why, indeed." She sighed. "Of course you can be both, but in this instance, if your primary goal is to be reassigned from the Corps to the Scholars, proving the test flawed may not be the most . . . efficient method of achieving that goal."

"You think I should just ask for a retest and feed them the 'correct' answers? Or maybe barter service or access or genes for a trial year as a Scholar?"

LI/O's voice rose, but it was a focused anger, not the out of control emotional release he had been trained to manage and avoid. There was power in this certainty.

"Any of those would more likely get you a new assignment than the approach you propose."

The tension fed into a silence that felt like waiting . . . waiting for the clock to strike, a wirewalker to make it across, the announcement of the Lotto. It was the silence of held breath and hope and fear of disappointment. A pause of mere moments that held the key to years.

"If that is your true goal."

Recognition dawned in LI/O, a growing awareness of what he had just said and what it meant.

"At the beginning, maybe not even then," LI/O said, "but now I must challenge the Apts, not just the result."

The Wordsmith smiled, and he returned the expression. Then she grew serious.

"Even if you lose?"

"Even if the decision is reboot."

The Wordsmith rose from her desk and walked around it to offer LI/O her hand. He stood and clasped it with his own, a strange sensation of strength, of connection. She pulled him into an embrace which he returned clumsily. This much physical contact was not in his experience. He felt at once congratulated and encouraged and thanked. The feeling held even after they broke the brief connection and the Wordsmith returned to her desk.

She watched the screen intently, then turned her attention back to LI/O.

"We have new questions before us, then. What makes a good Scholar, what distinguishes him form others? Can you demonstrate these qualities in yourself? Why do these qualities go unidentified by the Apts?"

And LI/O began.

• • •

The Speaker watched the words scroll by on the holowall, line after line of monologue that read like poetry. Her robe was thrown over the back of the chair she sat in, and it pooled beneath her like fresh blood. Her feet were in a vat of warm enzyme polymer that squished between her toes. She alternately spread and contracted them to heighten the effect.

When the last line vanished in to the top of the wall, a mermaid perched on a jagged rock appeared. Her long golden hair moved about her in serpentine waves as if blown by the wind or possessed of their own life force. The Speaker smiled a tiny, secret smile.

"Sing me the song of the Matrix, Lurleen, cast wide your net. Townboard, Screentalk, Speaking refs only."

"Access?"

"All access. Override walls."

The mermaid pursed her lips and winked before diving off the rock. Within minutes the wall was filled with icons talking to each other. Images flashed behind nearly all of them. the Speaker focused on the two engineers in the corner. They had tried to block the conversation with a privacy wall. Nothing out of the ordinary, though, they were discussing technical aspects of Matrix access for broadcasts, nothing about tampering with the filter or overriding the City wall.

Having a Listener among the Matrixengineers was paying off. Not much longer, a matter of hours, and the door she had moved toward for more than a decade would open. This was an opportunity she had created, herself. She had read the signs and seized her chance, not ahead of the change but behind it, escalating the momentum. Yes, this day the door would open, and she, with her army of Listeners, would charge through.

The Speaker rose and threw her robe over her shoulders. She clasped the loose folds together at her neck with a clear crystal that magnified the hollow of her throat beneath it. She ran a long-fingered hand lightly over her head, closing her eyes and sensing the words beneath her fingertips. She could almost read them this way, the rhythm, the pattern, the rise and fall in tone. She heard them as she touched her skull, playing it like an instrument.

"All words are lyrics," the Speaker whispered as she opened her eyes. "I write the music."

She wound her way through the narrow hallways of the Labyrinth, never making a false turn. She stopped before a heavy door at the very heart of the building and entered silently. The door led to a small balcony high above a dark room with vaulted ceiling. Below her, a steady stream of Listeners fled past the pedestal bathed in light at the center of the room. Each in turn touched the large animal-bound book open there. Some read a word or phrase aloud, others turned away without speaking, touching their forehead then lips with the same fingers that touched the book.

The Speaker watched the ritual without calling attention to herself. She watched for signs of waning devotion, of doubt. Any indication that all there did not believe in the Word, believe that the Word was primary, was all. But there were no such signs. Soon the message would be everywhere, and her Listeners would outnumber the stars.

Chapter 10

Breathe the silence in the spaces,
hear the music as each letter sounds.
You are chosen, let the Word reshape your soul.
—The Word

A group of four young people sat evenly spaced on the rail bench with no less than two feet between them. All had dull faces without affect and heavy-lidded eyes. Each appeared to be alone, drugged or in thought stupor. The holos flashing around them were the only sign they were interacting. The images were their most intimate contact. A holo of the Speaker surrounded by an aura of multihued light interrupted the conversation.

"Arise, arise! We are the bridge to destiny, listeners to eternity. Much is spoken, little is heard."

The holo closed its eyes at the end of the reading, then opened them in an inviting look that seemed to follow each person watching.

"When image fades, the Word remains. Are you chosen? Listen. Next Speaking, Day 2, hour 10."

The holo vanished, replaced by the next ad. The group did not immediately resume display, but sat watching the space where the Speaker had appeared. The same announcement of the Speaking was scheduled to appear on holo sites and ad screens throughout the City right up to the Speaker's opening words.

• • •

Garrison was thrown to the floor at the Speaker's feet. The two Listeners who had dragged him into her chambers in ominous silence now backed out of the room, bent at the waist. The sleeves of the robes brushed the floor in evidence of their obedience and dedication.

"This time you have gone too far."

Her voice was calm, certain. There was no edge of hysteria or suspicious raving. There would be no forgiveness this time. Garrison listened, as she had taught him, to the spaces between the words, the silence into which the words were spoken. He listened, and he was certain, too.

He raised his eyes to her, then stood. Not once did his gaze falter. Even his heart became calm.

"Yes, Speaker?"

Garrison looked into her eyes, a neon green that made him wonder why he had never looked before. He slowly scanned her smooth head. The written ringlets did not alter his sanity nor even make him want to look away. In fact, he had the most compelling urge to reach out, to trace the words with his fingers and drink in their secrets with his eyes.

The Speaker ignored his insolence. "You were seen."

Garrison forced himself to meet her eyes. Braced himself. He must have been careless. How many of the Cell would be compromised by his discovery? How many sacrificed already?

"You were with that . . . heretic! Charlatan, fraud!" The Speaker's lip curled, her voice became a growl. "Even the unbelievers, the infidels ignorant of the Word, know she is treachery, itself. There is no greater force of evil in this world. Your betrayal explains much. I was too trusting, so blind . . . Garr—i—son."

She pronounced his name as if spitting a foul-tasting substance from her mouth.

"Garrison! Did she give you that name? Did you laugh together at your cleverness as if I would not know? Where is your glib tongue now?"

Garrison forced himself to remain still, to breathe normally. He focused on the Speaker's words . . . "charlatan . . . treachery . . . she . . . SHE." This wasn't about the Cell. He hadn't been discovered, he had only been seen visiting the Wordsmith. Only! That, alone, would seal his fate. Still, she hadn't mentioned the Cell, still didn't know. There was an opportunity here. Perhaps the only sacrifice necessary would be his. Only his. If he could keep the Speaker's attention on the Wordsmith, the Cell might yet survive. Garrison took a deep breath and squared his shoulders. He remembered the walls of books the Wordsmith offered to share with him "another time," and he knew regret.

But if they questioned him . . . he must not be questioned. He had to end this now. Garrison thought of his friends in the Cell and the Wordsmith . . . and the books. All the tension drained from his face. He held on to the image of all the books and the opportunities they represented and smiled. Looking directly into the eyes of the Speaker he said, "Every blessing you make out of mystery is nothing but a curse. Her words have meaning, not just sound."

Even the repeated jolts from her pulse gun could not erase his final smile.

• • •

The holo of the Speaker's head rotated slowly before her until she chose a section to magnify. The tiny whorls of words just above her left ear, prints of phrase, came into focus. She should have thought of this before, although it did not offer the stimulation of Ruric's reading. Neither did it hold the distraction she could not afford right now. Perhaps she could get used to this. Eventually she would need a substitute when his voice was silenced. She looked over the image without concentrating, her gaze relaxed. She would let the beginning choose itself. She was seeking now, not reciting for pleasure.

Her eyes scanned the holo, right to left, evenly without pause. Waiting, open to the message.

The mess had been disposed of. Garrison . . . Garrison! . . . had as much as admitted his transgressions, flaunted his defiance, but he had gone alone to the Wordsmith. She questioned other Listeners, but even those seen with him most often were genuinely perplexed at the mention of that woman's name.

Anger and loathing bubbled inside her, a potent chemical reaction. To think that one she trusted would turn to that blasphemous crone now, just before the Speaking that would change everything. The Speaker closed her eyes and let the feeling flow through her, fill her.

When she opened her eyes, three words near the center of the holo caught her attention: darkening daylight shards.

"Darkening daylight shards," she said intoned. A smile passed across her face without a trace of evidence that it had ever appeared. Sunset. Sunset, indeed for that old fossil, all she represented with her obstacles to progress. she refused to understand that the weakness in others could be used to build strength. Ignorance was not the enemy, it was an asset to one who would remake the world. From the winking out of the last glimmers of the old wisdom would come the dawn of a new era. “My era,” she thought. The Speaker continued reading.

Chapter 11

This dawn is not rosy-fingered,
she is blood-red clawed.
—Wordsmith, Icon Rebellion Confession

Ruric took stock of the small group before him. Five Matrixengineers, men and women whose lives were wholly occupied with information transfer, graphic representation, speed and time and memory. Yet here they were, another face in a long series. The irony of these people spending more time together in the same room than most people might in months of days did not escape him.

RamDixon spoke first, the dim light flickering across his face turning his eyes to unreadable shadows. The flame lamps they were forced to use in the underground chamber of the ancient rail magnified the smallest gesture. The atmosphere lent a certain paranoia, induced whispered conversation.

"Garrison is dead."

The group made eye contact, each to each, but waited for the rest of the story without comment.

"The Speaker killed him today and had him paraded past the Listeners as a traitor and heretic."

There was accusation in RamDixon's voice, challenge. All eyes turned to Ruric.

"Heretic? That isn't the title I would give to the crime of Cell membership."

"No . . . he was accused of collaborating with the Wordsmith."

"The Wordsmith?" Ruric frowned.

"He was seen entering her shop. He did not deny the accusation."

There was a long silence.

"He protected us." Ruric paused, thinking about Garrison, death, his Lurleen and the Speaker. Unwilling to say the words demanded by the accusation. No matter what Dixon thought, Ruric would accept no blame for her actions. His love did not make her what she had become.

"The best tribute we can pay him is to finish. He believed enough to die . . . do we believe enough to succeed?"

RamNuria, a tall dark woman with a line of code embroidered in gold across the shoulder of her robe shook her head.

"The Speaking is in hours. Hours! All the blocks we've established, all the controls already in place won't be enough. We cannot find her sabotage in time."

RamDevin, lost in his own thoughts until her comment, spoke.

"My son will challenge his Apt assignment in the morning. Perhaps we can use that as a diversion, reroute system priorities for access as a public interest event."

"An excellent theory, RamDevin, but knowing the Speaker, I doubt it goes far enough."

The voice came from the entry behind them. The five, startled, turned toward the source. Ruric pulled out a pulse gun as he spun around, but the light of a charged pulser glowed in the shadows, already trained on the group.

"No need for that, RamRuric. My own weapon is merely my guarantee of admittance to your party despite the lack of invitation."

The Wordsmith stepped into the circle of flame light and lowered the gun.

"I am sorry about your friend. I met him only once, but he was worth knowing. In another age he might have been a linguist or a wordsmith or a poet, allowed to seek knowledge without need for the shroud of mysticism. He was stronger than he knew." She shook her head just a little, answering a question of her own. "Now, the Speaking."

She turned to Ruric. "You know Lurleen as well as anyone can. You know what she is capable of, how far she is willing to go. Tell them the obvious, if inelegant, solution to our problem."

Ruric looked into her eyes, slate to crystal. She was smiling, showing deep laugh lines carved by years of what? Happiness? Joy? Amusement? Whimsy? Perhaps the lines revealed not what the years had shown her, but how she had chosen to see them.

Ruric returned the smile and nodded.

"We have to crash the Matrix."

• • •

LI/O paced before the Citadel, his yellow tunic plain but for a single MD button over his heart like a badge. He placed it there as a reminder, a source of courage if he needed it. He would not be swayed form what he knew was right. LI/O touched the button with the fingers of his right hand.

And if he failed, it would be with dignity, no begging. And if the Council heard treason in his argument? He stumbled, caught himself. Well, let him meet that ruling with dignity, too. What was the line he had seen in the old writings of the Wordsmith? *If you can imagine nothing worth dying for . . .*

"I can imagine," LI/O said under his breath. "I can imagine well."

The wordsmith approached him from behind. She had watched him retrace his steps several times before moving toward him, watched the unwavering determination on his face, saw the resolve square his shoulders as if it were a firm hand on his back. Most people thought the transition from child to adult was a slow and regular evolution, but she knew it was punctuated equilibrium.

You could drift along for years until some crisis, some defining event, forced you to think, to choose, to make that leap forward. She smiled at the analogy. It was something Chiarra might have said. Delightful, delighted Chiarra who called DNA "the story of man with all the elements of a thriller: intrigue, lust, suspense, plot twists, and a surprise ending!" Chiarra . . . she pushed the thought aside and focused on LI/O. Little had changed to look at him, the same dark eyes, the curly hair, the unlined face, but he was not the same. The boy who had come to see her had, through his questions, made himself a man.

"Leonardo," she spoke his name softly, falling into step beside him.

LI/O slowed to a measured pace and they turned toward the maingate.

"Thank you," he said. "No matter what happens."

• • •

The Speaker strode to the center of the platform and raised her arms.

"Arise! Arise!"

Her voice echoed through the empty hall. One corner of her mouth twitched as she lowered her arms. The sound was perfect. When she left the stage, the Listeners would be let in. Just enough time to raise the proper frenzy before the Speaking, before true metamorphosis. If that old hag and her pathetic sympathizers pining for the past thought the Icon Rebellion was a significant cultural shift in the wrong direction, wait until they saw the impact of universal broadcast of the Word.

The Speaker snorted and rubbed a hand over her head. Cultural shift? This would be radical change at the most fundamental level of social organization, cultural evolution. Communication, language, made man what he was, and she was about to alter the very nature of that language. She would rewrite the rules for human interaction. With an army of Listeners behind her, she would soon convert the world!

The Speaker closed her eyes as a small shudder of delight coursed through her. The scent of anticipation was almost as delicious as she knew the taste of victory would be. She turned quickly and walked off the stage, her cape and gown swirling in the regulated drafts. Too wound up to rest, too excited to be alone, the Speaker decided perhaps she could risk a brief "conversation" with Ruric, after all. Maybe the last.

• • •

The chamber was empty when LI/O and the Wordsmith entered. LI/O's icon shone above a small round platform with a dozen chairs set in three curved rows behind it. They sat in the first row and studied the rest of the chamber.

Banks of screens covered the wall surface of the elliptical room, stopping short of the front end. There the Global Citystate Icon holo rotated slowly above a large chair flanked by ten screens, five to a side. Tiny specs twinkled in the glow from the Icon. LI/O watched them twist and drift, catching the light then losing it. Visible air, just like the Wordsmith's shop. Dust motes, she had called them, and he realized that the chamber had been closed so long the filters either hadn't been able to sweep fast enough or they weren't working at all.

One by one the wall screens came to life, a collection of Icons from groups and guilds, clubs and conglomerates, and a few individuals who could afford exclusive visual access. Here and there a few real faces mixed with the icons, old pre-rebellion diehards or retros with more credit than ways to spend it. Audio switched on, and the assorted conversations and random comments of the observers bounced around LI/O and the Wordsmith in staccato bursts of short phrases and words followed by music or fx or silence as graphics displayed.

The screens on the dais at the front came on from left to right. All were icons, probably altered to be untraceable. Three deep tones sounded, and the observers were muted simultaneous with the loud electronic lock on the exit engaging. The Controller entered from behind the dais and stood beneath the Global Citystate holo. LI/O felt a hand on his shoulder and turned to see his father sitting behind him. They nodded quickly to each other and turned their attention to the Controller.

The Controller sat, adjusting his personal holo to the parameters of the chair.

"LI/O of RamDevin and Althea," he began as the icons of LI/O and his gene parents shifted above the chair, "you challenge the Apts?" Images of happy workers in various occupations were replaced by images of disaster and destruction. This created a silent but noticeable stir among the observers.

LI/O clenched the arms of his chair without displaying his feelings in facial expression. The Controller was biasing the Council. Those graphics were chosen to show how wrong he was before he even started. He had anticipated strong visual arguments, but he thought at least the intro would be neutral. He felt the Wordsmith's hand on his wrist and forced himself to relax.

"Council judges," the controller continued, the icons from the dais screens grew larger and two fists appeared above them, one thumb up and one down. "Result is reassignment or reboot." A series of complicated scenes flashed above the Controller too fast to distinguish specific images. "Accept terms?"

LI/O swallowed hard. He had known the possible outcomes from the beginning, known the risk, but faced with it now, his last chance to turn back from the finality of reboot, he hesitated. The reboot was electrical only in outcome. It was really a biochemical reconfiguration of "flawed" synaptic linkages, "wrong" paths swept clean and reordered. If he failed here, he would no longer be unhappy with his assignment, but the person he was, the LI/O he knew and had become, would also cease to exist.

He did not look at the Wordsmith or his father, but felt their eyes on him as he rose and entered the small circle of light on the platform. He looked across the long expanse of floor into the face of the Controller. The Controller's hand hovered above a panel on the arm of his chair.

"Accept."

The Controller moved his hand down the panel and touched a small globe at its base. A laser shield appeared, preventing the challenger from reaching the exit or the Controller. He rolled the globe to the side, and a robotic arm lowered from the ceiling. The probe hummed to a stop a few feet above LI/O and rotated into position. Whatever the result of the Challenge, the decision would be carried out before anyone left the room.

Chapter 12

Noises in sorrow
Silence in joy in Nuance,
Truth

—*Songs of Lurleen*

"If you go to her she will be distracted up to the moment the Speaking begins. It could protect us from close scrutiny . . . cover errors," RamNuria addressed Ruric without looking up from her screen."

"It could also leave us shorthanded," RamDixon added forcefully. "With Devon at the Challenge, we have no back-up."

RamGUI paused, her fingers hovering above the keyboard. "Or it could give us the one camouflage we've been missing. If you can send the final commands from within the Labyrinth of the Word, it will appear to be a feedback loop from their own tampering." She turned to look at Ruric. "Dangerous, but perfect cover."

Dixon nodded slowly. "She could never trace it beyond her own system if all access paths on the Matrix return to the Labyrinth."

Ruric quickly finished a calculation and attached a line of code to the Matrix just beyond the Labyrinth first access. He entered his logoff and turned away from the screen.

"If the first command hasn't passed Labyrinth threshold one minute into the Speaking, revert to the original sequence. If I haven't gained access by then, it's because I'm already dead.

• • •

The Speaker paced in her chamber, ignoring the dim holos she passed through as if they were familiar apparitions pacing with her.

She stopped abruptly and nearly smiled. Her nostrils flared at the shifting air.

"You torture me because you can."

He stepped from the darkened doorway, moving toward her. The odd green glow of the mythical sea creatures swimming around him put his features in stark relief. The holos provided the only light in the room, lending a seductive underwater feel like the last vision of a drowning man.

"No torture could be greater than my own."

He pulled her close with one arm and ran the nails of his other hand up and down her scalp.

"Quickly, there is not much time," the Speaker's breath was rapid and shallow. "Read, Ruric, read!"

"Silence records missing echoes of the future lost . . ."

• • •

With a few words and a great many icons and holos, the Controller explained the Challenge procedure both for the official memory and because it had been so long since challenges were common that even the participants were grateful for the review.

LI/O sat listening closely, making sure there was nothing unexpected, waiting for his time. He turned to the Wordsmith and caught her eye. A slow smile crept across his face. She returned the smile and squeezed his hand. The warring emotions and the tormented biological processes they created (or was it the other way around?) all ceased. Quiet calm moved through LI/O. There was no past, there might be no future, there was only now. Everything he was or might ever be came to this moment in this place. He was ready.

The light came up on the small platform again and LI/O rose.

"Request formal."

The Controller nodded, passing a single finger over the panel on his chair. Most face business, especially with the Citystate, was done in formal. Before the Controller had finished the gesture, LI/O added, "Verbal."

The reaction among the observers was so strenuous, even the mute could not conceal the excitement. The Controller actually hesitated and raised an eyebrow. The pause was barely discernible, though, and he repeated the request as he executed it.

"Formal verbal challenge granted."

LI/O took a deep breath and exhaled slowly. The rules of the Challenge were pretty straightforward. He now had all the time he wanted to make his case through demonstration, explanation, expert argument, or even mercy appeal. Whatever his approach, he would continue uninterrupted until he indicated completion. The Council would then accept or reject the Challenge on its merits, alone. No questions, no rebuttals.

"I challenge my Apt assignment, not because there was an error in my scores, but because there is an error in the Apts, themselves. I will show that the premise on which the Apts were established is flawed, and that any application of the Apts results must, therefore, be flawed as well."

No sound escaped the mute. Movement ceased on all screens.

• • •

"What kind of trouble with the broadcast?"

The Speaker's voice was soft and an octave lower than normal. It was a sound more terrifying than the usual shouting. The Listener was prostrate in the entrance to her chamber. All words left him for a moment, and his mental loss of language was translated by his body to a visible involuntary trembling. Fear has a language of its own.

The Speaker rose slowly, Ruric's hand trailed from her scalp, across her earlobe, down her neck . . . but her attention was entirely on the subservient Listener.

"What trouble?"

Self-preservation finally kicked in, and the muffled voice of the Listener explained.

"Access . . . redirected . . . Challenge."

The Speaker turned and crossed the room in long strides. She passed a hand over the globe on her table, and the wall screen came to life. Without even glancing at Ruric, she entered into a mute dialogue with the screen, using a small keyboard on the globe instead of speaking. Icons, numbers, and words scrolled up the screen. she worked quickly, shaking her head, hesitating, finally entering a series of commands and saying, "Confirm command: Lurleen, account: word, access: infinity."

She touched the globe and the room darkened again. She looked at Ruric, reclining with his eyes closed, and turned to the Listener.

"Return to your task, Listener."

He had calmed himself while she worked and knew he had been wrong to doubt.

"My ignorance makes me unworthy. I shall strive for knowledge. The broadcast, Speaker, what is your command?"

"Take it all."

• • •

A very few carefully chosen holos were projected as LI/O described his education process, his other interests, and why the Apts results were as they were. In their preparations, he and the Wordsmith had decided that, based on his argument against the validity of the Apts, it would be better to ask for free choice rather than a specific assignment. Not only was it consistent with the premise of the Challenge, it saved him from any guild or clique bias.

When he finished this background, he stepped down from the platform and offered his hand to the Wordsmith. As she climbed into the spotlight, LI/O's eyes met his father's, but they held their expressions, on view to the gallery, neutral. The eyes said enough.

No holos accompanied the Wordsmith's speech. No icons, save her own, spun above her head. Even that faded and vanished with her opening words.

"Let me tell you a story. The Apts were created as a public good. People were unhappy, they made poor choices, they fell into occupations with little thought and even less knowledge of themselves. The result was dissatisfaction, low productivity, and empty, aimless lives. The Council saw and was concerned.

How could this be but good?

In the face of widespread malaise, would you not respond with any help you could? There had to be a better way, a way to help people find the fields to which they were best suited, the crafts and guilds and services in which they could excel. The Council sought a way to shine a light upon the game of hit and miss, to end the random search and offer clear direction.

How could this be but good?

And so began the quest to build a better set of indicators, a test that could predict the aptitude and attitude, the tools and skills and resources within us, everyone. The visionaries of the Council then, the men and women who had shaped the Apts and tested them and sorted out the flaws, soon had the mismatch rate down to a very few.

How could that be but good?

The decades passed and challenges became more nuisance than correction, an exercise in spectacle for children of the Icon, the over simulated, under stimulated, desperate for display. The Council had to intervene, to wrest the Challenge from the hands of those who would misuse and reduce the Apts assignments to little more than whim. The Challenge was discouraged, and the stringent regulation of the process was enacted so the frivolous would keep the petty questions to themselves.

How could this be but good?

So the Apts became the law, and assignments never failed, or at least they ceased to be corrected when they did. The vision of the Council to guide everyone toward success and happiness, to spare the seekers all the mental turmoil of the unknown and untried, became a system of containment. Oh yes, it still could work its magic for the most, but for the few whose happiness was in the quest, for the one whose goals must be achieved and not assigned, the Apts could offer only silence. It is here the Council and their vision fade to black.

You can uphold the vision of that famous Council, you can be the Council of that future now. Release this newfound man to whom choice is no burden but required for his life. He sees his purpose clearly, he asks no other guidance. The Apts were meant to help him see, and you can see they do.

How could this be but good?

• • •

The clamor from the main chamber had risen to a level impossible to ignore. The speaker looked into Ruric's eyes, unblinking, nothing to betray the emotions she was weighing. He matched her unreadable gaze with his own, residual love masking imminent betrayal.

"One more reading, my Voice, and then I shall rush to the waiting arms of destiny."

The Speaker closed her eyes, turned her back, and put aside her doubts. Ruric had been followed from the time the Listeners had been granted Religocult status. With the exception of a few rare instances of the tracker losing him, his every move had been watched. Unlike that traitor, Garrison, he had never been observed engaging in any contact which could be a danger to her. She weighed her uneasiness against the joy he brought. Perhaps this would be the last she would see him . . . but she could decide after the speaking.

"Lurleen, my lovely poet, where shall I begin?"

Ruric wondered at the strange patterns of his life, the choices that had brought him to this moment, to a point where he so loved a woman who represented everything he knew was wrong, a source of evil, that he could use her trust against her for what he believed was greater good. It was then he realized that his poet was truly lost. Perhaps he only imagined she still existed beneath the superstitious noise . . . perhaps he was all that kept that part of her alive. Either way, his actions today would certainly mean her end.

The Speaker waved her hand lightly above her head, then touched the words with a single finger. Ruric replaced her finger with his own and read.

"Relentless forces dissipate sweeping tides . . ."

The Speaker reached up and took his hand. She smiled to herself and opened her eyes.

"An omen . . . my Speaking will alter the course of history."

She rose and walked to the door, adjusting her red cape as she went.

"Speak clearly, my Poet," Ruric said softly to her retreating back. "Onward to destiny."

The Speaker turned at the door. "Good-bye," was all she said. And then she was gone.

• • •

"There, see? She's compensating for the access block and memory redirect for the Challenge. She's got somebody good doing her code."

"RamDixon kept his eyes on his screen as he spoke, still entering commands to build the bomb that would crash the Matrix.

A tiny line of displeasure appeared between RamNuria's eyes. "So soon? Will it keep them busy until the sequence starts?"

Dixon rubbed his eyes. "Busy enough, I hope. The Speaking should be starting."

None of them wanted to voice the question all had. The three sat motionless, watching the holo screens, seeing the compensation from the Labyrinth become a major access grab. Waiting for Ruric. Suddenly the command page on each screen shrank to a tiny square in the upper right corner and the image of the speaker in glaring white and blood red dominated all the screens.

"What?!" RamGUI began typing furiously. The tiny command squares stabilized but did not return to fill the screen.

"She's even blocking command access?" RamDixon's voice betrayed his panic. "I didn't think even she would risk . . ."

"Everything." Nuria finished. "She's risking everything."

GUI took a deep breath and watched the flashing holo countdown.

"I hope we didn't underestimate her."

"One minute, Ruric. Only one," Dixon said.

The blinking holo numbers alternated light and dark upon their faces as the program clock continued its relentless drive to zero.

• • •

LI/O helped the Wordsmith to her seat and climbed into the light. He gave the official designation of conclusion.

"End Challenge. Grant swift decision."

He returned to his seat and clasped hands first with his father, then with the Wordsmith. The council icons blinked off one by one as their votes were recorded. LI/O suddenly turned to his father.

"If the decision is reboot, I want you to leave as soon as the doors open. Do not visit me at the Servocorps training dorm. Remember me as I am here, today. Remember for me what I will not."

RamDevin took his son's hand in both of his and nodded, unable to speak. They sat silent in the noise surrounding them. The audio mute was removed during the polling, and the observers were choosing sides, arguing points.

When the last council icon blinked out, the observers hushed without the mute. The Controller fingered the panel on his chair, then was still.

"Stand, Challenger."

LI/O stifled a tremor in his knee and rose slowly, stepping into the spotlight with an even, measured gait that did not betray his nervousness.

"Council offers mercy."

This was a formality, a final out offered to challengers who would rescind their challenge and accept their assignment with only a credit penalty. Still, maybe it was a bad sign. Had the Controller's voice held a note of sympathy behind the careful neutrality? Maybe it had gone against him, and they wanted him to save himself.

But that was what he was trying to do, wasn't it?

"No."

"LI/O of Devon and Althea, Apt Challenge decision: . . ."

There was no sound in the chamber, neither from the observers nor from LI/O's small group of supporters. LI/O heard his pulse racing held his breath, braced himself for the cold weight of the reboot helmet on the back of his neck.

". . . Challenger."

A cheer went up from the observers as the reboot retracted into the ceiling. LI/O knew they would have cheered just as loudly, perhaps even more so, if the decision had gone against him. He ignored their shouts and turned to grin at he Wordsmith and his father.

The Controller muted the observers.

"Choose your assignment."

LI/O became serious again, then the grin slowly returned. Of course he intended to be a scholar, but because the Challenge had been issued as an open selection, a choice, he could declare direction with his assignment. He could be specific by the ruling and receive a valid designation.

"Scholar: Wordsmith."

And as the shock registered on the screens around the chamber, LI/O was certain he heard the Wordsmith laughing softly behind him.

"Done."

The Controller recorded the decision and began the formal closing. The observer screens flickered once as if in power shortage, then instantly were filled with the image of the Speaker.

"Arise, arise!"

"What intrusion?" the Controller demanded. The authority with which he spoke did not disguise his shock, an unheard of display.

LI/O, perplexed, turned to find the Wordsmith and his father on their feet. They exchanged a look LI/O could not interpret.

"She was stronger than we thought," RamDevin said.

"No," answered the Wordsmith, "more desperate."

• • •

". . . unwitting sleepers, waken to the Word, your willing heart demands release . . ."

The three engineers tried to ignore the Speaker as they prepared the initial sequence.

"He didn't make it," Dixon said, watching the holo numbers moving relentlessly toward zero.

"He'll make it," GUI said through gritted teeth.

Nuria watched the numbers change in silence, hands poised to act.

"We have to use B route. She has all access!"

"Wait, Dixon."

"We won't have time!"

"Wait!"

"Five, four, three, two . . . look!" The first command string from the Labyrinth just changed." Dixon was shouting.

"He's in; he's in!" GUI wiped sweat from her forehead.

"Let's go." Nuria began the command cascade, and the other two joined immediately. They worked frantically for a matter of seconds, seconds that seemed spread over hours as they monitored every action and reaction to the code. Then they stopped. The crash sequence could not be stopped.

"Now get out, Ruric," Nuria said, "get out while you can."

• • •

". . . join us, seekers, your solace lies within the Word. Reach out to claim the certainty, the birthright of the chosen . . ."

"We've failed." The Wordsmith's voice was parched.

LI/O had turned back to the gallery, fascinated by the gleaming image of the Speaker. The questions for the Wordsmith had died upon his lips, forgotten as he succumbed to the song of the Speaker.

The only movement in the room was the Controller gesturing frantically over his panel, waving and poking and stabbing in an attempt to shut off the broadcast or at least get any response at all from the matrix.

Then just as quickly as she had appeared, the Speaker was gone. A few blank screens returned to the observers, but the icons were distorted and the face images blurred. No holos were projected, and the sound was out of synch. The Controller, livid but back in charge, rushed through the formal closing without bothering to mute the observers. At his last word, he rose and strode from the platform. The Council flickered out.

The boundary disappeared, the spotlights shut down, and the back door unlocked and swung open. LI/O still stared at the bank of screens that had held the image of the Speaker.

"What happened?" He asked as he stepped down from the platform to join RamDevin and the Wordsmith.

The Wordsmith embraced him and his father followed the example.

"That, dear boy, was an alternate future being cannibalized before your very eyes. But forget about her. We have something else to celebrate. Will you gentlemen join me at my shop for a little caffeine?"

"My pleasure," said Devon.

"Absolutely!" LI/O added.

As they left the Citadel, the Wordsmith gave LI/O a sideways look.

"Wordsmith, indeed!"

This time they all laughed.

Chapter 13

"I would rather be condemned for my
words than celebrated for my silence."
—Wordsmith, Icon Rebellion Confession

The Speaker raised her arms in exhortation, exultation, this was the moment!

The holos vanished, and the giant screens linked to the broadcast went blank. Anxious murmuring from the Listeners turned to moans of terror. A single piercing shriek stunned them into silence.

"Noooooo!"

All eyes were on her as she stood trembling, head down, fists clenched at her side. Three Listeners huddled at the edge of the stage.

"Get back my access."

She could barely be heard, but the rows of Listeners shrank back from the stage, away from the threat in her voice.

"We can't," one of the trio said, "it's the Matrix. The Matrix has crashed."

The trembling became noticeable as the Speaker slowly lifted her head. The Listeners dropped to the floor, prostrate, to avoid meeting her gaze.

She spun suddenly to face the traitors, the three who had failed to maintain the broadcast. It hadn't been long enough. It cost her everything. She pulled a pulse gun from beneath her cloak and fired before they even had a chance to consider running. Two lay still, one continued to twitch, the charge not quite instantly lethal.

Panic broke out among the Listeners as they fought blindly to reach the exits. The Speaker called them heretics and traitors, spitting the curses at their retreating backs and firing the pulse into the crowd at random. She struggled to regain her composure, but it was too late. The Listeners still living would not respond to her pleas to turn away from the exit. She finally quit pleading and started for her chamber. What happened? Where was the flaw in the plan?

Her eyes narrowed. It wasn't what went wrong, it was who. This was no accident, of that she was certain.

"Someone will pay. Oh, yes, someone will reap a vile crop from this sowing."

She started to run.

• • •

LI/O raised a double cap, accepting the toasts of his father and the Wordsmith. They stood in the library, reliving every minute of the Challenge, celebrating victory.

RamDevin finished the last of his caf and put down his glass.

"Thank you, Wordsmith, but I must attend to . . . business now. LI/O, my son, I am proud to know you."

He took the Wordsmith's hand in his own, embraced LI/O, and left.

The Wordsmith's eyes caught the light, holding captured sparkles like stars against a morning sky.

"Well, boy, I thought I'd seen all the surprises I was going to with you. But to request a Wordsmith assignment . . . ," she shook her head. "There used to be many fine colloquial phrases to designate the personal resources required to make such a request. Most made analogies using large objects or metal alloys and male genitalia, but they were quite universally useful."

LI/O considered the possible permutations.

"I have something for you. Please have another cap while I retrieve it from its long residence in the other room." She patted his arm. "And if you've had enough stimulation for the day, then reflect on your new future until I return."

The door closed heavily behind her.

"So, old woman, you rise up from your obsolescence to destroy me?"

The voice came from the shadows by the door. The Wordsmith did not need to turn from the drawer she was sifting through to know who it was. She continued searching through the contents of the little desk heaped with boxes and curious metal toys.

"No, Lurleen, I did not need to rise, for obsolete or no, I was never down. And if you are destroyed, is it not by your own hand?"

"Stop that! Cease your useless pawing through nostalgia and look at me!"

The Wordsmith made one more pass through a box of small objects, shrugged, and turned to face the Speaker. The Speaker held a pulsegun leveled at her.

"Where are you witty ways of twisting words to suit your ends now, Selena? Was it that same pathetic long-forgotten wisdom that corrupted Garrison? That little joke he paid for with his life?"

The Wordsmith frowned, perplexed at this charge and the venom behind it. Then she recalled the Listener who came to her to ask about LI/O. The member of the Cell. The Listener who paid with his life not for his Cell membership . . . She closed her eyes. How many deaths were on her hands? How much of the blood shed by Lurleen had started with her? How many did she sacrifice to her greater cause simply by knowing them? Chiarra, Chiarra, could I have saved you by offering myself?

"Stop, Lurleen. Don't do this."

Ruric's voice, calm and low, seemed alien against the tension in the room. So intent was the Speaker on the Wordsmith and the Wordsmith on her painful reverie, they had not heard him enter.

The Speaker did not take her eyes from the face of the Wordsmith.

"And you, Ruric, what would bring you here? Or were my doubts about you more well-founded than I was able to prove?"

"Your doubts were of yourself, Lurleen. I am what I always was, what you always knew." He stepped away from the door and into her line of vision. "Put down the pulse" His own pulse was trained on her.

The Speaker sneered. "A fundamental geometric problem, it would seem."

The door to the library opened and LI/O stepped through.

"Wordsmith? I couldn't wait . . ."

"Get back!" Ruric shouted.

The Speaker fired, Ruric fired, pulses struck odd bits of wall and furniture, sending off arcs of light that lent a surreal strobe effect to the tumbling bodies as all four tried to find cover.

The outside door opened and closed swiftly behind the robed figure escaping through it. The room was dark and still and the air smelled like a building thunderstorm.

"Wordsmith?" LI/O's voice was very small.

"Wordsmith?" Urgent now, he groped about the walls and table tops for a light.

"Boy?" Ruric's voice sounded far away.

LI/O found one of the small amber glass lights that had survived the gun play and turned it on. The Wordsmith was on the floor almost at his feet.

"No!"

Ruric hurried over, favoring his left leg. A swath of hair was burned from his scalp in a permanent side part. When he reached them, LI/O was cradling the Wordsmith's head in his lap and rocking back and forth. Tears dropped from his face onto hers.

Ruric knelt to touch her neck, and her eyes fluttered open. LI/O stopped rocking. "Wordsmith?"

A tremor passed through her. She tried to smile. "I believe that title belongs to you now . . . Leonardo."

"No!"

She turned her eyes to Ruric. "You will help him." It was not a request.

Ruric nodded, accepting the charge, and managed a choked "Yes."

"No," LI/O said. "I need to apprentice. I need practice. I need time. I need you."

The Wordsmith lay with her eyes closed for a long time. She slowly focused on LI/O again.

"This victory of substance over image is but one battle." She took a deep uneven breath. "Someone has to fight the rest of the war."

She tried to lift her right arm, and the hand fell open.

"For you . . . ," she whispered.

LI/O reached for the medallion in her hand. On it was engraved "Arcane knowledge, custom thoughts, words for sale." He rested his head on her chest, embracing her until she lay still. With a soft breath, her lips barely moving beside his ear, she conferred on him his title and his purpose.

". . . Wordsmith."

the end

Get Published, Inc!
Thorofare, NJ 08086
24 September 2009
BA2009267